The Coffee Story

Peter Salmon is an Australian writer now living in the UK and running The Hurst – The Arvon Foundation writing centre once owned by playwright John Osborne. He has written for television and radio and has published short stories. *The Coffee Story* is his first novel.

Peter Salmon

The Coffee Story

SCEPTRE

First published in Great Britain in 2011 by Sceptre
An imprint of Hodder & Stoughton
An Hachette UK company

1

Copyright © Peter Salmon 2011

A CIP catalogue record for this title is available from the British Library.

ISBN 978 1 444 72470 7

Typeset in Sabon MT by Palimpsest Book Production Limited,
Falkirk, Stirlingshire

Printed and bound in the UK by Clays Ltd, St Ives plc

Hodder & Stoughton policy is to use papers that are natural,
renewable and recyclable products and made from wood grown in sustainable forests.
The logging and manufacturing processes are expected to conform to the environmental
regulations of the country of origin.

Hodder & Stoughton Ltd
338 Euston Road
London NW1 3BH

www.hodder.co.uk

To Kerry

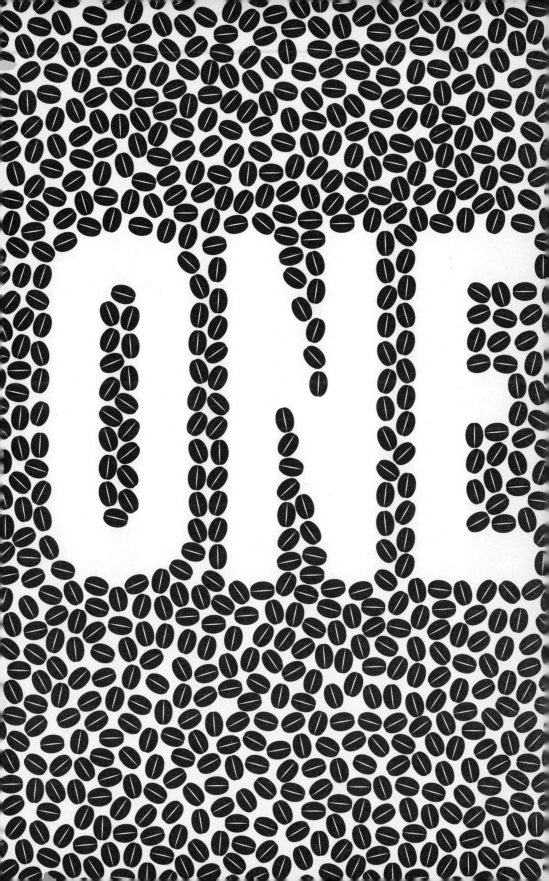

The coffee here, thank you for asking, is the worst fucking coffee I have ever tasted, and that's saying something, considering the shit my second wife used to make. A man who in his prime could have had any coffee bean and any woman in the world, but who went and fell in love with that pallid slip of whatsit with her flat shoes and floral prints, her grey eyes and moral certitude, and Christ alone knows how she used to get rid of all the flavour.

I used to say to her, Moira, Moira my dear, it takes seven years of good harvesting, bent backs and the love of God to squeeze all that flavour into the bean, and you four minutes, a kettle and a coffee spoon to take it all out.

My first wife used to make perfect coffee every time – I mean it: that goddamn woman could make International Roast taste like Harar longberry, without betraying the slightest effort or interest. God, I loved that woman's coffee. She hated my guts, it's true, regarded her coffee-making talents as evil in so far as they brought me pleasure. She tried to make bad coffee for me – she tried to burn it, make it too weak or too strong, she even introduced foreign substances, pills and liquids, you'd have to admire her for that – but out it would come, every time, spinning in the cup, perfect coffee.

So, as in some cheap melodrama, she had to choose whether to destroy her gift or give it to someone else. She ran off with a bean-picker from Brazil, a bean-sprayer from Guatemala, a Bodem maker from Paris, a Monacan prince, who turned out to be gay, and finally a moist Cuban revolutionary who grabbed me at gunpoint in a bar in 1953 and told me, with a twinkle in his eye, that my wife had been doing for him three times a night what filthy capitalist pigs like me were doing to Cuba, and just as violently. Carlo was a passionate and ugly man, with darting eyes set deep below a single thatched eyebrow, eyes that could pick out a false consciousness or a weakening of the revolutionary spirit just from the way you held your cigarette or tied your laces. He had large lips and spat into his hands constantly, SCHRUNKKTH, SCHRUNKKTH, depositing a livid green substance all over his palms and down his wrists – THE PHLEGM OF THE REVOLUTION! – a substance he deftly removed by shaking hands with anyone he met, leaning deep into their faces and telling them, in a rheumic rumble, of the coming of the revolution, *Which side are you on, brother?*, until they bought him a drink or gave him a cigarette, or fled the building in a shower of pamphlets and expletives, *¡Viva la revolución! pig-fucker!*, SCHRUNKKTH, SCHRUNKKTH, *¡Viva la revolución!* What was left of his opalic excrescences ended up caked on the crotch of his trousers or spread on the nethers of passing females.

I ducked out through the kitchen as he led the crowd in a chorus of 'La Lucha Continua', one of his hands gripping a beer, the other gripping my first wife's backside. This was the revolution to him, this was it – group singing and

4

group hugs, torn flags, pamphlets hot off the presses and filled with exclamation points, photographs of tilled fields, drawings of smiling children and dead capitalists. It was the dream of free alcohol and free cigars. Carlo was that most fearsome beast of revolution, the man of passion, the man who had not read Marx, who didn't give a shit about the economics of the thing, but who had a gun and would shoot you in the heart if it offered him a chance of fucking your wife.

'La Lucha Continua'!

Carlo shot himself three weeks later, when he found out that my wife had had a change of political heart, and started doing to one of the Rothschilds what Stalin had done to the Politburo.

Messy divorce. She and I. Me and her. The first one's always the hardest. Lawyers and lawyers and lawyers. The papers were full of it. The great courtroom drama of 1955–6. That and the Rosenbergs'. We ended up going for irreconcilable differences as it turned out that we had cheated on each other almost simultaneously, me with a buxom sandwich-shop girl in the foyer of our New York hotel, her with some pimple-faced bellboy while I was downstairs buying her bagels.

Some pimple-faced bellboy, 'Who must,' screamed my lawyer, 'have been about fifteen years old!'

We spent four months sitting on opposite sides of a teak courtroom, tearing each other to shreds via Steves and Bobs and Marcias until she got half my fortune and I got half her jewellery. This turned both of us on so much that we spent the next three days screwing each other in a mock-Georgian bathtub until she left, without paying half of the bill. I was already seeing my second wife at this point, Moira – Moira meaning 'destiny'.

That's Moira beside me on page six of the *New York Times*, looking, as the caption pointed out, sombre and dignified. Sombre because her new lover had just asked her for a hand-job in the male toilets, dignified because she had refused. My second wife, Moira, whose name meant 'destiny' and whose coffee tasted like shit.

Listen, my second wife was a gentle and caring woman, who spent her entire life on the verge of tears. Her defining gesture was a timid half-step backwards with which she could disappear from a conversation for three weeks at a time. Her skin would become translucent, the lightest dust would fail to stir in her presence, and I was left to pile up accusations against myself until the weight of their collective horror dragged her back into existence, and she pressed her body against mine in the night.

She would always kiss me harder than usual when she returned, her tongue large against my teeth, her legs wrapped around my knees, her belly pressed against my hip. She would stare for hours at my face, looking for something she had convinced herself would be there. Then tears would fill her Irish eyes and I would feel her lips upon my chest, her tiny hands inexpert but honest on my cock. We would make love gently, slowly reintroducing our bodies to each other, careful not to offend. When we had finished she would rest her head on my chest, her hair smelling of camomile and lavender, and tell me softly about our love. Then she would get up gently, brush the creases out of her oversized floral nightie, and go and make the coffee. Which would, God help us, taste like shit.

Oh, Moira, what I wouldn't give now for one more taste of that dreadful, shitful brew. This is how the coffee is made here, my love: they place half a teaspoon of freeze-dried into a litre of tepid water; half floats on top, the other half becomes a kind of trace element. It's then sub-divided among about a thousand patients in a pageant of polystyrene – and make sure you piss it out regular, friend, or we'll be going in there by force. We have tubes you've never dreamt of. We don't want you to caffeine yourself out of that drug haze for an instant or you might start yelling at the nurses, which would be a waste of time, anyway, a waste of fucking time, because they all have the selective hearing of a kindergarten teacher. You fart as much as you like and they'll talk to you about grapes; you swear at them and they top up the water in your flowers.

But for now I don't care if they serve me coffee so weak you can read a book through it. Bring me one more cupful, you saccharine, sacrilegious bastards. We may be in for an all-nighter. I have much to say and don't intend dropping till I've said it.

This is my coffee story.

I should have written it years ago, of course. I fucked that up like everything else. I should have written it before my lungs turned to black rubber and left me arse to bed-sheet twenty-four hours a day in this Hicksville hospital, surrounded by grinning ingrates in white starch, who like nothing better than emphysema because it gives their lives a moral centre, a clear case of bodily punishment and reward. The fuckers. May they all get inexplicable terminal illnesses and die in agony and moral confusion. Especially you, Dr Lovejoy, because what the fuck kind of a name is that anyway, and piss off with your gold watch and your gold teeth and your gold-rimmed spectacles, because it's not so long ago that I had two Jags too, and more women than you'll ever run your clammy hands over.

My coffee story has nothing to do with either of my wives, Moira meaning 'destiny' or the other one. It's about Lucy and I'm sorry I brought them up, but I'm dying, and it's not true that your life flashes before your eyes: it breaks off in chunks, a wife here, a wife there, Africa bloody Africa, the sound of bullets hitting flesh, the Italians, the Americans, the Cubans, the first lump beneath a testicle, the broken coffee-table, the dead child, the cars driving off with your happiness in the back, Lucy Alfarez, Lucy Alfarez, Lucy Alfarez, the bloodstained shoes wiped by a hand-kerchief, the handcuffs, the dossiers. The terrible burden of hidden guilt, the terrible burden of guilt revealed, but always, thank Christ, the smell of coffee, bean, powder and brew, drunk from cup, *ibrik* or *cezve*, bubbling black, steaming on a bedside table, or pale and iced, gulped down in haste to kill the beating behind the eyes of too much whisky, too many cigarettes, or sipped slowly slowly on a too-big bed, legs entwined around the legs of another, or in a café beside the Bois, a shanty in the Fatih district, at the womanly join of the Tigris and the Euphrates, a shiny glass box on Fifth fucking Avenue, but always the first sip sending a sword of heat down the gullet, the spine, making it just about possible to keep going, making life just about liveable.

A proper drug, a drug you can trust, something ballsy and historical, not like the anonymous white drugs in anonymous white capsules they give me in this anonymous white room, drugs to get me up, get me down, keep me more or less the same, *Much of a muchness, Mr Everett!*, drugs that come in little plastic cups or in hollow glass syringes – they may have made them pretty but it's still the same Magick as in the Middle Ages: they don't fool me, these jumped-up goddamn apothecaries, even though I know they will win in the end. They will settle me comfortably into some cosy morphine haze, and leave me to die grinning inanely, I know that, and hats off to them for doing so. Christ, I've had a happy life!

My happy life! Background information as preface to merry yarn. Who or what was Theodore T. Everett? THE TRUTH AT LAST! What made him tick? What were his loves, his hates? Did a heart of gold truly beat beneath that gruff exterior? And why coffee? A condensed autobiography in lieu of three vellum volumes. Here to here to here.

Born, our dying narrator, of cosmopolitan conception, in 1920, to the fifth generation of coffee merchants trading under the name of 'Everett and Sons Coffee' (1832– present), named after the founding father of the business, the bewhiskered and rapacious Mr Oliver Everett and his two lesbian daughters Lisbeth and Fran – the youngest of whom, Fran, now has the poetry she used to tuck into her stocking tops studied in schools and universities across the known world, where they are found to have anticipated the breakdown of the self in high modernism or something. You are no doubt familiar, etc. Elder daughter, Lisbeth, the untalented, destined (Sapphic imperatives notwithstanding) to be the great-great-grandmother of said narrator, did, on father's orders, marry her cousin, also Everett, and begat Simon of the Big Nose who, with Constance, begat Percival Everett, future shaman, mystic and suicide, advocate of William Butler Yeats and colonic irrigation, who did, they say, glow with rosy ardour and who did, they also say, beget some five score children of whom only one was legitimate, that being my father, Oliver the Second, heir to the Everett quintillions. The fat fucker.

He was conceived, so legend has it, in the salubrious environs of the first-class compartment of a Trans-Siberian railway carriage – his father, Percival Everett, future shaman, mystic and suicide, finally directing a few billion billion of his erstwhile spermatozoa towards the ova of his no more willing missus, Adelaide of the Suitcase, who had her first dose of morning sickness less than five minutes later, perched above a shuddering pre-Soviet sink, desperately wiping her genitals with an embroidered silk handkerchief, initials PE. The evidence of ticket stubs points to Christmas Day 1898 as the likely date.

Listen, cells grew and split, split and grew, forged towards organhood. Helixes gripped and tore, tiny spirals of bad breeding coming together and encoding the zygote with as many repulsive attributes as could be mustered. The train passed through Omsk and Novosibirsk. Adelaide heaved into hand basins. Within her, antinodal follicles on the walls of semi-permeable membranes advertised the possibility of hair, while stubby limbs emerged, pop pop pop pop, from four evenly spaced points on the embryo's torso, each of them, arm and arm, leg and leg, curling rapidly outwards and resolving themselves in frayed extremities. What else? Head, shoulders, knees and toes, knees and toes. And then? Genitalia, Lovejoy, genitalia! There's no escaping it! The penis of my father, oblivious to its fate, edged its way outwards from the arc of his already bloated belly to drift serenely in the amniotic juices, like kelp in a rock pool. And hear me, one and all, as that noble train groaned into Vladivostok, carrying its genteel cargo of pre-revolutionary Russian bourgeoisie, there came into the world the Central Nervous System of Oliver Everett the Second.

Eureka!

Months passed. Eight, nine and, migod, ten months. Eleven. Can you imagine?

Adelaide stayed serene, went mad, wept, sewed, spewed. She found God. She became an atheist. She pricked her stomach with darning needles and bit huge chunks from seventeenth-century bed heads, spitting the splinters at her husband like poison darts. She gulped down castor oil, cod-liver oil, petroleum, wiped her mouth with the back of her ruffled sleeve and cast the empty container into the fireplace with a roar. She cut her pretty hands open with pieces of stained glass and wrote *j'accuse, j'accuse, j'accuse* five thousand times on her husband's vanity mirror in blood, in lipstick, in rouge, before collapsing on the ground like an injured bird, mute servants standing round her sobbing body like disciples in a religious fresco, one turned towards us with his palms outstretched, *O miserere*.

Eleven months. Twelve.

Twice a week her legs were spread out in stirrups of leather and wood to allow babbling physicians, proto-Lovejoys, with pockets full of iodine and leeches, to peer at her intimates, poke at her clefted clefts, and scribble, shrugging, into notepads. They told her the child was not ready, was incomplete, was still growing. Midwives multiplied around her increasingly inflated form, shooing away the know-nothing doctors, jostling for position and the promise of instant notoriety. Adelaide was prodded and jabbed by phrenologists, cabbalists, ascetics, Chelsea witch-doctors, and then, at dusk, by horny young medical students from Tottenham, who mistook her for the Cosmic Mother, and fell as acolytes to their knobbly knees, sucking greedily at her podgy toes, licking out her belly-button, and, perhaps, *why not?*, adding their own fecund liquids to the unholy brew.

The tubby homunculus finally made its move during the last New Year's Eve party of the nineteenth century, chewing its way through its own umbilical cord at three minutes to midnight and squeezing its thirteen-pound body head first into the world when it was sure that the Victorian era was on its last legs, and that there was a good party in progress. It may have been smoking a cigar. It may have run an approving eye over the arses of the midwives.

Legend does not have it.

Adelaide of the Suitcase was not displeased to be rid of

her fat cargo and, forgoing the temptation to eat her newborn, remained in the house only long enough to see that the child was thoroughly slapped by all present (Eliza, her personal valet and long-time lover, taking particular pleasure in this operation), before packing all of her belongings and three packets of Everett's finest Brazilian Roast into a tweed porter, nailing a note on the outside of the darkened coal shed (wherein Percival, legend does have it, was shagging the coalman's daughter) and fleeing (with Eliza), to deepest deepest darkest darkest Africa.

The note said: 'Dear Percival. Fuck Off.'

Adelaide? Were you there, Adelaide? In deepest deepest darkest darkest Africa? Was that you I heard, deep in the night, outside the window of my antediluvian *tukul*, your crinoline frock rustling along with the crickets, as I desperately held the end of my childish penis in my ten-year-old fist, praying that tonight, dear God, tonight please don't let me leave the yellow stain, Father will be so angry, again he will – did you hear him, Adelaide, did you hear the blows, night after night, was that you and your jodhpurs-wearing lover listening to that son of yours you had the good sense to abandon rain blows on his own son for the crime of micturition? Are you listening to me now as once again I hold my childish penis, because once again I leave the stain, can you believe it?, a grown man, on my pyjamas, on the sheets, because in the night I dream of you, and I dream of water, I dream of swimming clear of all this cancer and all this phlegm, and I feel it releasing as I dream, feel it warm and then cold, and wanting to move, but I can't move, and hoping like fuck, like fucking bloody fuck, that in the morning I'll be dead, and I won't have to face those plaster-cast nurses with their school-book discretion, with their gentle lifting of my cock, and their measured wipes with their sterilised towels.

There, there, Mr Everett, that's better, isn't it?

This is my coffee story.

Pater. Mater.

My mother, Mama, is best understood by the aligning of two photographs, herewith designated pre-Everett and post-Everett. The former shows a proud, defiant woman, seventeen years old, staring straight out of the photograph, all boobs and chin, all shoulders and mouth. All forehead, hair held back by an arabesque of pins and clasps. All eyes, twinkling above flushed cheeks. All bodices and brooches and ruffs. Big-boned for a teenager, full of hope and cakes and sunshine and life.

At what point did he break her? At what fucking point did he break her?

Was it the day that he and her father, my maternal grand-father, retired to the latter's study, a room that smelt of teak and leather, of journals touched by generations of men, leaving her, Emily, sitting in the next room, the female room, holding a trembling porcelain teacup in her thin white hands, the muffled sound of male voices in her ears, voices discussing the division of the property, the price of the goods, the quality of the merchandise? Did she break there and then? Did the bodice pull tighter, the cup tremble more?

Or was it when she was summoned into the room itself, Come here, Emily, into her father's room, summoned to meet her unsuitably suited suitor, to pledge her troth, to gaze through blurry eyes at that mountain of turgid flesh that was to be her destiny, her *moira*, her meaning, her love. Was it then? Did she break there and then?

Or was it later, did she hold on until later, as she was being led up the aisle (the pins in her hair starting to slip beneath her veil), wearing her mother's dress (did it smell of her? Something borrowed, something old?), placing one tightly laced boot in front of the other, unsteady but moving ever forward, too much class to struggle, too much fear to run? Did she start to go then? Did her breasts begin to sag? Did they descend with each step?

Or were they pummelled into submission that night and every night after by the dead weight of his heaving eighteen-stone body, his huge stomach and tiny cock, spending itself quickly into her, one jerk, one bull's-eye to make history, to make me, one coffee spoon of cum to make a world.

The woman in the second photograph is my mother. Blank eyes. Flat breasts. Slumped shoulders. And if the chin remains upright it is for the purpose of keeping the mouth shut. The photograph is badly lit, and out of focus, a cheap metaphor, let's be honest, for my mother's need to hide in the shadows and for her mind never being completely clear.

And that's not all. One cheap metaphor deserves another. The shadow that covers her in the photo is that of my father. He is standing above her, one fat hand on her slender shoulder. He is looking off to the left, towards the servants' quarters, towards the room of my nanny, towards the corseted but pliant Mrs Smithers.

He was, of course, screwing Mrs Smithers. I am not given to suspense. He was also screwing the first cook, Mrs Duncan (!), and the seamstress, the waifish Miss Todd. And, apparently, her second cousin, Adam, presumably on the pretext that immense wealth and overarching obesity can only resolve itself in the lewdest varieties of corpulent activity – screwing small boys on horseback, for instance, a story whose retelling would only become useful to me as an aphrodisiac for my first wife, for whom all things were sexually stimulating, unless you happened to be her husband, in which case you were forced to combine Dante with the *Kama Sutra* in order to get a reaction.

With my second wife, Moira, it was enough to say, I love you, and regarded as beside the point to say anything else.

She: Say I love you. He: I love you. She: I love you too.

That and hugs. Her cooing, me bored. I asked her to hit me once and she wept for an hour, then went walking about the garden in a terry towelling nightgown for half the night, leaving me to masturbate until the fact that it was inappropriate overcame the fact that it was good, and I stopped and went to sleep. When I woke the next morning my Moira was gone, leaving only her body next to me as a reminder of her absence. It was more than a month before I felt her arm across my chest, her legs around my knees, her tongue against my teeth.

She: Say I love you. He: I love you. She: I love you too.

Moira and I were married in the fifties, both of us sober – unlike when I married the first one – but then it was a sober time, 1957. Lawns were cut as neatly as the hair on a returned soldier. Bakelite was manna. Nobody died for an entire decade. There was no death. There was no cum in the fifties – no smegma, no shit, no piss, no pus, no toe-jam, no ear wax, for an entire decade. Everyone drank instant coffee.

Instant! What would you have made of that, Kebreth, my old Adere china, as you chewed the pulp from the *tera bunna*, rubbing the black bean against your coffee-coloured skin, feeling its oil across the too-short lifeline on your palm, its juices running down your wrists, into your shirtsleeves? You rubbed it on my face and hair on my fourteenth birthday, the night you made me a Communist, rubbed it on my face and said, Teddy, how does it feel, my coffee-coloured young man?

Do you remember, you gave me my first taste of Abyssinian *chat* the week before they crowned Selassie, and to a ten-year-old *chat* was like cocaine, and I can still remember every moment of the ceremony, seven hours of the passing of orbs, of scarlet robes and crimson, of pink umbrellas and Evelyn Waugh.

All hail, Haile! All hail, Haile!

I ran from the car as soon as we got home to tell you all about it, about the marching bands and the lions and the photographers, and you held a finger to my lips and asked about the lepers, *fuck you*, the lepers that Haile Selassie had removed from the city and dumped on the outskirts, dumped in the forest, and you told me, laughing, laughing, that lepers liked little white boys, liked to hold them in their twisted limbs, GOTCHA, and sometimes their limbs broke off, CRACK, because they're so sick, because they're already dead but not dead, and it's so hot in here, so goddamn hot, I keep telling Lovejoy that I need to be kept cool, how hard is that, to be kept cool?

Oh, Kebreth, the lepers still come to me, pouring through the walls in the dead of night, limbs twisted like Ethiopian trees, coffee-coloured hands covered with sores. They sit around my bed and watch me drown in sweat. In the night they touch my feet, my ankles, my wrists; they rest against them softly, fluttering against the skin. If I press harder they move away, if I relax they return. My bedsores have finger-prints, scaly whorls pressed into their purple ridges – you could dust me and find a million lost lives printed on the parchment of my skin. And Lovejoy wonders why I never sleep and my shit is turning yellow.

Kebreth Astakie was my father's contact with the Galla people, and he was fluent in Amharic, Harari, Arabic, English, Italian and Marxist-Leninism. His hobby was attempting to lead the employees of Everett and Sons Coffee into insurrection by assassinating my father and placing the entire operation in native hands. We became firm friends.

His plan for the insurrection was a combination of Socialism and Bombs, and he spent every waking hour collecting as many varieties of each as possible. Socialism and Bombs were big in those days, of course. Everyone had kitchens full of explosives left over from the Great War, and those who didn't could send away for an instruction kit from any reputable comic-book company and make them themselves. You can't go wrong peddling patriotism. There were days when you couldn't bump into anyone in an overcoat for fear of being blown sky high, and Ethiopia was well stocked by Yemeni gun runners who carried TNT in the saddlebags of their camels, the occasional accident leaving humps strewn across the Djibouti railway, from Gelille to Dire Dawa.

Kebreth would come to our *tukul* in the middle of the night, easing my window open, banging his clumsy head clumsily against the eaves, Teddy . . . Teddy . . . pressing a finger to my lips, his face illuminated by a flickering candle, and tell me where he was going to plant the bombs that would blow my father to smithereens and set in motion the wheels of Pan-African emancipation. Here, Teddy, do you see, where the wood is torn away beneath this window, see? I know someone, don't ask me who, you don't know him, nobody does, that's part of the plan, who can make a bomb just this size, a little smaller, a little bigger maybe, depends what you want, with a timer, a detonator, a wick that you light with a match, Teddy, which you set with a switch, that will blow down half the house, half the bedroom, just his side of the bed, the daddy side, he sleeps on the right, I've checked, I've done the maths, he will die in agony and moral confusion, except maybe he won't die, he'll be maimed, he'll be scared, he'll be warned, he'll tell them all.

And then Kebreth would name me the day, the hour, the minute of the blast, the signal, how to get my mother out, *She's already dead by then, Kebreth!*, where to meet afterwards, what to bring. They will come looking for us, Teddy, you and me, but we will have guns and we will shoot them, me and you, they will see that we are brave, us, *we are brave*, and we both repeated the word 'brave' to each other as a mantra, a secret talisman to make us stronger, braver, and Kebreth did get stronger, he did get braver, as strong as one of Selassie's lions, as brave as one of his tigers, while I remained a coward, which is why he is dead and I am still alive.

After Kebreth had gone I would crawl back into bed and imagine our house being blasted to smithereens. Kebreth would have given me the password that afternoon, pressing a scrunched ball of paper into my hand as he walked past. I would be calm, like in the movies, going in to get my mother (*She is a slave to capitalism as much as we, Teddy, read Rosa Luxemburg, read Sylvia Pankhurst, read Trotsky, read Mill, read Nearlyright Bakunin*), and leading her to a safe place, with me and Kebreth and Johnny Weissmuller, all of us peering through the leaves as the explosions began, African drums *tumtumming* across the sward, watching as our stupid home was blown to pieces, the trees around the perimeter turning black like the limbs of lepers, twisting and breaking off, crack crack crack.

And I would run into the wreckage after the last explosion to see my father lying there on his back, a quivering lump of man blubber, the four-poster bed flattened around him, a cartoon villain with smoke coming from his hair, the incendiary force of the revolutionary fires. And I would hold his head in my hands as he recanted, apologising with all his heart to me, to my mother, to all of humanity, for the inequities of the capitalist system, for the dark stain of imperialism that blighted half of the known world, and especially for beating me when I peed, and I would say, *Haha!* and cut his head off with my whittling knife, holding it up by the hair as the workers cheered and declared me their leader, Kebreth my high priest and Minister of State.

The March of Socialism awaits the bare feet of Harar!

He was a tall and rigid young man, Kebreth. You would have liked him. He had a mind that was completely focused on the idea of revolution, and a body completely unsuited to the task. His body was an assemblage of ill-fitting parts, rather than a cohesive whole, limbs of-themselves but not yet for-themselves, so that the butt-simple revolutionary gestures of raising a fist, flicking back a forelock or pointing towards the glorious future became for him long pneumatic ceremonies, circumlocuting through a series of inappropriate stations before reaching, or almost reaching, their goal.

Are you getting all of this? I'm talking about my child-hood. Listen.

Kebreth Astakie was my father's contact with the Galla people. He was twenty-four years old, and had been briefly educated in Sudan at the behest and the bequest of one Lord Benton, who was linked by some felicitous and possibly suspect consanguinity to Gordon of Khartoum. Benton had observed Haile Selassie, then Ras Tafari, prancing about Europe with his lions and his tigers, had been mightily impressed with the regal bearing of the diminutive prince and, by extrapolation, the obvious nobility of a nation that would disgorge such a noble (*noble* is Kebreth's word, sneering, *noble*), such a noble monarch. So Kebreth was plucked from Harar and left for ever the poverty of his noble native land for the neat lawns of the Gordon Memorial College, only to return four months later, *Screw Lord Benton!* driven by the smattering of Thomas Paine and dialectical materialism he had picked up from some Sudanese nationalist or other, a single question, *What is to be done?*, honed in his mind to crystal sharpness.

The Harar he had left was a world of natural hierarchies, familial, sacred, tribal, with complex damasks of religion forming elaborate knots in the brocade – here Muslim, here Falashan, here Ethiopian Orthodox, Coptic, Jain. Karl Heinrich Marx undid them all, unstitching the shop-worn tapestry, and the Ethiopia he came back to was one of power and exploitation, the reification of values, commodity fetishism. The knots had been unravelled. He could make the necessary connections. He saw his father working sixteen hours a day and sleeping on a dirt floor and, yea, the young man grew angry, at his father's obsequiousness, at his father's pride in such enslavement (a father of-himself, says Kebreth, to a ten-year-old white boy, but not for-himself).

He would talk to his father angrily at dusk, Lucy and I listening as we crawled through the undergrowth, Kebreth explaining, explaining, explaining, extrapolating from the base to the superstructure, the superstructure to the base, his father shouting back, *Respect, respect, respect, you are young, it will pass, boys used to sit with their backs to their fathers as they ate dinner, that was respect.* And occasionally his mother, wailing, desperate, *You're killing your father, Kebreth, you know that, don't you, you're killing him, does that make you happy?*

This happens at night, dark, foreign, Abyssinian night, and the arguments always end with Kebreth storming out to sit beneath the *kojo* tree, tripping once, twice on the journey, then lighting an English cigarette and making notes, *In the future We Will, when the people Then It, after the revolution Then They*, on the reverse pages of the cash journal I had stolen from my father.

Kebreth Astakie was my father's contact with the Galla people, and his secret was bombs, which he bought from Yemeni merchants and Somali traders. He would meet them at Dire Dawa station while he was selling my father's coffee. All the buying and selling at Dire Dawa was done in secret, the buyer and seller sitting opposite each other with blankets over their hands, communicating by touch to prevent the others knowing the prices. Along for the ride, sitting among the sellers of salt bars, earthenware pots, beer and grain, I would watch Kebreth selling the coffee and scratching his bollocks with one hand, and buying guns and bombs and books of Lenin with the other. Bullets, *chat* and gold were legal tender, but bombs were Kebreth's own thing. And because he spoke as many languages with his hands as with his tongue, and because he grew the best *chat* in the whole district of Harage, Kebreth always got the best price for my father's coffee and for his own explosives. I helped him carry them home sometimes, grenades and the like, safer for me to hold them in case he tripped.

It was Kebreth who approached us the first day we arrived at the plantation outside Harar, the ten-year-old Kwibe Abi two steps behind and silent, have I mentioned Kwibe Abi?, Christ, look at us standing there as they approach, my fat father and his fat suitcase, his cream suit stained already by the sweat that was to pour off him for the next four years; my mother, her body already observing an obverse curve to the body of my father, a suitcase of her own as befits; and me, also in a suit, ten years old and already insane inside that doe-eyed English head. Plus the body-guard Holbrook, I don't want to talk about Holbrook; my father's mistress and housekeeper, Mrs Smithers, I don't want to talk about her either; and my private tutor, the opium-addled Mr Birtwhistle, who had been employed by my father the week before we left and who was to flee shortly after we arrived, having delivered precisely one lesson to me on, migod, the Politics of the Anthology, with particular reference to Palgrave's *Golden Treasury*, which he felt had enshrined the notion that poetry was an anachronism, a concept he hoped to put to the sword with his own experiments in Imagism, me nodding quietly and wondering what six times four equalled.

I dedicate these ashy leavings to you, Birtwhistle! This smudged and fanciful palimpsest, this dark glass through which to

We had come via Southampton, Djibouti, Aden, Dawe, and then been wedged into the back of a dilapidated Model T Ford, *The seventeenth car ever bought in Abyssinia, sir!*, by a constantly smoking dwarf, who peered at the road through the shaking steering-wheel, singing a single interminable song at the top of his voice, for forty interminable miles on what passed for a road. Dire Dawa, Kombolcha, Harar. Through the gates, a quick lap of Feres Magala Square, chased by the entire population of Africa brandishing chickens, and out again, then twelve miles north to the coffee fields, the offices, living accommodation and sweet sweet fields of *caffea* plants of Everett and Sons Coffee, Ethiopian Division. The car disgorged us, *bleugh*, leaving the six of us standing there in front of our new abode, bewildered and confused, like something out of Buster Keaton, our ties and hats flung sideways by the departing car, a cloud of dust swirling about us and settling gently into every crevice, where it would remain for the next four years, no matter how much we scrubbed.

We were out of our depth! We were complete fucking idiots!

Kebreth would imitate our arrival as entertainment around a fire some nights, the six *English* swaying in the car's back draught, him waiting until we had come to a rest, and then approaching us like an African in a movie, *Hello, misters! missus!* and offering to carry our bags, *good no?!*, knowing instinctively that the fat man with the fat head wouldn't recognise him the next day when he was to be introduced as his translator.

Kebreth and Kwibe carried our bags in for us, Kwibe upright and silent, Kebreth bowing and scraping cartoon style, *Come, sirs, is good house, yes! Priest he was here but now go inside walls, city Christian again, God be praised!*, and then dropping our bags a little too heavily on the uneven floor, and in my memory he gives me a special wink when my father isn't looking, but that can't have happened, let's pretend it did.

The house, or *tukul*, let it be said, was not what was promised in the brochure. My father had decreed – in any number of letters sent to the local Ras – a stately pleasure dome. What he found was a ramshackle series of holes held together by thin, rotting wood, appropriate for its surroundings but far from all the wet dreams of Empire that he had entertained as the lackeys were packing his suitcase. It had been rebuilt with old wood pillaged from a local Orthodox church. The church had been built clandestinely when Harar was a Muslim fortress, with the purpose of gently re-educating the infidels in the error of their ways through the moribund agency of touring missionaries. It had fallen into disuse after King Menelik, impatient with the clumsy efforts of these servants of Rome, had, according to Kebreth, come up with a better way of reintroducing Christianity to Harar, bursting through the walls in 1893, suppressing all resistance and declaring the third holiest city of Islam irrevocably Christian by the simple expedient of taking a piss off the top of Harar's chief mosque on to the chastened infidels below. Salvation was delivered! Covert churches would be no more: let's build some that God can see!

It was felt that wood of such holiness would be eminently perfect for such eminences as the family Everett, so about twenty minutes after the church was torn down it was rebuilt in colonial style by a group of builders who had absolutely no idea what colonial style was. Evidence of its sacred origins abounded. Lumps of gold and brass flecked the walls above the sink. An upturned *tabot*, the replica of the Ark of the Covenant, served as a wood store. Roughly hewn church pews served as roughly hewn *chaises-longues*. Above my parents' bed there was a soft brown outline where a cross had once hung, a stain through which my mother's soul would one day pass on its way to heaven. The walls themselves were stuffed full of saints and martyrs, why not?, eternal witnesses of the vicissitudes of the holy Ethiopian Orthodox Church, whispering to each other during the night, I could hear them, debating the true nature of Christ, the benefits of adopting the Coptic creed – it was a mini Council of Chalcedon muttering from dusk until dawn, *in duabus naturis inconfuse, immutabiliter, indivise, inseparabiliter*. Amen.

The energy that would be spent over the next three years in stopping the whole misshapen dwelling collapsing seemed to me almost as much as the energy Kebreth would expend in attempting to bring it down. From our first day there to our last it was as infested with humans – builders, joiners, plumbers – as it was with termites, as it was with saints, and when I think of it now it is always with a black body attached halfway up a wall, mending a hole, righting a gutter, nailing on a block of wood of ambiguous utility. It was a living thing this house, this ex-*ex cathedra*, and it still makes my skin crawl.

It was empty when we got there, utterly sick-in-the-stomach empty. We spent the next four years trying to fill it, but our things never took possession of it, never got a grip. Bookshelves would fall from the walls they rested against, our beds would slide across the rooms during the night, mirrors would crash to the floor and hat stands would topple. It was as much as we could do to stand upright. I can still remember lying in bed at night and seeing how the water in the basin on the bedside table sat at an angle, the moon reflected in it and sliding off to the side of the bowl. In his more mystical moments the blind seer Tekle Tolossa would tell me it was the saints of the Coptic Church, Raguel, Samuel, Libanos, that lot, wreaking polite revenge on us for the destruction of the church, or perhaps it was a Badu giving us the Evil Eye, not that he believed in that sort of shit, but grandfather clocks don't usually fall by themselves, do they, Teddy?

Below the house – the *tukul* – stretched our Kaffa Kingdom, six thousand hectares, with row upon row of *caffea arabica*, row upon row of happy *gabbi*-wearing natives, shaded by bright, happy umbrellas as colourful as circus tents, Oromos, Amharas, Somalis, Muslims, Christians and Falashans, picking the coffee berries, washing them in the long trays, and smiling beatifically at the glory of their lot. How many were there? Hundreds? Thousands? No idea. They came and went, and as long as they came there was no need to count them.

My father was angry, standing there in the dirt the day we arrived, beatific natives or no beatific natives, and he stamped his angry English foot angrily in his anger. Furniture should have arrived, we'd sent it ahead, servants should have been waiting, we'd made arrangements. What the fuck is this shit hole? Where the fuck are we to sleep?

Beds, sir, beds, I will get for you! They are Africa beds! Very good, good beds. Good for man woman jiggy-jig. Another wink. *I get!*

Kebreth, you prick. You'd spent the afternoon reading Montaigne.

I go now, sirs . . . Much heavy bag, sirs . . . my poor back, sirs, and then a proffered hand coin please!

Later, the others around the fire would laugh as Kebreth mimicked my father's slow, slow, ever-so-slow turning out of pockets, the slow peer into his fat hand, the picking out of the smallest coin there and the handing of it, so, so slowly, to the grinning servant.

At which point Kebreth would produce the tiny coin out of his pocket, a single *bessa* worth little when my father gave it to him and nothing a year later when Selassie introduced *matonas*. Kebreth kept it in his breast pocket, a *bessa*'s worth of luck is better, I suppose, than nothing, and sure enough when Holbrook shot him four years later, he hit the coin. Being worthless, however, the *bessa* allowed the bullet to pass through its soft metal and lodge in Kebreth's heart, killing him instantly.

Kwibe got no coin but then Kwibe didn't get shot.

I spent that first night lying awake on lumpy mattresses that Kebreth had taken from his father's junk pile, *Soft soft mattress, sirs, proper filled with oryx pelt* (bullshit!), *proper comfy, yes* (no!), and feeling the whole of Africa against our thin English flesh, prickling our pale English skin.

The mattresses are better here, I'll give them that. Standard issue. Mine has the number 46 stamped in blue on one corner; I discovered it the day I fell off the bed sideways – you do that when you plan to make a run for it, when it all gets too much and you decide that a bullet in the back has got to be better, the gowns are open back there after all, my skinny white arse gradually getting smaller as a guard calmly takes aim and shoots. But it's the doing that's the difficult bit, *isn't doing always the diffi-*

cult bit?, and your great plan of leaping up and high-tailing gets wrapped up in the bed-sheets, and all you find yourself doing is falling to the ground, god, it hurts, hitting the tiles bang with a clatter of old bones and loose teeth, having to lie there until they come and get you, and say, *There there*, and then you're back in bed, new sheets and talcum powder, and that's the end of that.

(It gives the lepers something to laugh about, and it is to the sound of their chiacking that I fall back to sleep, and return to Ethiopia.)

It was three days after arriving that I caught Kebreth going through my father's papers, spreading them out on the floor in front of him and copying the relevant figures into a blank ledger. Kwibe was sitting atop my father's desk, his legs swinging backwards and forwards as he watched his manic mentor scribbling note after note. Kebreth stood as I came in, *Aha, the son, come in, child, come in*, some of the papers sticking to his feet, a couple to his elbows, lifting me on to the desk as well, *You can watch from here.*

I should have called out, of course, but there was something in the situation that made me instantly complicit, and without a thought I found my own legs swinging backwards and forwards in rhythm with Kwibe's.

The problem, as Kebreth saw it, was that, in the absence of a coherent Pan-African nationalist movement, filthy capitalists such as my father, *such as you, Teddy*, were exploiting the conditions of poverty that existed among his people, and it was therefore the duty of all right-thinking individuals such as Kebreth, *Such as you, Teddy?*, to attempt to lay the ground work for a revolution that would destroy such iniquities, or was it inequities, and lead to a new and better society where the dictatorship of the proletariat could be ushered in and the workers could seize the means of production in a fair and equitable manner, which would allow for free exchange of needs and abilities, which would eventually lead to a coexistence between the formerly oppressed, such as Kwibe here, and the former oppressors, *such as you, Teddy.*

My role would be vital in all of this, eventually as a representative of the new breed of culturally aware post-revolutionary bourgeoisie, but for now if I could help him copy out some of these papers and steal him the odd blank journal then that would be very much appreciated.

The excitement of kneeling beside him! Both of us on all fours, knees and elbows, pencils in right hands, documents held in left, Kebreth would pass them to me, *This section, Teddy, here to here, exactly as they are written,* and I would copy them, exactly as they were written, meaningless figures to me, I did not enquire of their meaning, but there was a deeper meaning, I could sense that, $2 + 2 = 4$, but it also meant something more profound, the 4 was not shared universally, the 4 belonged to some-body, the 4 belonged to my father and Kebreth wanted some of the 4, maybe all of the 4 to belong to everybody, everybody except my father. My father had had his turn with the 4, and now it had to be taken from him, and us kneeling there was the start of taking it away.

Kebreth breathed through his nostrils when he concentrated. There was, I don't doubt it, something erotic about us both kneeling there, our bony arses raised in the air, one white, one black, the smell of each of us mingling in that tiny room. The papers were passed backwards and forwards between us, but our hands never touched and that was deliberate and therefore more intimate. The only sound was our pencils on the paper and the *thud thud thud* of Kwibe's feet against the desk, right, left, right, left. It was Zen, it was tantric, and when Kebreth grabbed all the papers and said, *Stop now* – having smelt the wind and known my father was coming – it was like being pulled up from under water or waking from a dream.

The papers were returned to the drawers, Kebreth and Kwibe disappeared without making a noise, and my father opened the door to find me standing there quietly having, unbeknown to him, begun my revolutionary activities, and engaged in my first ever act of treason. I stand before him, now and for ever, a traitor.

Herein a definition . . .

Traitor – from the Latin *traditorem*, 'one who delivers', specifically Judas, who delivers the Saviour to the Romans. Dante reserves the ninth and last circle of hell for treachery, beneath lust, gluttony, violence. Giants guard its mouth, symbolising the spiritual flaws of those who inhabit it. Cain is there, traitor to his brother and, by extension, his father – even the first father was betrayed by his son. And Antenor, who opened the gates of Troy, betrayed his city to the Greeks. And Ptolemy, murderer of his guests, you shouldn't do that, *mi casa es su casa, compañero*, and finally Judas himself, and all of them encased in ice, because what is it that enters into the bones of the traitor, what is it that will make him shiver every night while the others sleep?, the ice in the marrow, the sickening cold of it all, and if I did have the strength to pad my way to the toilet it is, above all, the prospect of that cold floor beneath my feet that stops me, that icy moat, a perfect Alcatraz.

BUT WHAT WERE WE DOING IN ETHIOPIA! Good God!

Listen.

We were in Ethiopia for the coffee. My coffee story is all about coffee. Lucy and coffee. My coffee story is all about Lucy and coffee.

In 1928 Everett and Sons Coffee was THE BIGGEST

34

COFFEE PRODUCER IN THE WHOLE WORLD! We owned Brazil, baby! Peru! Guatemala! We walked around with our thumbs hooked beneath our braces, our chests out, and our hips thrusting hither and yon. We were in the full strut of Power! We were as jaunty as gamecocks! We danced the cakewalk, bro, and our women were slim of ankle!

But (and here the music modulates, here a shadow fleets across our horizon) the people of the Americas, they were getting restless. Brazil especially. Self-determination and all that. And, gosh, the Americas were a long way away, what with ships! And, gosh, the emancipation of the slaves had raised labour costs! And, gosh, the Depression! Would people still want coffee now that they couldn't back it up with food? My father and my great-grandfather, Simon of the Big Nose, would have meetings DEEP INTO THE NIGHT, whisky and cigars, while moving flags on a map, dropping ash as they did, on Argentina, Panama, Belize, Mali, Niger, Chad, me sitting in a corner watching them, my father's great bulk throwing Russia into shadow, like in the political cartoons of the day, he should have had **Fat Cat!** emblazoned across him, the ever-seated Simon's nose obliterating Indonesia and the Philippines. They were like gods to me in those moments, my father and great-grandfather, exchanging opinions and figures as obscure and murky to me as a passage from the Book of Deuteronomy, and if the son of Ibrahim Salez – have I told you about Ibrahim Salez? – and I would find ourselves spending the fifties and sixties charting revolutions on other maps it was to their example I nod.

It was in that room, on one of those nights, I heard the word 'Abyssinia' for the first time. Simon had found himself sitting next to Ras Tafari at Cambridge in 1923 when the Prince had received his honorary degree (Engineering? Media Studies?), and had uttered that golden word for any entre- preneur – 'modernisation'. Sure, they were abolishing slavery too – they all did in the end, what with Progress – but, still, closer, cheaper, better. Everett and Sons Coffee already had a growing concern there and, Your Highness, we feel that we would be well placed to assist you in making your ancient and venerable Empire into a Modern State, have another glass of wine. To offer a step up out of the dreaded mire of African commerce. Yes, Your Highness, it would be an honour to visit your Great State. Personally? Of course.

So Simon of the Big Nose found himself, two years later, again sitting at the right hand of the Crown Prince, receiving an honorary Order of King Menelik II (Fighting Lions? Defending Axum?). Ethiopia is poised to become the leading country in Africa, and, dear sir, we feel we could help make Everett and Sons the leading coffee concern well into the future, have another *tej*. To offer a step up into the very highest echelons of African commerce. Yes, it would be of interest to me to assist in any way. Personally? Of course.

So, as my father and Simon circled the map, their little flags continued to gravitate towards the Horn of Africa. Might it be possible, speculated they, to attend the forth- coming Coronation of Ras Tafari and use the upsurge in universal goodwill to establish a foothold and do some goddamn business?

My great-grandfather and my father agreed that it would. Everett and Sons' most exotic blend yet! Produced for a shilling less and sold for a shilling more, you couldn't argue with the maths. And for the percentage we would have to turn over to the Abyssinian government we would have the right to Tafari's profile on every packet, facing that of the founder as their silhouettes gazed at each other in mutual admiration.

There would, of course, have to be an Everett on the ground, given the deviousness of the African. Given the reports we were hearing about Grandfather Percival and his addiction to various cults, various women and various emetics, it was felt that my father was the only person for the job. Take your family, Oliver, that wife of yours and that son. It will be good for the boy. IT WILL BE GOOD FOR THE BOY!

Oh, Simon, do you know that I look like you now? My nose is not so big, sure, but it's your features that ended up stamped on me, not the fat fat face of my father, or the dark eyes and melancholy expression of the sybarite and Great Masturbator Percival, and inside that little boy in his shorts and tunic was a wizened old man who would be beaten out of there limb by limb. Will it be good for the boy? It will be good for the boy.

We arrived in October 1930, a month before Selassie's Coronation.

1930! You remember 1930! It was a funny time. Things were happening. The surface of the Earth was expanding, *shazam!*: you could feel it through your feet, tickling your carbuncles. Listless young men, second sons, would-be

Crusaders, felt it through their feet and it made them want to fly, and soon they were putting fragile planes built from canvas, chicken wire and potato skins into the sky, and the sky, no matter how you looked at it, was a thin tissue, and for every six column inches in *The Times* on a hero who had gone further, flown higher than anyone ever had ever before, there were twelve column inches on some poor bastard who had proved Einstein right, space was curved, and if you hit the top of the parabola there was a fair chance you'd come down just as fast, accelerating towards the rising ground at thirty-two feet per second per second, leaving a black stain on the ground for Kansas farmers to gather round and shake their Kansas heads.

Or the humans were travelling downwards, down into the earth, sweet Mother Earth, digging at her for coal or oil, diving down into the sea in submarines, diving bells, scuba gear. Everyone found themselves wearing breathing apparatus and a pair of flippers. Oxygen was something to be prized. Red-faced explorers broke the surface of the ocean, flicked back their collective forelocks, and told breathless reporters that down there were creatures that needed no oxygen at all!

Every day another boundary was crossed, another boundary imagined then crossed. The exploits of explorers were the television serial of the day. Ten-year-old boys watched their maps filling with new countries, their kitchens with new machines. Old women told them in trembling voices that a newspaper printed in New York could be read in San Francisco three hours later, sent down by radio waves, so it was certain that the world would end next Thursday. But the next Thursday would only bring a new advance in hair technology, so the old women were left to tremble on. About radium. About nylon. About women parliamentarians. Leon Trotsky released the first volume of his autobiography to sensational reviews, *Chapter One, Childhood is looked upon as the happiest time of life. Is that always true? No, only a few have a happy childhood. The idealisation of childhood originated in the old literature of the privileged* . . . and for the first time ever they milked a cow on an aeroplane.

The President of the United States spoke to the President of Chile on the telephone and both agreed that the world was getting smaller, but they were both wrong. It was getting bigger, filling with too much stuff. Every day, Teddy, too much stuff.

Then the Lowell Observatory announced the discovery of a new trans-Neptunian planet and the galaxy itself expanded.

Imagine that.

Upwards downwards across. Everyone everywhere was in motion. The *nouveau riche* hit the Depression and fell from the sky like dying aviators. Lucky punters put their money on the backs of horses and the fuckers won and could afford Vionnet ballgowns and strawberry jam and Lincoln Model Ks. J. P. Morgan launched the largest yacht in the history of the yacht, the *Corsair*. It was 343 foot long, and it sat on the surface of the water and didn't sink. You could do that if you were J. P. Morgan. And you could sail it around and look at things, so many new things to look at, new places, new lands, new markets, rough slabs of wilderness that had just enough room for a five-star hotel, a road or two, a wine rack.

Dizzy times. Stalin said that. Everyone had a headache. Champagne hangovers. Pre-menstrual tension. Lots of people really needed to shoot someone. The newspapers filled to bursting with gangsters, union busters, private detectives. I would cut out articles and paste them into my scrapbook. Policemen, professional killers, amateurs. Anything about guns – what boy doesn't like guns? A CID man shot an American anarchist at an anti-Fascist demonstration in Brooklyn and was himself shot. Two women in Warsaw fought with pistols at dawn after woman number one caught woman number two in a café with her husband. Negro Pullman J. H. Wilkins was found dead, hanging from a tree, a single bullet lodged in his throat. One of my father's bodyguards shot a seventy-year-old Galla woman dead for stealing a bag of coffee.

At the time they thought it was the last convulsions of the Great War but in truth it was the first convulsions of the next. You can't discover new planets without people getting jumpy. And there was the Depression, of course. Suddenly everyone was a something. You were rich and capitalist or poor and socialist, or National Socialist, or Fascist, why not? And you hated the others, not a weekend kind of hate, but a hatred to your marrow, and the marrow of your class. Capitalism didn't seem to be working. CAPITALISM DIDN'T SEEM TO BE WORKING. There was a huge void, and a rush to fill it. I can still see my father sitting there, eating one of his endless breakfasts, full English and then some, *The Times* propped up on his enormous gut, grunting obscenities about Commies, and no doubt there were Commies coming up from t'pit grunting obscenities about him.

Kebreth, bless him, really needed to shoot my father. He was reading the newspapers too. English, American, Italian, Chinese maybe, who knows? He had learnt to make the necessary connections. It was him who told me to cut articles out and make a scrapbook. There will be a war, he told me, just you wait. The last phase of capitalism, that's what we are seeing, Teddy, you better believe it. He showed me the guns under his bed, pistols and rifles: he let me hold them, he made me hold them. *Just in case.* Dear God, a pistol held outstretched is the heaviest thing in the world to a ten-year-old. I remember looking down its barrel, trying to stop the end sagging down as my wrist began to burn. Gunmetal is so soft and heavy. It was the wrist and the inside of the elbow that would start to hurt first; then the barrel would start to shake and my trigger finger would start to shake and get pins and needles. Kebreth would stand beside me with a second gun, also outstretched, his arm straight and strong, and he would count to ten, fifteen, twenty, then shout, NOW, and we would both scream, BANG. And my father would be dead.

Fuck you, Kebreth. Burn in hell.

Years later, when I had my own gun, when I was as rich as fuck and I needed one, I would take it out of the bedside table in the middle of the night and stand there with it outstretched and count five, ten, fifteen, twenty and hear Kebreth shout, NOW, and I'd blow the bedroom mirror to smithereens, because you can do that when you're rich, but

Moira didn't like it so she left me, *Goodbye, Teddy, goodbye*.

If you were rich in the thirties you were really fucking rich. You'd dodged the Depression. You hadn't known you were going to: you'd lain awake at night and waited to sink, but each morning when you woke up you were still floating on top, you could still breathe, there was still light. And if you had any sense you started to move, to travel across the thin meniscus to safe ground, dodging the drowned as you went.

So my father gathered us together on Southampton Pier at the end of March 1930 or was it April?, the invitation to Selassie's Coronation burning a hole in his pocket. We were to go to Alexandria first, before proceeding. The previous week he had seen a lecture by Professor F. A. Hughes on the recent discovery of the tomb of Ra Ouer in Egypt and had decided he wanted a piece of that action too, goddamnit! My father was neither an Egyptologist nor a man given to lectures, but in those days it was almost impossible not to find yourself at one sort of public presentation or another. Hughes was spouting on about Egypt, Featherington about the Antarctic, Quincey about the lost civilisation of the Maya. My father had been dragged along to see Hughes by Ibrahim Salez, Cairo merchant for Everett and Sons Coffee, and, to my father's delight, pimp of some repute, Arab women being prized for their passivity by the European type.

He was a burnt match of a man, Ibrahim Salez. Thin and bent with skin like waxed paper and black black eyes. He wore a goatee and a fez, and was valued at dinner parties as an interesting piece of exotica, something baroque to match the candlesticks. He loved coffee and hated Jews. This too was considered advantageous. His hands were covered with black hair and liver spots, and at every possible opportunity he would place them under my arms, *let me go*, and hoist me into the air, telling everyone how much I'd grown, look at our Teddy, look how much he's grown.

Then he would put me down and stare at me, head cocked to one side, fez askew, and take a small metal box out of his pocket. From which he would take a small white tablet. Of salt. See Teddy, my young man, salt. Spice of the ocean, mother lode of the desert. The human body is seventy per cent water, Teddy, and so is the Earth, and seventy per cent of the ocean is salt, you see what I'm saying. Would you like some of my salt? It's fine salt. God's own. You want to grow up big and strong like your father

BIG AND STRONG

like your father, don't you, Teddy? He is a great man, Teddy, a very great man, and your mother too, she is a beautiful woman, Teddy, your father is very lucky, with a boy like you and a beautiful wife like that, a beautiful beautiful wife who I want to fuck fuck fuck, I know you know that, you used to watch me watch her as she crossed the room, staring at her calves, her breasts and arse, and you would go red with anger and shame for your poor mother, but maybe you were wrong, Teddy, looking back, you know what old men are like now, they look and they look, anyone will do, and besides, she was no real beauty your mother, let's face it, so who are you kidding, you fucked-up old man?

43

Listen. When my mother and father were out of the room Salez would give me liquorice, which was a shit because I hated the stuff. It was hard and bitter and I swear he always brought it out of the same paper bag that he must have kept in his sock, given the taste. He told me liquorice was man food and it would put hairs on my chest when I was big and strong.

And not just on your chest!

Ah, Salez, you thin, pickled man. When you left the room they said you drank your own urine and shat standing up. But who cares?, because you sold shitloads of coffee, and the day you died we might as well have bombed the Middle East for all the sales we would get in the future.

(And here I am at his funeral, grown-up, big if not strong, standing in that baking Cairo heat, a fly playing about my lips, looping away and back as I shoo it with my hand, Nasser's police watching me, watching everyone, noting down our names, was that the first link in the chain that put me here?)

This is my coffee story.

Salez had convinced my father to see Professor Hughes because Salez could convince my father to fuck goats if he wanted to. My father respected Salez more than any other man he knew because Salez could get him laid in the middle of Cairo in thirty seconds flat, and if that's not worthy of respect then what is?

Photographic evidence reveals Hughes as a stout, balding man, with a red face and a large moustache, set below a bulbous nose. A big pink walrus. Dandruff and ear wax. His bald pate was given to scabrous growths, which he would pick at while he spoke, placing them on the lectern in front of him as they came away. It is said that his lectures tended towards the interminable, and were as dry as Cairo sand. Although unsuspected at the time, it was later revealed that he was an itinerant dabbler in the occult, theosophy in particular, and it is rumoured that as a young man he might have porked Madame Blavatsky, and as an old one, the wife of Bertrand Russell.

Salez had some plan – Salez always had some plan – involving swapping gold for coffee, coffee for girls, girls for tobacco and tobacco for gold. At various points he and my father would dip their hands in and scoop out some money, which would end up in a bank in Egypt. You don't need to know the details. I swear, your honour, I never did.

My first wife did Egypt at one stage. Call it 1949. She painted the bedroom yellow and blue and drew the eye of Osiris above the bed, which is just what you need. We couldn't bang for two months without invoking Cheops, and when we did it had to be tantric, which bored you to tears, kneeling on the chest of drawers or balancing on one leg, and your back ached for days. Foreplay was a tarot reading, and premature ejaculation could happen any time in the first three hours. The whole house was awash with Pre-Raphaelite paintings, there was incense everywhere, and our bedroom was festooned with caftans and bags of runes. The bedside drawers were full of amethyst and Benzedrine. My wife investigated the genius of nations and eras, the accumulated wisdom of the centuries, all gathered together in pamphlets put out by the Theosophical Society. She took to organising dinner

45

parties at which her lovers and their wives sat around on beaded cushions and listened to her quote from books on alchemy, Rosicrucianism and Jung. She told me, for instance, that in Egyptian medicine the body was divided into thirty-six parts, eyes nose teeth arms, et cetera, each with its own demon, and the demon had to be expunged for normal functioning, Quaaludes being her expunger of choice.

I'm down to about twenty-three parts and counting.

Fortunately my father cared not a whit for such things. The thought of him engaged in tantric sex is terrifying. For him, amulets of gold meant gold that happened to be in amulets. His notes from the lecture consisted of a single pound sign, gone over a hundred times with a blue Parker.

He had coffee with Hughes after the lecture, Turkish blend 7. Hughes picked his scabrous head and talked to him about the burial practices of the pharaohs, or voodoo shit, as my father called it. My father asked about conversion rates. Ibrahim Salez asked where the best place was to get laid in London.

Number 27, Dorchester Street, Savile Row, Salez, you old prick. Ask for Candy. There's always a Candy. Sometimes she's fifty and sometimes she's fifteen, and sometimes if you're lucky she's got a penis too, but whatever's the case she'll blow you for a tenner and

and then we're packing our suitcases, because we're hitting the dark continent, baby, to plunder the lands and steal ourselves some primitive merchandise, and my mother is fluttering around me, breasts flat in a tear-stained blouse, forcing socks and knickers into my hands, and discreetly coughing blood into her lace handkerchief and

and my father is

and we're pulling out of Southampton the six of us, and I'm ten years old and I've wet the bed for three weeks in a row so the salt in the wind burns my legs where the welts are

and I spend every night holding on to the sides of the bed and vomiting, green, yellow, blue, like I do now, practice for lying in your own piss and shit and vomit and wishing you could die, but you can't because the body doesn't want to die, you have to kill it to make it stop and who has the balls for that, or the strength?

There are thirty-six parts of the human body, each with its own demon. To cure any part of the body, for instance the lungs, it suffices to invoke the demon and tell it to get its shit together. This is not, however, easy. Reciting the prescribed formulas once may not be enough. It may be required that the formulas are recited again and again, like a mantra, with increasing urgency, increasing volume. In extreme cases the patient may wish to howl and tear at the sheets. Or cough up bits of the afflicted areas, such as, for instance, the lungs. For the benefit of the nursing staff it is requested that any stools discharged be no greater than ten centimetres in length, and be released at twelve fifteen precisely. Catheter bottles should be filled no later than three p.m. Any effluence over and above these limits is the responsibility of the patient, and re-consumption is not out of the question, the dying body becoming as self-sufficient as the universe, nothing gained and nothing lost, this is your own personal ceremony of the dead, you your-self are the worms that will take your flesh, and we will stand around and chant our mantras, noting that bell-ringing remains the province of those who can still raise their arms and morris dancing is restricted to those patients still able to maintain an erection.

I have decided to fall in love again! Seek a few immanent and tangible agonies instead of these transcendental and abstract ones I find myself dealing in. Something close, meaty and female for my crippled soul to get its teeth into. Every jailbird needs a sweetheart, *She stuck beside me through thick and thin, did the missus, never doubting that this day would arrive, and all credit to her.*

I have decided, therefore, to plight my troth to Siobhan, the freckled red-haired nurse with the red hair and freckles, who sticks a thermometer up my arse at eleven o'clock, two o'clock and five o'clock, plus seven o'clock on Sundays. Half an hour later she brings me my food, half an hour after that my drugs. Sometimes she pats powder on to my bedsores and tells me not to scratch, they will never get better if I scratch, which is sound advice, although I do have lung cancer, so it seems less of a problem than she makes out. I don't tell her this, though, as it would break her fragile heart.

Yesterday Siobhan accidentally brushed the back of her perfumed hand against my crinkly old frenulum and I knew right then she was the girl for me! Today she has a beige sticking plaster on her right heel just above the shoe line, and I swear to God that given the chance I could peel it right off and eat it.

She has the same smile as a woman I proposed to in a bar in 1962, Sestina her name was, the fifteen-year-old daughter of a Cypriot diplomat, with Lucy's eyes, no hips and a bad perm, who had shown me the Pyramids and the Sphinx and the Nile, then matched me gin for gin for six hours in an alleyway bar, until I slumped to my knees and asked her to marry me, *Marry me, Sestina!*, and she went to the toilet and never came back. They found me three days later, fifty metres into the Mediterranean, trying to swim to Cyprus, which is a hell of an ask but you don't know if you don't try, Christ alone knows how I got there, but later I heard that they had given her name to a drink we invented that night, where you put a burning coffee bean into a glass of vermouth – they still call it the Sestina – and she had become the richest woman in all of Cypriosity, seven times married and not balking at an eighth.

I knew her because her grandfather had hidden in Ibrahim Salez's basement during the 1953 coup, as did Salez himself, the pair of them huddled behind wine barrels for six weeks eating mice and salami until their opponents, whoever their opponents were, I can't remember, it doesn't matter, found them and tortured them to death on suspicion of being members of the Muslim Brotherhood, one of whom had tried to shoot Nasser the day before. Were they, weren't they? Sestina told me that her grandfather admired the Pyramids as an advertisement for the advantages of slavery, and had thrashed her with a switch at the age of five for saying money was silly. Salez had hit her too, but Salez just liked to hit girls.

Listen, forget that, Salez was there to greet us when we arrived in Alexandria in 1930. We had spent the last 450 years trawling the coast of Tripoli, watching the yellow land roll past us, my father turning bright red in the Arab sun, my mother fainting at every possible opportunity, and me throwing up my entire bodyweight every half-hour. The Bay of Biscay, the Strait of Gibraltar, the beaches of Algeria and Tunisia, Libya and Morocco, the port cities of Málaga, Constantine, Palermo and, finally, Alexandria – I traced our route in vomit, and salute these places even today for embracing my bile in the spirit in which it was offered.

Salez met us, *movie-style*, amid a throng of JOSTLING HUMANITY, all of them eager to take up our bags, carry our stuff, procure for us camels. Salez stood among them, his fez jaunty in his home town, his goatee relaxed, his piercing eyes softer, rounder, and those hands, which darted about in foreign climes, resting gently in the pockets of his baggy trousers. He was no exotic chattel here. He was a powerful man, at ease, the emphatic gesticulations with which he would charm the ladies of London unnecessary here and thus relinquished. When he picked me up to tell me how I had grown, he did so not with the eccentric flamboyance of a foreigner but with the easy assurance of a man whose very body was a part of the land, and whose feet trod in the steps of his ancestors.

(Twenty-three years later, when they cut off his fingers one by one, pulled out his tongue and his eyes, tore his hair away with their fists, he asked his killers to bring him to this very beach head, so that his blood might mingle with that of his people. But the killers knew that such a pungent brew was liable to produce new life, avengers of his martyrdom, so they put him to death in an aeroplane hangar, its concrete floor absorbing nothing, the blood mopped away the next morning.)

(this very beach head where, the year before their deaths he and Sestina's grandfather had stood and watched King Farouk recede on a luxury yacht and into the pages of history, the pair of them feeling there and then a chill down their spines where the blades would later run, but business was still good.)

(and then not so good.)

Salez, fingers intact, hair parted to the left, put me down and offered me some liquorice. He told us how wonderful it was to see us, although we had come at a bad time. Locusts! The air had been full of them for weeks. They had gone now, but they would be back, rest assured, stripping the crops, driving the devout to suicide, or into the streets to watch the end of the world. My mother turned white, but she was too scared of foreigners to faint.

(But not, alas, to die.)

Alexandria! City of coffee! The air was filled with the sound of *ibriks* coming to the boil, eight, nine and, migod, ten times. Eleven, can you imagine, and on the twelfth boil being poured into an egg-sized cup, so so strong, no sugar, no milk. Everyone knew their coffee. Everyone had at least ten pots, brewed their own brew, had their own *kahweh* room in the back of their house.

Someone go up to heaven and tell God this is how life should be!

That night, or the next, or maybe the one after, Salez took us into his *kahweh*, assigning my father (in his stupid canvas pants, in his ridiculous canvas shirt, in his insane undersized fez) the place of honour nearest the stove. I was next, followed by a gradually descending hierarchy of locals and itinerants, winding their cushioned way along the wall to the arched doorway, until this age-old meritocracy reached the most anonymous and downtrodden of them, hunched in the shadow of the eaves, their murmured *Bismillah* greeting unacknowledged and unanswered by the host. My mother wasn't invited. My mother wasn't there.

The coffee stove sat in an alcove at the far end of the room, amid a vast collection of ornate, ostentatious copper coffee pots, their quantity, ornateness and ostentation conferring on Salez a munificence that was a cigarette paper less than God's. The stove itself was tended by Salez's slave, another marker of our host's manifest magnificence, who Salez called Susu. He was a slim Bedouin, not much older than me, who went about his duty with a seriousness honed by generations of coffee-makers.

Herein an evocative description of Susu making coffee. You can almost smell it!

Susu began by arranging the lumps of charcoal on the

stove, blowing them with bellows to produce the ideal heat. He then filled the largest and most ornate of the coffee pots with water, and placed it on the stove, athwart said lumps. He drew, with great care but little ceremony, a knotted rag from an alcove in the wall within which resided, *Bismillah*, the coffee beans. He warmed them in an iron ladle, turning them red, filling the room with the acid tang of newly roasted coffee. He then ground them carefully in a mortar before adding them to the hot water, which he brought to the boil three times, spicing it with saffron at the exact moment it reached a rolling boil, the whole process taking him half an hour, three-quarters maybe, but to all of us in that room time and space were desert creatures, wide and unhurried.

The young Teddy Everett looks on, fascinated. Until then coffee has, for him, been a mere commodity, a nice-tasting commodity, sure, he'll grant you that, but still a bunch of stuff in boxes, shipped, packed, sold, traded. But at this moment, staring at the boy Susu, he comes to appreciate the intensely personal relationship between this black gold and humankind, the cultural significance if you will, its place within a series of rituals stretching back into THE MISTS OF ANTIQUITY, and it is a lesson he will carry with him for ever, finding its apotheosis in a series of television commercials he will green-light in the 1960s featuring a cut-price version of Peter Ustinov, blacked up and in a fez, extolling the virtues of Everett's Brand C.

While the coffee was being made, Salez fed us dates dipped in butter, which, he said, tasted like a woman, and he told us of the time that he found his wife in bed with an *araba*, one of the men who carries coffee kits in his saddlebag, and who will boil up an *ibrik* on the roadside. Salez had his wife and her lover tailed by one of his servants, who added a sleeping drug to their coffee – the *araba* always drank a coffee before sex to give added drive to his member – which caused them to fall into a deep sleep after their lovemaking. As they lay in each other's arms, Salez and his servants entered their chamber and wrapped their sleeping bodies together, still clenched, in a bolt of muslin, which they placed on the back of the *araba*'s own mule. This they drove through the town. Salez laughed as he told us of them waking up on the back of the mule, their lips still pressed together, their naked bodies struggling against the muslin, hearing the jeers of the villagers who followed the mule up the hill on the edge of the town, to the cliff beside the sea where, after Salez had beaten the two-backed beast with a stick, they were thrown to drown.

My father sat laughing on his cushion, tears rolling down his face. Praise be to God.

Susu did not laugh. He was making coffee, bringing it to the boil again, then transferring it to the grandest of all the coffee pots, then into the little cups. The first of these he drank himself to show, as Salez explained, that there was no death in the cup, a ritual not practised by my current medical hosts, and then moved down the hierarchy of cushions, each of us receiving the small half-filled cup with a *Bismillah* and drinking slowly from it.

Round after round of coffee came to us, and Salez enumerated every one of his sexual crusades, as decorously as could be asked of any coffee-house storyteller, pausing only twice, once to turn about on his cushion, as all the others did, to offer his prayers to Mecca, and once to produce a large, vulgar hookah pipe, which Salez claimed had once belonged to Salah-ed-Din himself when he was Vizier of Egypt, before he done what he done, *let bygones be bygones*, and which he filled with equal parts tobacco and hashish, passing it around the top of the hierarchy, which meant me too, going up on coffee and down on the smoke

and then more coffee and more sweetmeats

and then sleep and

my father

with my head on his lap and him

with my head on his lap and him

stroking

I think he was stroking

my hair

I think my father was stroking my hair

He was stoned, of course. My father was stroking my hair but he was stoned, of course, and I'm glad Kebreth shot him in the fucking heart and let him die.

Through drowsy eyes I watched the denizens of Alexandria shuffle out of Salez's *kahweh*, in order of importance, until there was only Salez, my father and me, and Susu the slave, the mortar between his legs, grinding more beans, inflating the bellows to heat the stove again and again. More and more coffee came, and Salez would not stop talking, eventually forgetting who we were and shifting into Arabic, the guttural turns of the language being softened by the hashish or the dates, and my head swam with foreign words, with foreign poetry, and I think that as I fell asleep I saw Ibrahim Salez undoing the cord of his trousers and moving towards the stove and towards Susu but I can't be sure, I may have made it up, I can't be sure.

The next day! The next day was a big bright sunny day in the Middle East filled with big bright happy people bartering for big bright happy goods in the marketplace beneath Salez's window. The smell of coffee and cardamom filled the air – not to mention dust and limestone! – and when I woke up my mother was in the bed beside me, her knees curled up under her chin, looking seventeen again, but gaining ten hard years the moment she opened her eyes. She held me against her breasts, and I heard her heart beating, not the steady pulse that must have filled my ears as I grew inside her, but an uncertain, reluctant beating, as though each contraction might be the last, as though it might just decide to stop.

But is there anything you need to know here, any insights? We still haven't made it to Ethiopia, we bumbling Everetts, the story still hasn't been born. Lucy is still waiting for my arrival – she is lying on her back and watching the kites circle, killing time until I get there, awaiting her entrance, and I want so much to see her, I miss her so, so I'm not going to stay in Alexandria a moment longer than I have to; I'm not going take you through the rest of the journey. Forget Jeddah, still awash with money and cholera from the recent *hajj*, where Mr Birtwhistle took copious notes for his never-to-be published treatise on what he called the Mussulman. Forget Aden with its Universe Hotel, and its Hindu women stacking endless coffee sacks (one of the women buckling before me under too much weight, the sound of her shins cracking staying with me still). Forget Djibouti, with its gun-toting sailors and coolies and its fourteen-year-old prostitutes made up to look like forty-year-old French women. You'll have to go there yourself like I did, when I returned in 1962, after the fall of Algeria, when the place was full of forty-year-old French women made up to look like fourteen-year-old-prostitutes. And you'll have to take for yourself the twenty-six-hour train ride from Djibouti to Dire Dawa, with its inexplicable stops and antediluvian toilets, me being passed backwards and forwards every half-hour from the thin thin lap of my mother (her knees pressed tightly together, white spots where they joined) and the bulky thighs of Mrs Smithers (ever parted and yielding).

I want us arriving in Harar, gaining our first view of the walled city through the window of the seventeenth car ever bought in Abyssinia, *Faster, driver, faster!*, faster past the city and up the hill to the plantation, to the fields and the coffee-pickers, row upon row, and up up up the hill to our *tukul*, affording luxurious views, a heady aspect, a developer's dream, faster up to Kebreth standing there with Kwibe Abi, watching our car pull up, and I am standing

57

beside him, old as I am now, watching the scene occur, my eyes closed in a hospital bed, seeing the small pink face of Teddy Everett in the back of the car, wide-eyed and innocent, a lamb being led up the hill by his Abraham, not knowing that the instant he steps from the car history will throw him down and press its knee into his chest, take out a rusty scalpel and gouge away at his face to leave it torn and haggard, blow smoke into his lungs to make them hard, press down on his cock to make it soft, and fill his head with a million demons that will still be clawing away at him as he draws his last breath. I hear the crunch of leaves beneath the wheels of the car, and watch as Kebreth steps forward and opens my door.

Hello, sirs!

Ah, Kebreth! That my father had employed a fervent Marxist-Leninist as his intermediary is proof positive that he didn't know shit from clay. It would not have occurred to him that his English orders were being transformed into lessons about imperialism. That the small gatherings of villagers sitting at Kebreth's feet at day's end were discussing the incarceration of Gramsci rather than how many beans they had picked flew right over his bulbous head. Looking back, I truly believe he was surprised that the natives could speak, let alone talk politics.

Stupid people think people are stupid. First law of business.

Gramsci was big news among the bean-pickers that year, as the Italians sat paring their nails on the Somali border, waiting for the signal from blackshirt Benito that the Second Roman Empire was ready to take the stage. That the invasion was imminent even my father knew, but hadn't his

58

grandfather, Simon of the Big Nose, managed to keep his massive snout in both the English and South African troughs during the Boer War? Coffee is the most capricious of commodities, no country can be without it, and the Everetts are nothing if not adroit. And these people were Italians, who don't mind the odd cup. Besides which, Mussolini would have struck my father as someone you could deal with. The Miracle of the Punctual Trains was not easily overlooked.

I would watch Kebreth all day, stopping people at their work as soon as they were unsupervised, standing in their way and cajoling them, drawing the socio-political power relationships in the air with his clumsy hands. And they would nod, *Yes yes, we are puppets of rich landowners and totalitarian schemes, pawns in their game fated to wear the yoke of oppression by the greed and avarice of the rich*, then meetings would be called and nobody would show up. I would go and watch the blind seer Tekle Tolossa stand in front of a crowd of four people, maybe five, and speak in his deep, sonorous Amharic, his wife standing beside him, bursting into song and clapping. Tekle told me that his wife always told him there were three times as many people there as there were, and he would say, Don't you think I can hear the clapping? and she would reply that only a handful of them were clapping, the rest were plunged deep in thought by his wisdom. And he would throw back his head and laugh.

Afterwards, Kebreth would sit me down over a feast of *wat*, the lamb stew raising a curtain of steam between us, and tell me of the hunchback genius Gramsci, who became a fantastic figure to me. I saw him as some kind of maniacal spider, scuttling at the feet of looming cartoon dictators. And then he told me that the forces of evil (that was his word, evil, the forces of evil) had locked Gramsci up in the even more fantastic Penitentiary for Handicapped Prisoners, and sometimes Lucy and I would run into the forest and build playhouses and play prisoner and guard.

Sometimes I was evil, sometimes she was.

Kebreth was always ahead of the papers in his information – a mystery to me even now, laid out on hospital bed 46, the all-knowing Buddha of the bedpan, as wise as an Oriental, but I do know it amused him to tell the blond-haired son of the bossman about the insidious evils of the capitalist system. Christ, I need a coffee. He took me aside one day and told me that Mussolini had said of Gramsci, 'We must stop this man's brain working for twenty years.' I nearly wet myself. It was the biggest thing I had ever heard.

Years later I would wedge a chair back against the door of my office to hold it shut and march backwards and forwards barking orders like Mussolini: *Ma che cosa e questa libertà? Esiste la libertà? In fondo, e una categoria filosofico-morale. Ci sono la libertà, la libertà non e mai esistita!* and then digging away at him as Gramsci, *Sono un pessima a causa dell'intelligenza, ma un ottimista per diritto* and it wasn't because I was mad, I was sane, it was just something to do, why not?, but one day I stopped, I can't remember why.

Here to here to here.

Listen. Gramsci went to jail, I lost my virginity, my father died, Kebreth got shot, the Italians invaded, I ran away,

Kwibe led a mighty army of his own invention, I was chairman of the board, then, seventy years later, I got cancer and died.

That's my coffee story.

I lost my virginity on my fourteenth birthday to the sweet sweet Ababa, the gargantuan wife of the Falashan coffee-picker Tekle Tolossa, who dug her fat fingers into my slim shoulders and threw me down in a barrel of *arabica* coffee, bouncing me up and down midst the oily beans, my hair changing there and then from blond to black because of the coffee oil or because I was becoming a man, or because their hut was swathed in black dust like the stuff I cough up now, dust she shook from the roof with every bounce, BANG BANG BANG.

And she called me sweetie baby honey sweetie as the coffee beans got caught in the crack of my skinny arse, underneath my testicles, in my ears. And I said *yes yes yes*, because that was all I could think of, apart from *Get these beans out of my arse*. And when she had finished she held me tight against her panting body stroking my oily black hair, *baby baby baby*, until she stopped panting, and then she beat the crap out of me, to teach me some goddamn respect, boy, because you may be the heir apparent, sonny jim, you may reek of frankincense and myrrh, but listen, honeychild, we're all of us the same down here, put your finger there, boy, and we're all the same up here, put your hand on my chest, here in our hearts, we're all the same black white rich poor, only some of us give it away for love and some of us give it away for money, and you'd better choose which it is going to be, honey, sugar, honey.

And then her husband comes home, her husband Tekle Tolossa, who is a blind man and a seer, a man descended, so he tells me as I sit shaking at his dinner table, eating his bread and dying for a piss, a man descended from a race of princes so fucking glorious, so fucking glorious, that your father would not be fit to lick their royal arses, not in a million years.

Then he beat me up as well, because even if he was blind, he wasn't that blind, and I heard them making love as I ran home.

Lovejoy! Lovejoy! Bring me a fucking coffee, Lovejoy! Let me get hard again, Lovejoy! Cure me, Lovejoy!

My coffee story is not about the blind seer Tekle Tolossa, or his fat wife Ababa, it is about Lucy, but they are all still there, all necessary. Kebreth will be there too, required, by the inexorable necessity of history, to die heroically as an elderly young man, dying stupidly and pointlessly, as if there's any other way, thank you God.

My coffee story is about Lucy, and Lucy knew her coffee. She knew how to plant it, grow it, test it, pick it, dry it, roast it and grind it. She knew an *arabica* from a *robusta* at twenty paces, and could pick out a *caturra* bean in a barrel of *arushas* like a princess feeling a pea beneath her mattress. Think about the best coffee you ever had and Lucy could make it better. Not only that, the best coffee you have ever had would have made her apoplectic with rage, with white anger, and Lucy when she was angry was the most formidable sight I have ever seen, she was the whole biscuit, five foot eight of blind fury, balling her coffee-stained hands into fists, spitting *chat* and coffee

62

beans in a stream of invective, who ever knew what it was about?, a single pearl earring swaying on her left ear, the earring I gave her on her fifteenth birthday as we sat among the *caffea* plants, sat facing each other with our legs entwined, chewing coffee beans and wondering what we could set fire to.

Let me tell you about Lucy.

Lucy Alfarez walked out of the jungle at the age of fourteen with a silver lighter in one hand and a coffee bean in the other. It's 1931. We've been in Ethiopia six months. Various servants and bodyguards have arrived, and a few desultory pieces of furniture are sliding monotonously around our house, including the bed that my mother had retired to on the day of Selassie's Coronation, and in which she had now been for five months.

I spend most days sitting on the steps, whittling misshapen animals out of misshapen wood, a forgotten child of the ruling class, my private tutor already gone native and lost, wandering the jungle in search of Rimbaud or Kurtz. My friend Kwibe Abi always two steps below me, a forgotten child of the working class, his doleful eyes staring ahead, back ramrod straight, waiting for the moment he would be pulled to his feet by destiny and become a symbol of Ethiopia, *pax* Abyssinia.

Lucy's dress was white, her hair and eyes black, her nails blue. She had red lips black eyelashes. She had bare feet with high arches, and they were covered with dark rainy-season mud.

She was the most beautiful thing that Teddy Everett had ever seen, and his littleboy dick stood straight up. The Everett cock is not given to poetry. It was his first ever boner, and was greeted by the emerging Lucy with a roar of delighted laughter.

Teddy Everett was, by now, not unused to the traffic of the incomprehensible coming out of that undergrowth. He would sit on the porch of his house, whittling blocks of wood into blunt, indistinguishable creatures – the dorcas gazelle, the bohor reedbuck, the cheetah, the Nile croco-dile – or into blunt indistinguishable effigies, copied from the saints adorning the wall of his *tukul*, Frumentius (white wood, the bringer of light), translator of the Bible into Ge'ez; Moses the Black (dark wood, former Egyptian slave), who renounced violence even at the hour of his death; and Tekle Haymanot (misshapen wood, wings on his back and only one leg), who stood, unidextrous, for seven years. Teddy would watch the forest open and close its doors on all manner of life forms, animal and human, emerging from the darkness, blinking, into the sunlight. If it wasn't hyenas or oxen breasting their way out of the woods, it was beggars and indigenes, or steady trains of Christian priests, carrying their *tabots*, portable Arks of the Covenant (we have the real one here too, Teddy, sssh), celebrating the Epiphany, the Assumption, the Birth, colourful processions of men in gold and pink and red, some wearing turbans, some carrying umbrellas, others spinning golden walking sticks in their long-fingered hands. Ethiopian crosses – golden and baroque – hung around their necks. Coffee-picking halted as they walked by our house, chanting, singing, murmuring softly to themselves, to each other, the backs of their heads softening to receive incantations from the one behind. I asked, Kebreth, Kebreth, what are they saying, what is their song?, and he pulled me close and said, Teddy, Teddy my little prince, some are liturgies, some are hymns, some wax and gold poems, some are discussing the comfort and the power of faith, some the sacrilege of polyphysitism, some the Arcana of the Falashan, but mostly Teddy, Teddy my little prince, they are discussing how pissed off they are about the destruction of their church to build your *tukul* and what they would do to your father if they had a few nails.

Kebreth tells me that after the revolution nobody will need religion any more, not Christian, be it Orthodox Ethiopian Monophysite or Sacrilegious Ethiopian Polyphisite, not Muslim, Hindu, Jain or Vedic, not even Judaism, because, Teddy, everything the spirit needs will be here on Earth, religion is an opiate, see Marx, *A Contribution to the Critique of Hegel's Philosophy of Right*, Book 3, Chapter 4, it's all there, the Gospel truth, these men are deluded, they are fools, they think that holiness is to be found in crosses and arks, worse, that these crosses and arks are symbols for something outside life, unattainable until after you're dead, which is how those in power teach them to suffer, to not question or oppose, but heaven is achievable on Earth, Teddy, and and and

And I looked at them, Kebreth talking talking beside me, and I saw the sunlight reflecting off their gold crosses, playing across the red of their turbans, and saw their long beards and heard their soft voices and and and

And I think I was just impressed. I think I failed to make the necessary connections.

Kebreth's view, give or take a few ideological differences, was also my father's. HISTORY TEACHES US THAT POLITICS IS A SPECTRUM ON WHICH THE FURTHEST EXTREMES END UP LOOPING BACK AND TOUCHING. My father asked the local Governor to please get these bastards off his land, they stop the people working, I already have to give my workers time off for fast days they're that weak with hunger, fucking country, but that's by the by, just get them out of here, and the Governor bowed low and pointed out that long before this land belonged to Everett and Sons, and long before the land was cleared for the production of coffee, these men, these holy men, had been observing their ritual walk, praise be to God, on this very track, amid these very trees, after all, sir, listen, is not this the very land where Prester John sent news to the Pope, yes, the Pope, sir, telling him of a Christian Utopia, right here, sir, right where we are standing, sir, so I could not stop them, even if I wanted to, sir, the very stones would cry out, sir, and and and, and my father said, How fucking much?, and the Governor bowed low, blinked twice, named his figure, and the processions stopped. According to my father. It was his favourite after-dinner anecdote!

Lucy Alfarez, ignorant of the holiness of the track on which she walked, emerged from the Ethiopian forest at the age of fourteen carrying a silver lighter in one hand and a coffee bean in the other. Whittling ceased. Blood rushed to genitals. She stopped on a bare patch of earth at the edge of the forest, reached inside the waistband of her underpants, fossicked, blinked twice, and pulled out a cigarette. With one hand, she flicked open her silver lighter, lit her cigarette, and flicked shut the lighter. She lifted her head, blew out a plume of blue smoke, and watched it assumpt, high above the Ethiopian trees, all the way to heaven. She lowered her head and looked hard at the skinny boy sitting on the porch, his penknife poised above a block of wood. She saw the boy slowly press the block of wood down against his shameful crotch. Lucy Alfarez stared hard at the block of wood, hard at the skinny boy, and then, in a gesture that was to stay with the skinny boy until he was an old man, she threw back her head and laughed, and laughed and laughed, filling the sky with her laughter as she had filled it moments before with her smoke. The boy blushed bright red, the blood rushing from his crotch to his cheeks. And the boy found himself smiling. For the first time since he had set foot in Ethiopia, the boy was smiling.

Well.

Where had Lucy come from where was she going what was she doing? She would not say. Not to Teddy, sitting there blushing, or to Kebreth, who came striding striding striding out of the crops, *Hello hello*, or to any of the women who came to peer at her, mothers at the front, picking her up and turning her around, she's just a child, and wiping her nose and cuffing her behind the ear, god knows why. Woman stuff. Or to my father, who came bullocking past me down the stairs, fat rolling in the noonday sun, *Get back to work! Get back to work!*, no, not to him, especially, though he asked her again and again, in case she knew something (what?), in case others would follow (who?) and fuck up his little principality. He was as scared of the jungle as my mother was.

He grabbed Lucy and put her under his arm, lifted her off the ground, and carried her back into the house, a dead weight, legs hanging down, amused, not moving as he placed her on a chair and rounded on her.

What is your name, little girl? Silence. Where are you from, little girl? Silence. Tell me! Silence. Silence even when he lifted her from the chair and placed her across his knee, her tiny breasts against his thighs, the back of her neck in his fat palm, and thrashed her with his belt, slap slap slap, as he had thrashed me many times before. But Lucy, sunshine, she didn't even cry, she didn't make a sound. Even when, after his arm had gone numb, he put her down and kicked her out of the door with the sole of his foot, his thin beige sock against the welts on her arse, she still didn't cry or stumble like baby Teddy always did, no, sir, she just put her shoulders back, her head up, and walked out the door, to the silent cheers of the coffee-pickers, *Fuck you, strap man, fuck you.*

Lucy Alfarez sat on her sore arse and told me my father was a bastard. This is the start of the coffee story. Get rid of the rest. None of it matters. I'm sorry I. Only I. She is four years older than me, a foot taller, and smokes a pack of cigarettes a day, more if she can get them, and she always can, everyone gives Lucy cigarettes, just to watch her smoke them, like they give her coffee and chocolate and *chat*.

Lucy Alfarez shakes my hand and tells me her name is Lucy, and that my father is a bastard. She also tells me that she can play the harmonica and light her own farts, both of which are new to me. She tells me that she is also a magician, *would you like to see?* She holds a coffee bean in her right hand and challenges me to take it. I try to, she closes her hand, and when she opens it the bean is gone. She takes it out from behind my ear. I press the wood block back down against my crotch. She tells me the trick is to distract the audience, to make them think of something else (it is true: I am thinking about her slim beauty, her dark eyes, the wood block rough against my cock). Make them look here, she says, waving the thin fingers of her beautiful left hand, and do the trick here, she says, waving the thin fingers of her beautiful right. She picks another bean from behind my ear with her left, and giggles. Then she lights two cigarettes in her mouth and gives one to me, Here you go.

Lucy smoked ivory-tipped Marlboros and my first one nearly killed me. Lucy smoked ivory-tipped Marlboros and, ironically, as I lie here dying of lung cancer, the first one nearly killed me. I sat on the stairs that day and hoped and prayed that each time I sucked on the end of it, drawing the smoke into my lovely clean pink lungs, that it would go out and I would be able to hide it from her when she wasn't looking (behind my ear!), but it didn't go out, and she never looked away, because Lucy never looked away, always, always those eyes, a magician's eyes, so I had to smoke the whole fucking thing, ivory tip and all.

I blew the smoke downwards, so my father wouldn't see, but he was probably still trying to get his belt back on, fat fingers struggling with the intricacies of the buckle. (Later, when he was even larger, he would lie on his back and get two servants to buckle him up, one pulling hard on the end of the strap, one fixing the buckle. Despite the frequency of the operation – my father, driven to exhaustion by the heat would beat my mother and me at the slightest provocation – the servants always took a long time to buckle him back in, which my father always ascribed to stupidity on their part, but Kebreth told me that they simply enjoyed watching him roll around on his back, like a beached whale. More oil on the wheel of the revolution!)

I spent the afternoon showing Lucy around Everettville and becoming addicted to cigarettes. And maybe it was the smoke in my lungs or maybe the first stirrings of love, but I was the new *Chrysostomos*, the golden-mouthed, words spilling from my mouth in a torrent of bullion. I've never been much of a talker!

I told her that the Everetts had snuffled their way into Ethiopia under the reign of Simon of the Big Nose, who, in the thrall of Arthur Rimbaud (as businessman, not poet of the future) and Henry Ford (as poet of the future, not businessman), had seen the future and it was Harar.

Not that we were the first, I told Lucy. The French and the Italians were already there, the former represented by the house of Viannay, Bardey et Cie, the latter by the Bienenfeld brothers, Vittorio and Giuseppe, who, I explained, had arrived from Trieste in the 1880s, when it was discovered that the Berbera coffee of Harar was every bit the equal of Mokka. I informed Lucy that Simon's revolution was to set up this coffee plantation that didn't just rely on the local Galla population for workers but invited workers from all across Ethiopia, an Everett League of Nations, to cultivate the fields, pick the berries, remove their pulp, so that the Everett brand would arrive at Aden, already de-husked, shiny and new; regimented rows of plants had been laid down, washing and drying huts built, human people brought from every district, every creed, every religion. Money does that. Thus began the Everett's African Coffee Revolution!

With a stick in the sand, I traced a rough map of the city of Harar, the Gey, the Jugol, the 100 Mosques, Rimbaud's house, and the future site of the beer-bottling plant that I would help bankroll many years later, in a failed attempt at diversification. These walls surrounding 368 alleyways, walls five metres high, built to keep the Oromo out. This house where Ras Tafari had his honeymoon, him and the missus, we always goes to Harar, it's nice there, the people are so friendly.

I built a small mound to represent the Kundudo mountain on the outskirts, where the hyenas and feral horses roamed, and a man was a man, goddamn. Workers gathered around us as I ran Lucy through the sixteenth-century war of conquest launched by Gragn the Left-handed, who would always time his attacks during Lent when the people were exhausted, cheating bastard, and who held Harar for fifteen years before they built the wall AND SOME SAY HE HOLDS IT STILL. I pointed to the people, Amhara, Oromo, Somali and Gurage, explaining that they referred to themselves as Gey, 'Usu., the people of the city, their language Harari, a Semitic pocket within a predominantly Cushitic region'.

Finally, as rainbows curved across the sky, as angels descended with trumpets, and as the people of Harar began to sing and dance (the women ululating, the men blowing blues harps), I traced the extent of our holdings, the plant-ations in Giwara, below Koremi, outside Ejerso Gworo, birthplace of the Emperor, don't you know, the huts of the workers, here's where Kebreth lives, you'll like him, this is Tekle Tolossa's house, we must visit him, he is a blind man and a seer, he has a barrel of coffee beans in his kitchen, here is my house, my *tukul*, it was an old presbytery, the porch we sat on was the spire of the church, and we plan to expand this way and this way and this way, until we have established the greatest coffee-producing concern in the whole wide world! At which point the people threw me up and down in a blanket, cheering and clapping and crying my name.

Lucy seemed unimpressed. As everyone went back to work, laughing and slapping each other on the back, she lit another cigarette and wiped out my map with her foot, the dust gathering between her long brown toes. Then she spat a gob of tobacco on my desert lands, sending the ants scurrying.

Lucy spent the rest of the afternoon giving me Chinese

burns, which, like my erections, were my first ever. It had been quite a day! When she tired of this, she said I could give her a Chinese burn too if I liked, so I tried, I gripped her forearm in both hands and twisted her flesh this way and that, but Lucy just sat there quietly, smoking her cigarette, until I gave up in exhaustion and asked her to do it to me again, which she did until I cried.

Where had Lucy come from where was she going what was she doing? Women came from everywhere, picked her up, prodded her, held her upside-down and shook her by the ankles, Lucy calmly smoking a cigarette as they did so. Theories were tossed back and forth, proposed, discussed, rejected and then proposed again with subtle variations. The girl was deserted at birth. She was raised by wolves. She had come from the sky. Her parents were killed, her parents threw her out, she had no parents, she is an earth spirit, a sky spirit, what's her name?, *Lucy, she told the boy her name is Lucy*, she stuck out her hand and he shook it. They took her to the nearby watering-hole (here, sir, where baptisms have been performed since before the birth of Christ!) and scrubbed her and repeated their questions and stamped on her foot and tweaked her ears and she still wouldn't answer, but that comes later, for now she's mine, they can go away, for now and just for now Lucy is mine.

That night, after Lucy had gone to Tekle's, after Tekle had offered her a home, I lay in bed and thought about her her her, my stomach in a knot that I thought was love but which was probably caused by the cigarettes, which taught me there and then that love and pain are two sides of a coin, thus fucking up my relationships with women for ever. And as I lay there I touched behind my ear for a coffee bean that wasn't there and I felt alone, which taught me that the absence of the loved one makes you love them even more, thus fucking up my relationships with women for ever. And that night, for the first time in Ethiopia, I didn't wet the bed, thus learning that love makes a man of you, and your cock belongs to them, which, alas (are you getting all of this?), fucked up my relationships with women for ever.

And every night when I fall asleep I am back there, another Ethiopian night, every night. How many were there? Five years, so 1500 give or take, eight hours a pop, so 10,000 hours, as many hours as there are stars in the sky, give or take. I replay them again and again here. One night kept awake by a mosquito as loud as thought, another with some animal scratching at the cracked wood of the hut, one when my mother's dry-retching kept a randomness that made sleep impossible, one where I peed so much I shat myself, and one where I woke to find a fat fat bug sitting dead centre in the middle of my palm its cheeks puffed out like Louis Armstrong's. And always that first night of Lucy.

And always the smell of rancid butter and cow dung,

my father's shit, coffee and *awazi*. Voices in the distance talking in a thousand tongues, never shutting the fuck up or, worse, shutting the fuck up and letting in the sound of gelada baboons rutting and hyenas howling, a thousand thousand slimy things rooting, eating, shitting. Plants growing, I swear to God I could hear plants growing, bursting their sides with big fat growth, and then the night of circumcisions and then the night of gunshots, and then the night of Holbrook falling down on the veranda pissed, the night of Holbrook bringing back the head of a nyala, and the night of the man left tied to the tree after a beating, I don't know who, I don't know why, and this was the great seething mass that Kebreth hoped to tame with books, and me with money, and if the only sound he hears now is worms against his casket and the only sound I hear is the beep of machines and the sound of trolleys rolling down corridors, that only proves that money is better than books and all other things made of myths and paper.

I have never been so alone as I was on those nights. They think they have me alone here, but I know that the tube that stretches from me up into the wall is joined to a network of other tubes, stretching from other arms, sluicing out blood or pumping in sedation, so the whole hospital is a living thing, one giant organism joined at the veins, and I think to myself that if I squeeze this clear tube shut some other condemned fucker three wards down will die of a heart attack, and maybe thank me for it in heaven.

Kebreth loved the nights, of course. *It's the time of subterfuge, Teddy!* He told me he spent that first night watching our house, taking in the design, the possibilities, destroying it again and again in his mind, doors walls flying outwards, bodies flying outwards, the blue-winged goose perched on the eaves sucked into the flame, burnt crisp and trying to drag itself clear by a single charred wing. And in that heartbeat before the screams, that wing beat before the howls, achieving once and only once true and absolute silence. You see, Teddy, after that all hell will break loose, but that moment, that moment, there will be a silence made that will enter the heart of every man who hears it, and they will want it and need it and do any deed necessary to find it again; it will drive them mad with desire and they will chase it through every day and every night and it will be called Socialism and Pan-Africanism and it will be the peace at the end of a long long road, and he said a whole lot of stuff, Kebreth, always another bullshit scheme, and I believed it all because I was ten years old and I just wanted the noise to stop, and you can put that on my gravestone.

But no one was ever killed by Kebreth's bombs, except some poor innocent in reprisal, and with every subsequent explosion it was the same, Kebreth failing to kill my father, another young man taken away by Holbrook and shot, and when I think of my last months in Ethiopia it is the sound of bombs that comes back to me, some loud, as Kebreth accidentally blew up another tree, some soft, distant, muffled, as the first scuffles between the Italians and the Ethiopians began, gradually getting closer, but not a lot, and I was safe and sound in London by the time they rained down on Harar and finished what Kebreth had begun.

The hospital smells different today, more antiseptic, if such a thing were possible. Perhaps my nostrils are losing their lower register, the happy smell of sick dark urine and rotting human flesh that has been the glorious *basso continuo* of my olfactory life here. Today I can smell only the high, fluting tones of bleach and peroxide. This is either a good thing or a bad thing. Another bit of me gone, I guess. Bad, then.

There was a time when this nose of mine could distinguish between an *arabica* bean and a *robusta*, a *liberica* and an *esliaca*, or a *canephora* or *racemosa* at fifty paces, and then take a handful of one, a cup of another, a teaspoon of a third and a pinch of a fourth and produce a blend that would make you feel like a god and give you a hard-on for days. Now that's a magician!

Meanwhile, in the now, they have been trying to feed me toast. I take this as an encouraging sign. Last night I ate a whole triangle of the stuff, start to finish, crusts and all, to put hairs on my chest. Big and strong. It is my dream some day to consume an entire slice. Fanfare for the common man.

My love, the red-haired nurse, Siobhan, tells me that my vital signs have improved, a runic message that I don't spoil by enquiring into further. I like mystery in my women!

Yesterday she told me my blood pressure was higher, today she told me it was lower. I don't know which is better, nor do I wish to. I do know that the pressure band around my arm gets tighter each time she inflates it, and that one day it will splinter the bones in my fragile arms, but I always affect an air of stoicism in her company now, brave soldier, except when she inserts my catheter when I weep like a baby, overcome by pain and, be honest, certain sentimental attachments. She comforts me as I sob, which is all you can ask for, really.

Lovejoy usually appears shortly afterwards. He has taken to placing his hands in the pockets of his coat as he talks to me, rolling a coin in his fingertips, no doubt. I am onto him! My white blood count is down. Or up. He tells me that it is good that this is happening, whichever it is. I imagine him sitting in his bed in the evening, looking up from his copy of *New Scientist* and telling his doctor wife – she will definitely be a doctor wife – that my white blood count is down. Or up. They smell of soap, the pair of them. That I know.

For myself, I avoid turning the shards of information that Lovejoy throws out at me into anything resembling hope. I take the bread on to my tongue, my triangle of toast, but do so with ritualistic boredom, like when I would attend Moira's church on a Sunday, performing for her family without thought of a paradise to come. Hope would draw me out of this room, imply a future beyond it, and I'm just getting settled; my bedsores have nestled precisely into their respective grooves of linen.

I even feel an odd affection for it, this room, my restive

final resting place. The metal, the white walls. No bars on the window, which is thoughtful. They have given me back some of my stuff. There are boxes under my bed that contain more wisdom than you'll ever know, scraps of paper covered with bits of information gleaned from all the emotional ports of my human being, all thirty-six of them, together with not a little flaking skin. Audit me and be done!

I like to think Siobhan reads these scraps during the night, sitting beside my bed as I sleep, a single tear running down her pearly face as she silently mouths the words on the torn bottom halves of affidavits, the numbers scrawled on cheque stubs by interchangeable accountants, the mind-numbing paragraphs in the annual business statements of Everett and Sons Coffee. She weeps for what could have been if I were not a filthy diseased husk of a man repulsive to the human eye. It's my bravery she loves, I can tell. It takes all my strength to tell her with my eyes that she will, one day, find another.

I want to tell her that she has the same nose as my Latino secretary Marta, whom my first wife adored because she had made herself totally sexless, forcing my bejewelled angel to recognise with full force, and then exaggerate, her own wild proclivities, set in sharp relief as they were. Marta was there when we first got back from Cuba, dragging our love-less marriage from continent to continent to see if it stank as much in different locations. My first wife was still aflame from the attentions of Carlo the Cuban Revolutionary, I must tell you about Carlo the Cuban Revolutionary. Every time Marta entered the room my wife would go into a hot flush. And every time she left we would have to make love on my desk to prevent her murdering someone. She would cry Marta's name as she came, inadvertently at first and then, sensing a possible short cut, with gay abandon, turning her head towards the door behind which sat her Latin fantasy.

Marta's leaving in the evening became over time a studied performance. She would neither avert her eyes, nor stare, goodbye, Mrs Everett, and my first wife copying her, goodbye, Marta, only the shaking of her hands and the heaviness of the air giving anything away.

The night of the proposed ménage we invited Marta to dine with us at the Ritz. We spent the night listening to the scraping of cutlery on plates. My wife would occasionally sally forth into conversation, lobbing anecdotes towards us, and then lugubriously twisting them around to make them about sex. She discussed first boyfriends over the lobster bisque, the discovery of masturbation during Caesar salad, polyandry with the rainbow trout and potatoes, and finally the perversity of human desire over the cheese and crackers.

It was with the coming of the coffee that my first wife could stand no more, launching into a deranged panegyric on the pleasures of anal sex, Sapphism, nymphomania, S & M and glory-hole blow-jobs, before tearing open her twin set and throwing herself on Marta's disinterested body, an assault that Marta met defiantly, sexlessly, with a perfectly aimed upper cut, her signet ring leaving a scar on my first wife's chin that she would never lose.

Happy days, Siobhan, happy days!

But for now I prefer to talk about Moira, because she was my favourite wife, and I loved her and lost her, and that always appeals to a broad audience.

Moira was the third of twelve or fifth of sixteen or something. Farm people. Catholics. Her father had engaged himself conjugally with her mother every Christmas Day of his married life, producing, with admirable strength of character, boy girl boy girl year after year, deviating from his relentless production of alternating sexes only when he predicted drought and felt that a glut of three boys might be in order. Two or three had fallen in the war, *brave souls*, an event her father had failed to predict. They were celebrated in the dining room of the Callaghans by a collection of modest shrines, pictures candles rosary beads. Moira's mother would point at them solemnly whenever anyone uttered anything resembling a profanity, as if their death in the blood and shit of France had invested them with an abiding sanctity above and beyond us profane fuckers watching on.

Moira's mother had borne the role of human incubator with a determined fatalism until the arrival of the first set of grandchildren, which awakened in her the blinding realisation that she didn't actually like children all that much, and she let motherhood fall away with barely a shrug, leaving the raising of the last two or three (or four) children to Moira. She resisted all further attempts at impregnation through a regime of television, prayer and an imposing fortress of underthings, *Krak de Bustier*.

Family dinners were a riot of sons, daughters, nephews, nieces, an ever-expanding mass with only the occasional heart attack to cull the numbers, a brimming roomful of people who had nothing to say to each other but who must keep talking in case anyone accidentally said anything.

The largest portions at dinner were reserved for her father, with an indistinguishable group of brothers and brothers-in-law taking the next share. Grace was a Byzantine affair, with God being thanked for every possible favour he had bestowed on the assembled Callaghan multitudes. When I was in attendance, with my gold cards and silk socks, her father would open one eye and look at me as he thanked the Redeemer for when the family had survived on one potato, *not like some*.

Moira's father was a solid and ruddy-faced man who liked things boiled, hated blacks and the English, and who spent an hour a day on the toilet. His joke to me was 'What's wrong with tea, then?'

He was resolute in his belief that there was a God, and that God was a Catholic, so those who weren't Catholic were condemned to eternal punishment by the Devil, a short man dressed in red, with a pitchfork, who lived in hell. Mass was the best insurance against getting one's gonads flambéed, and he would throw himself into the gymnastics of the second half of Mass with a fervour undimmed by weekly observance for more than seventy years. When the rest of the congregation would perform the ritual of standing kneeling shaking hands and God be with you with a practised minimalism, he would fling himself around his pew as though the whole experience was new to him, a weekly revelation, and perhaps it was.

Legend has it that Moira's father even went through a

phase of clapping at the end of each Mass – a tendency the other parishioners could only defend themselves against by joining in, much to the bemusement of the Monsignor, who was eventually forced to take his overenthusiastic lamb to one side and point out that such percussive enthusiasm was the sort of thing that spawned the Baptists, you know, the one with the darkies.

Moira's mother, if less convinced of the certitude of the existence of the Almighty, was more certain of the things of the earthly realm. Whether, for instance, her children were showing the desired quantities of Humility, Charity, Willingness to Get Wed, Willingness to Get Pregnant, Willingness to Burst Forth with the Gift of Life. etc., and whether they were keeping in touch with the Church, with the Monsignor and with Mrs Bumfluff up the road who made the Cheesecake or some such crap, and whether her daughter Moira was serious about the divorcee she kept bringing to dinner.

Whenever I was there, the Callaghans would invite the Monsignor over for dinner. He was an ancient creature constructed out of soapy skin and melanomas, with enormous, thickly veined ears, and a nose from which thick tufts of ginger hair hung, swaying in the breeze. Dear god his God had made him ugly! One of his eyes was glass, and the other had acquired a thick film of milky residue, which, once, during one of the interminable Callaghan dinners, I had the misfortune to see drip out of his eye and into his soup, ripples of the white effluvia spreading outwards through the puréed pumpkin before being gently stirred in by His Holiness, as one would cream.

The Monsignor was as old as God, and had, by a lifetime of genuflecting and the giving of succour, developed a pronounced stoop, which meant that he directed all of his conversation towards your genitals, turning his head to one side and pressing his ear to your crotch to hear the replies. He was a man who, like Christ, found no human folly absurd, delighted as he was in the absurdity of life, to the point that Good and Evil had become unnecessary to him, and he spent much of his time subtly but decisively removing any reference to God from his sermons, which became, instead, half-hour anecdotes concerning juicy bits of local gossip, and his luck or otherwise, at the previous day's race meet. I believe the Callaghans used to invite him to dinner so Moira's father could convert him to Catholicism.

During dinner, the only word the Monsignor ever spoke was *mmm*. This was used to approve the quality of the cooking, as a question (with an upturning of the eyebrows), as an answer to a question (with a nod), and as a method of acknowledging the quiet beauty of the world itself. I have never been so close to murder. The instant he finished eating he would fall asleep in his chair, which meant the rest of us had to sit there squirming until he woke up, it being bad luck to wake a monsignor (Leviticus something

something). When he woke, *Mmm?*, coffee was served. Instant. Ehler's Brand A. Made by Moira.

Inevitably these evenings, invariably these evenings, always these evenings, would end with me being left alone with the Monsignor either to scare me off, or to work on my salvation. I would sit quietly in my armchair, my nails digging into the leather, as he gradually roused himself from another stupor. He would start with trivialities, as though we were having a conversation, before moving, so so slowly, on to the wretched banalities of his faith.

What a desiccated religion he was peddling! Such thin gruel. He presented the Mystery to me as though it were *The Times*'s crossword. The Afterlife as Boston. As he spoke the colours of Abyssinia would come roaring back into my mind, the reds the greens the purples, the singing, the dancing. Somewhere, at some time, in this *papier-mâché* religion of his, this flame must have burnt too, but not now. This was a religion of consolation, nothing more, and I found no consolation in it. I was so polite to him. I thanked him for his time and offered him another biscuit.

I have never ever worked so hard to get a girl as I did on those long nights.

The chaplain who visits me here in the hospital is young and fresh and smells of peppermint, and he knows I am a lost cause, hell bound at best, so he doesn't bother to talk about God, or death, or salvation. I'm not sure he's that interested in those things himself – last time he was here he spent twenty minutes asking me for advice on coffee machines, he and his wife have a new flat, I bet it smells of peppermint and I bet she does too, and he gives me a firm handshake as he leaves, knowing that next time he comes back there might be someone else on mattress 46 and not caring a jot.

Years later after we were married Moira told me that the Monsignor had, when she was nine or ten, taken her aside and told her gravely that her uncle so-and-so didn't believe in God. She was shocked, bless her, because she knew that if you didn't believe in God then you must be evil, she had heard stories, her mother had told her stories. So Moira lay in bed that night and thought about her uncle, and thought her uncle must be evil, and she set her mind to think of the most evil thing a person could be.

So she decided he must be a robber. She told all her friends that her uncle didn't believe in God because he was a robber.

Oh, Moira, my innocent and awkward love. Here I lie, like Jesus himself, surrounded by robbers at the Hour of My Death, wishing only to hold your awkward flesh in my withered arms. It was your awkwardness that got me in from the start, of course. I have always been a sucker for an awkward girl, a shy girl, the sort that never shits, the sort that turns on the tap in the hotel bathroom so you can't hear her pee. I have fallen on my knees before these women, knelt before the most ungainly, the most uncertain frames imaginable. I have pressed my cheeks against the blushes of shy girls, sixteen-year-olds in thick glasses who sneeze out of turn and can only talk about ponies, who play the cello badly and have no friends, and the heat of their reddening cheeks has sustained me more than the perfection of a supermodel. To kiss a foot shod in a sensible brown shoe has always appealed so much more than a perfect arch in a high heel, a skirt below the knee has always inflamed me more than one above. My red-haired nurse never makes me ache more than when she is in her mid-shin tunic, with tan tights and flat blue shoes.

And watching them unfurl in bed, these skittery angels, their rigid bodies beginning, clumsily at first and then with more confidence, to move with mine, their fists unclenching and resting speculatively on the middle of my back, perhaps reaching down to touch my buttock, their tongues gradually emerging and meeting mine, their polite fake orgasms turning, fingers crossed!, into real ones.

And the pleasure of leaving them! Of compounding their saintliness with a gesture of reproach, of rejection. The pleasure of tears moistening behind those thick glasses which

Never happened! I mean, Christ, what was I to them? A rich man, a novelty, but ultimately no different from the men in their childhood who would ask them to raise their skirts for a fiver, the men who made them rigid and scared to begin with, except with me they got dinner and maybe a trip on an aeroplane, plus the vague and unspoken possibility of salvation. Of pumpkins turned into carriages and dormice into stallions, a slipper that fits and will pad about halls palatial. But, Christ, the conversation they had to endure on the off chance of that, me moaning, ever moaning, *my wife, my wife, my wife.*

Lucy.

The psychiatrists of this world would point to the inept hands of my mother fumbling with my shirt buttons of course, the eternal search for clumsy women to lift and then destroy, your shame and anger, Mr Everett, dovetailing with the traces of your clattering and stilted pubescence. Let them. I don't claim to be psychologically complex. I don't claim anything.

I would watch Moira at these family gatherings, watch her being bruised at every turn by this gathering of morons, and with every declaration of her hopelessness I would fall more deeply in love. It's a good feeling! Treating her like a princess in front of them, lifting her above their wretched lives and idiotic intrigues, punishing them for trying to do to her what I had seen done to my mother. *I do not claim to be psychologically complex* but it gave me a satisfaction beyond words.

The heady pleasures of hubris! Who will speak up for the heady pleasures of hubris?! Of knowing that Moira and I would eventually get our comeuppance and fall from the skies, passing the dogged Callaghans on our way down, raising our middle digits as we went past, mine anyway, because they would never get so high, even their heaven was not so high.

Here to here to here

On second thoughts, forget them, they don't belong here, the Callaghans. They just confuse things, this lot. I'm having more and more trouble holding this together, there's too many people, too many fucking people, this is my coffee story, they don't need to be here, they can all fuck off, because my coffee story is about Lucy, it's about Lucy.

Lucy Alfarez walked out of the jungle at the age of fourteen with a silver lighter in one hand and a coffee bean in the other. It's 1931. We have been in Ethiopia for six months, my mother in bed for five of those, my private tutor Mr Birtwhistle missing, unmourned, for three.

To this day I wonder what became of Birtwhistle. No I don't. Yes I do.

He was a melancholy man, Birtwhistle, early twenties, bookish and bumbling, and I speculate that he was in love with my mother, based on absolutely nothing. He was an intellectual of mediocre intellect who had seen through the hypocrisy and cant of the world but found nothing with which to replace it. A man of borrowed ideas, desperately pressing any two of them together in the hope of producing a third, and never quite succeeding. He smelt of unfinished novels, unfinished essays and unfinished poems.

On meeting him in London, *This is Mr Birtwhistle, Teddy*, he had spoken through his pipe and into his beard about a proposed *roman à clef* on the emerging middle classes, their troubles and mores, that sort of thing. Later, in Jeddah, I think it was Jeddah, he told me his dream was to study the Muslim, or Mussulmans as he called them, analysing them as a type, a genus if you will, in order to discuss the deleterious effects of their, the Musselmans', inability to absorb the possibility of a tripartite God. Then in Harar it was all Imagist poetry and Ralph Waldo Emerson, plus vague rumours of a novel, a white man's version of Africa. It was also suspected that he might be working on a biography of my grandfather Percival, by that time ensconced on the island of Tinos practising the poetry and voodoo that was to make him a darling of American campuses in the late 1960s.

Birtwhistle brought with him on the ship a motley collection of 'improving literature', Nietzsche and Kierkegaard, tied up with string, which he flicked through occasionally, waiting for some aphorism to illuminate the genius he hoped was latent within him. He also brought a parrot in a cage, which the crew of the P & O *Rampura* threw overboard on the first night of our voyage just to annoy him.

(Birtwhistle, sitting by my rocking bed that first night, his narrow face lit by a flickering orange candle, tells me that sailors have been known to catch pairs of sharks, tear out their eyes, and then make them fight on the decks, throwing buckets of water over them as they thrash about and bite. These are the sort of men we are dealing with, Theodore. Their cruelty to my parrot is symptomatic of their deviance. I have lately become interested in phrenology . . .)

For Birtwhistle, Harar was Rimbaud's city, and to be following in the footsteps of the great annihilator filled him with an almost erotic energy. I think he dreamt of finding a lost scrap of poetry tucked into the city walls, left there especially for him, *Dear Sir, The world is fucked etc, love Arthur.*

He tried to tutor me on precisely one occasion, painfully awkward for both of us. Me at my desk, in our *tukul*, the sound of workers picking coffee in the background, me in shorts, socks, the whole palaver, him shuffling from one foot to the other in front of me, silent. Fifteen minutes of this and then 'Keats!' ejaculated forth in a mixture of inspiration and desperation. Followed by a forty-five-minute soliloquy on the failure of the poetic to learn the lessons of the prosaic, or vice versa. Palgrave's *Golden Treasury* was to blame. Poetry does not yield to the exclusion inherent in taxonomy. The only good life is the poetic life, the life of the mind, and it was people like my father, yes, your father, Theodore, who are sucking the human capacity for the aesthetic life out of the world. He supposed that I would do the same, oh yes, boy, you won't have a choice, by the time you are my age it will be too late, you'll have been sucked into the machine. Well, I proclaim the Overman, the meeting of Dionysus and Apollo! Plato be damned – the poet shall have the Polis! He slammed his hand down on the desk in front of me, a clear teardrop of mucus hanging from his nostril, making a small rainbow. I met your grandfather once, he said. The mystic. He was wearing a caftan. We talked into the night, and I saw in him the possibility of salvation. Africa! This is the birthplace, the seat of civilisation! Read your Conrad, your Rider Haggard. Burton, Stanley, Frazer. This is the cradle, the heart, the womb.

He gulped at a coffee, annoying me.

I felt I could help to save you, Teddy, guide you into the light. I have been working on a book. Prose and poetry and philosophy combined, our Western divisions broken down by this melting pot of a continent. Looking out of my tiny Salisbury window, looking into the base parts of my own soul, I have conjured up Africa. Drums and spears and fear. I came to bare my damaged soul and rebuild myself. But here . . . in this land . . . of . . . of . . . primitives . . . There is not enough light! The sun itself has not enough light to banish this darkness!

The drop of mucus fell from his nose and landed on the back of his hand. We both ignored it. I stared into his eyes and watched his brain searching for a new thought, something elevated, something profound, watched as it once again reached its limit and stopped. Never fall in love, he said.

He stopped on the hour and walked out, leaving me sitting there for another hour until I realised he wasn't coming back. The next morning he was gone, his books left behind – Nietzsche, some Pound, *In the Steps of the Master* by H. V. Morton, *The Tempest* and *Mrs Dalloway*, all of them with dumb-ass underlinings and annotations. *How true, how true.* I hid them under my bed until a year later my father fell on his arse trying to pull his sock on and discovered them, and had them burnt immediately.

I tried to track down Birtwhistle, years later, in the full flush of the crushing boredom you can only get from wealth, but never found a trace. It's possible my father had him rubbed out by Holbrook, BANG, but I prefer to imagine he simply wandered into the woods, his heart broken by his unrequited love for my mother, his damsel, his soul afire with the search for truth, ending his days worshipped as a god by the ululating natives, or boiling in a pot, straight out of *Punch* magazine.

And me? I took the journey you asked of me, Birtwhistle, you stupid fuck. More than you ever did. I analysed analysed analysed and in the end I will burn for it. If you're going to have a dream of Utopian Leftist Freedom, you're always going to end up in Western Capitalist Jail.

It was while tracing the fortunes of Birtwhistle that I started constructing my map, I think it was then anyway, all of those financial reports in all of those filing cabinets, turned upside-down, reversed, placed face down, the flowcharts and the graphs face down on the carpet, and each with a little number in the top corner, 1 through 264, so I could pack them away and then put them back together again. I drew from memory the contours of the Horn of Africa in my unsteady hand. Some of the pages took two, three, a hundred tries to get right, tracing again and again the curve of the land above Debre Damo, the sudden downward sweep of the Ogaden border, the jumpy escarpments where the Gambela National Park clattered against Sudan (I would place a cross on these pages: why is the border this shape exactly?, what wars were fought over this whorl of land pressed against my fingerprints?, who died and how?) and then crawling across it, the paper CRINKLING beneath my knees as I ran Matchbox cars across Addis to Awash, tracing the route back from the Coronation, and Birtwhistle I placed on a whim at the foot of Gara Mulets, just outside Harar, he wouldn't have got much further. Once I had him wandering about the Blue Nile like Livingstone, but he wouldn't have got more than a hundred miles on foot, nice to speculate, though.

I spent years crawling all over that map, looking for clues, trying to conjure these half-fragments of memory into some cohesive narrative, tracing my finger north from Harar to Adowa, west from Adowa to Abobo, south from Abobo to Kebri Dehar, and north again to Harar. There was a picture of Selassie on my wall, my fellow exile, my fellow returned head of the corporation, there was a picture of the sulphurous Danakil Depression on my wall, there was a picture of a gelada baboon on my wall, there was a picture of a young Balcha Safo on my wall – I met him once, an old man, riding off to fight the Italians. There was a jar of desert sand on my desk. A branch of a *kojo* tree.

I took a penknife from the basement mail room, a hundred floors below, and wood from the surrounding parklands, and took up my whittling again, my big-man hands even clumsier than before, carving my wooden animals and saints; I kept them in a pencil case when I wasn't using them, it was one of those ones that lets you slip the letters of your name into plastic slots on the side T H E O D O R E E V E R E T T, and I'd keep it in the top drawer of my desk so nobody saw.

My wives, the first one and then, later, Moira, would burst into the office sometimes, their only shared gesture, and find me building the Harar walls out of matchsticks, staplers, ring binders. My briefcase was the rise outside the walls where it all went to hell, Kebreth an English Waterloo soldier, Holbrook a Prussian, my father an Easter egg given to me by my secretary, Lucy a babushka doll. I was me, gun in hand, a real gun, towering over them, a god, able to change everything, and yet always playing out the scene exactly as it happened, BANG, BANG, BANG, BANG, and then curling myself up in a ball, the gun heavy, and Moira would hold me every time until she didn't care any more and she left me.

He's mad that Teddy Everett!

I would stay there deep into the night, as the offices below me sighed to sleep, my light the only one left blazing, a beacon of hope to passing sailors, me sitting cross-legged on the edge of the map, dropping ash from my cigarette on to it as my ancestors had once done, the burning embers spiralling downwards on to the volcanoes of the Danakil, and is that red wine staining Harar itself like blood?

Night after night flat on my belly gazing down at Harar, smoothing my tie down whenever it went askew, gazing down at those little figures from my past, and when I closed my eyes they would rise up above me again, Kebreth, Lucy, Tekle, Ababa, Kwibe, rise up and stand around my prone figure, chattering endlessly, accusations mostly, accusations exclusively, and more than once I jerked awake clutching handfuls of my paper kingdom, which I would have to flatten down carefully and repair.

As the sun began to rise over New York, and hence over the Chercher Mountains of Eastern Ethiopia, I would slowly, carefully, pick up my wooden fauna and place them in my pencil case, with Lucy, Kwibe, Kebreth and the rest. Then pack the paper up in numerical order and lie the sheets back in the filing cabinet, before quietly shutting the drawer and returning to my desk.

Did I ever go back there, to Ethiopia? No, I never went back there.

I was sitting beside the map when they found me, of course, years later, when they came to arrest me, that same map, those same figurines, me alone in my bedroom, naked, smoking, a cup of coffee going cold on the Gojam desert, they were so gentle with me, lifting me up, so gentle, so tender, giving me the privileged treatment reserved for the insane, and only one of them hit me, crunch, on the side of my head, because someone had to hit me for all I had done, knocking me on all fours like an animal, before lifting me up again, gently, tenderly, and letting me get dressed before they put the cuffs on, before they shoved me out into the flashbulbs, my bloody nose and my tears proof I had resisted arrest.

Lucy Alfarez walked out of the jungle at the age of four-teen with a silver lighter in one hand and a coffee bean in the other. Deep in the jungle, Mr Birtwhistle crouches, watching her through eucalyptus branches that he holds back with an extended hand, like in a movie. We can only hear his breathing.

He watches the girl from behind, running his eyes up those long, toned legs. Her skin is coffee-coloured, as, he thinks, all skin will be one day, once the races have truly mingled, the Intellect of the Overman combined with the Physicality of the Negro. He scribbles *Miscegenation!* in his notebook, next to the circled word *Berlioz!*, and below the crossed-out word *Lingam*. He searches his brain for a concept to capture this moment, but the odds-and-sods cupboard that is his mind is full of the girl's legs, those lovely silky legs, and the tune of 'My Bonny Lies Over the Ocean', which has been stuck there for a month.

Now the father is taking the girl away, the little hussy, what will he do with her?, would that the mother were free, I would take her with me. I think I am in love with her. He writes the word LOVE in his notebook, circles it and crosses it out. An affective fallacy. Has anyone explored that idea? I must think! I must go away from here and think! This could be it!

He lets go of the branch, and disappears back into the African jungle.

Did I mention I have only one testicle? Not easy to forget a thing like that. It was an unrelated cancer, a 1970s cancer, glitterballs and tubular steel. Moira discovered the lump, bless her, cupping my balls in one of her pretty round hands as she did sometimes while falling asleep, a protective, asexual gesture for her that left me wanting to bite a hole in the bedpost. The night she found it, *What's this, Teddy?*, was the first time I ever knew, for certainly certainly certain, that *I* was going to die, no one had told me before, the others made sense, but me?! I remember the fear starting in my bollocks, a tingle that turned to ice and ran up my spine and into my brain, rising to the surface intermittently over the next twenty years, never any nicer, often much worse.

It was a night of mirrors, that night, me squatting above them, Moira and I peering ashen-faced into that cold reflection, that cold and dreadful reflection, moving my testicles this way and that, holding them at an angle, holding them flat, looking for clues. And then, with Moira in a fitful sleep, me gazing into the bathroom mirror at three a.m., cold with fear, the lump between my legs weighing me down like a ball and chain. I would have sliced the damn thing off there and then, given a good blade, whipped it off and flushed it down the loo, job done. The next morning was the first time I'd ever seen a doctor, and I left five grams lighter, boom boom. But I still have all of my own teeth, boom boom.

Even now when the nurses turn me over to intrude again, my greatest shame is reserved for that redundant half-filled sack dangling beneath me. So many things to be ashamed of, but that's the one I'll have trouble telling St Peter about. Must we be so relentlessly flesh?

It wasn't long after the operation that Moira left me. It

was unrelated. It *was* unrelated. It was *unrelated*. *It* was unrelated. She sat me down one day, Teddy, I think we need to talk, and told me she'd had enough, don't say anything, you know what I'm talking about, and all I could feel was the space between my legs, everything about me was nauseating absence, and as she drove away in the back of that boxy taxi, it was that tiny lopsided weight hanging down that I could feel more than anything, the centre of my being, off to one side.

It was then that the cancer saw its chance, of course. It saw that the man with one testicle was a man no more, his woman had left him after all, and it started working its way through my body, belly, ribs and then lungs, check out these lungs!, and and and

The rest of me is catching up now, falling away, returning to dust. I am mostly bedsores. My fingernails are yellow, my toenails purple. My skin flakes until it is covered with a white cream, then it becomes itchy, until I scratch it and it flakes again. My face is shaved regularly by a disinterested male nurse, and each time I feel the blade getting closer and closer to the white bones beneath as the skin gets thinner and thinner. My eyesight remains perfect, untested as it is over distances of more than three metres. My brain remains my best feature, never sleeping, never stopping, grey with fear. Presumably bits of it have gone too, but I guess I'll be the last to know. Boom boom. Maybe there was a far richer story in there than the one I am telling. Other obsessions. Some great Colombian story about the assassination of Gaitan, of Rojas and La Violenzia. Other girls I fell in love with and lost, who weren't called Lucy, and other Lucys who I met and who didn't destroy my life.

By the time Lucy arrived my mother had already become supine, unlovable, and those who would deign to love her, the Birtwhistles and Salezes of this world, would have had to forage beneath a mountain of quilts and eiderdowns for the merest glimpse of any part of their beloved below the Adam's apple. She had taken the heat of Ethiopia and clasped it about her, keeping her enemy close, falling in and out of sleep to the drip drip drip of her own perspiration on the uneven floors.

This was Ethiopia to her, this was it, a bed in a room no bigger than mine now, surrounded by lopsided walls within which incomprehensible black saints scrabbled around in the night, and to which clung incomprehensible black sinners, fixing the camber of a door frame, watching her from the corner of an eye, the nameless Other, the smell of their sweat. Faces at windows, gazing in unselfconsciously, as at a zoo, observing her behaviour and discussing it. A language impossible to understand ringing in her ears despite all of those French lessons at school, *Quelle heure est-il?*, *Il est trois heures et quart*.

Sniffing the wind, taking the temperature of the future, doing the maths and coming up with a result that was fucking horrible at best, my mother had retired to this bed the day of Haile Selassie's Coronation, never to emerge.

It was a hell of a day, Selassie's Coronation! You should have been there! Everything everywhere was in a state of high excitement, preparing for the glorious ascension of this glorious Lion of Judah. Decorations were laid out, banners and posters. New roads and new cars to go on them. Ceremonies of every conceivable religion in every conceivable colour, from the most ancient religions, the Christian Monophysites, the Jews, the Muslims, down to religions that would be born that day and gone by sunset, they called themselves the April the Thirders, syncretic and given to wailing, retiring to slim beds at midday in the hope of conceiving a child on this holy, holy day.

The trip from Harar to Addis Ababa took us a day and a night, the same Model T Ford materialising again on the day of our departure, the same dwarf behind the wheel, singing the same interminable song. My father sat up front, me and Holbrook in the back, and no one can drive that fast.

Selassie had spent the night in the Royal Cathedral of St George, praying with the Archbishop. It's proper serious, what he's doing. He's the 225th monarch of the Solomonic line, stretching back to the Queen of Sheba's night with the King. His wife Menen prays beside him. Yesterday they were watching the Duke of Gloucester unveil a statue of Menelik II; tomorrow he will be the Lion of Judah. All those internecine battles are over! The pretender, the apostate, Iyasu seen off! The physical but not spiritual descendents of Menelik gone! They say that as Emperor Haile Selassie never revealed the man behind the crown, he became regal to his core, but I like to think that at some stage during the night he squeezed Menen's hand and said, Goodness!

He has spent three million quid on the knees-up – it was a lot of money in those days, but the Empire was glorious – and invited the great and the good of the world to watch, my father and his son included. He has, they say, the Ark of the Covenant with him, so God has an invite too. For some, *Salut, my Rasta friends!*, this is the most important moment in history.

Did you ever think of me, Emperor Selassie? Do emperors daydream? As you sat there for year upon year, observing visiting dignitaries bowing and scraping before your velvet throne, did Teddy Everett ever cross your mind? The small boy you glanced at during your investiture, later the powerful man who bought and sold your coffee? I thought of you often, the friend I never had, the enemy I never defeated. I thought of that glance, a millisecond of my life, and what is life but a collection of milliseconds, and who knows which will carry any weight, now and at the moment of our death?

I ran from the car as soon as we were home to tell Kebreth all about the Coronation, about the marching bands and the press photographers, and he spat out his *chat* and said, What about the lepers, fuck him, the lepers Haile Selassie had removed from the city and dumped at the outskirts, and they liked little white boys, liked to hold them in their twisted limbs GOTCHA and sometimes their limbs fall off, Teddy, because they're already dead but not dead and and and

They are my night-time companions, the lepers, instead of sleep, they crowd around my bed and check that I am getting the facts right, they whisper in my ear the order of things, they argue about causes and effects, about whether my mother chose of her own free will to swallow the word 'death', or whether it slipped down in a moment of weakness, the once healthy are always weakest when they are sick, we who are sick are always much stronger and and and and

And amid the bustle of life in the grip of a single idea, an entire population transfixed by this regal moment, my mother, who had never once felt at one with the rhythms of her surroundings, who had never once found herself part of a common humanity, sank like a stone. When I came home from the Coronation she was in bed, one of her headaches, and she would stay there for the next three years, beneath the faded outline of an absent cross, tended only by my silent friend Kwibe Abi, until she died and she was dead.

Let me tell you about Kwibe Abi.

Kwibe Abi always came out of the forest quietly and sideways, emerging as though the forest itself had dreamt him up, generating him out of its own superabundance, a succulent leaf made flesh. He was as silent as the trees, Kwibe Abi, and to this day, I cannot remember whether he and I ever spoke to each other. When I think back to him, I always see him, silent and sullen, sitting just over there, just to one side of whatever was going on, silent. Me sitting on the porch, Kwibe Abi sitting under a tree nearby, sitting at the bottom of the steps, sitting on the second bottom step, sitting on the same step as me, but at the far end. I liked to whittle blocks of wood into animals, he liked to whittle too, but I never saw what he made. I don't think he ever made anything, *nada*, nil.

He was an inconclusive whittler, Kwibe Abi!

His parents were both dead. This was a given fact and required no investigation; I was ten years old, so I didn't investigate. Our games were wordless, had no rules. They would simply begin, a ball being hit against a wall, a branch being thrown, and then they would continue until they stopped. I don't remember laughing while we played, we were in deadly earnest, but the game had no discernible point, other than keeping us playing. He was an orphan, I was soon to be one and Time, not being linear, but curved, had chosen to throw us together at that point, at exactly that point. Of course, once I became an orphan I would be in charge of the third largest business in the world, and Kwibe Abi would be running through the forest with tears in his eyes. But such is the fickleness of Fate!

Why didn't they ask me about that at the trial? I was only trying to overturn the fickleness of Fate!

Kwibe would usually come over in the afternoon, the

sun smacking us around the head, and he would start to draw curves in the sand with a rock, or would throw me a wrapped-up bunch of eucalyptus leaves to use as a ball, or would take off both his shoes and start to run. I can't remember the games starting, the game just was.

Then in the evening he would be there again, and we would watch the sun go down, listen for the hyenas, pretend to be hyenas. Or just lie there under the *kojo* tree and look at the stars, and Tekle told us that those constellations were Cepheus and Cassiopeia, King and Queen of Ethiopia, father and mother of Andromeda, think on that, Teddy Everett, think on that, Kwibe Abi.

It was not until later that I found out that Kwibe was looking after my mother during her, shall we say?, convalescence. When my mother had first taken to her bed it was Mrs Smithers who tended her, when she wasn't having sex with my father!, but as the sex grew more frequent, her ministrations for my mother became correspondingly less, until my mother would go whole days without food, water or company.

Which is the more essential of the three? Discuss.

I would only go in for my goodnight kiss, a simple blessing, a quiet prayer. In the beginning she would ask me about my day, but the sheer monotony of my answers, the sheer monotony of the days, eventually rendered the ritual pointless. As though the prayers weren't.

Sometimes I would show her the animals I had whittled, tell her the stories I had made up for them, but the stories were made up and reality had too much of a hold on her for her to find any pleasure in the fantasies of a small boy, even if he were her own. All stories are lies, and she had given herself over to the truth that life was terrible, and those of us who tried to ignore it were hypocrites. *Which is another story I've made up, another lie.* She never thought that, but I think about her all the time and have to give some reason for her inertia, so why not something grand, why not another big fat lie on top of all the rest?

The change from Mrs Smithers tending to my mother to Kwibe Abi doing so happened seamlessly, almost un-noticed, unnoticed. It seemed the most natural thing in the world, whatever that means. The boy without a mother, the mother without . . . just without. He would take her food and water, three times a day, I saw him through an open window, walking into the room, placing the *wat* and the water beside her, walking out. He never spoke, she never acknowledged him. Later he would come back and take the empty plate, the empty glass, rinse them, dry them and put them away. We passed once, he taking away her evening meal, me going in to receive my nightly benedic-tion. We paused face to face, Kwibe and I, the same height as each other, wearing the same clothes, his face black, mine white. Then he walked on and I went to kneel by my mother's bed, to feel her hand on my head, *Angel of God, my guardian dear, to whom His love commits me here, ever this day be at my side, to light and guard, to rule and guide*, and we spoke our separate *amen*s.

(And God in his heaven did listen to the prayers of the boy and his mother, and He did send down said Guardian Angel to keep and watch over them and from that day forth they were never plagued by any misfortunes, no bad dreams plagued their nights, and their lives were spent in gentle bliss, each sufficient to the other, each dying at precisely the same moment in each other's arms, thus to enter heaven together and dwell for eternity.)

When I went back outside, Kwibe Abi was sitting under the *kojo* tree, throwing a twig into the air to try and make it catch in the branches, and I sat beside him and did the same.

When I close my eyes I am still lying there with Kwibe Abi, beneath that *kojo* tree. There were lots of *kojo* trees, of course, it was bloody Ethiopia, but, listen, they were all contained in this one. No doubt the Buddha parked his arse beneath any number of Bodhi trees before he saw through the veil. So it is under this tree that Kebreth sits, it is from this tree that I break the branch I am whittling when Lucy arrives, a splinter from the True Cross, and it is from this tree that Kebreth's body will swing, eventually, one day, back then, as a warning not to fuck with the House of Everett.

It was from this tree that big fat Tekle Tolossa, the blind man and the seer, broke a branch and taught me to whittle, not that I ever could. Tekle told me that the manifest world is an illusion, *pace* Buddha, *pace* Lenin, and that within every manifest thing, this branch, Teddy, there is the possibility of other things – a horse trying to escape a block of stone, a hyena clawing at the *kojo* wood that can be animated with a few deft cuts, perhaps even a good man inside this wealthy fucker I see before me, Teddy, *tee-hee* – and Tekle would run his knife blade around the bark, into the meat of the wood, a single line drawing out the creature within to sit flat on his palm, newborn and breathing the light air through its nostrils.

You see, Teddy, a hyena! And Tekle would press the middle of his creation with his thumb to snap it in two, drop it in the dust, and wipe his hands together laughing. Gone. Life is transient, Teddy, my son. Remember that and all else follows.

Not transient enough sometimes, Tekle, not transient enough.

Tekle would sit beside Kebreth some evenings, I can see them now. Kebreth scribbling, Tekle's blind eyes staring out across Harar, the silent seer, listening to Kebreth's pencil moving across the pages, taking it all in, nodding his assent occasionally at some piece of wisdom, raising an eyebrow at some piece of foolishness. *Inside Kebreth there is a hero trying to get out, maybe.* Tekle would leave without saying a word, but you could almost see the cord of understanding between them unfurling as he walked away.

As I fall asleep Kebreth keeps writing, filling page after page after page, the thoughts of a man soon to die, the last thing anyone needs. When I wake I am in this hospital bed and Kebreth has been replaced by a blank white wall, utterly effaced, the only writing here the chart at the end of my bed, my self-portrait in numbers and statistics.

I should have died years ago, Kebreth. Cancer is no way to die. I hate dying of cancer. How long have I been here? I keep forgetting to ask Lovejoy. If I could just get a fixed point of reference, something to map my deterioration by. If it's been five years then I'm doing all right, the decay seems reasonable, nothing out of the ordinary, but it may have been five weeks, in which case I am slaloming to hell with abandon. Lovejoy looks the same as when I got here, I think, but he doesn't have a worry in the world – he falls asleep as soon as his head hits the pillow, no ancestors scream their stories in his ear. When he is not here I obsess about time constantly; then, when he arrives, that rude pink face of his makes time stand still and I find myself asking about getting my gown changed and some more moisturiser on my arse.

Siobhan brings me a whole piece of toast and a glass of water, silently, and I do not acknowledge her presence. I am thinking about Lucy.

Once, back in 1931, on the other side of the world, I lay in bed and thought about Lucy. I'm eleven years old, my stomach in a knot that I thought was love but which was caused by the cigarettes. I had left her that first night with Tekle Tolossa and Ababa, they had taken her in, setting up a small cot in their front room, *The Lord has delivered us a child.* Did Lucy lie in bed and think of me? I like to think that she did; I know that she didn't. Every time I try to recall her face it becomes more blurred. Or I view her in flashes, incandescent moments. She can only be captured in gestures, my Lucy. Her gestures were aristocratic. She was the one true aristocrat among us: her fingers should have been bowed by heavy rings, her chest crossed with lace. She had freckles on her chest, and I would watch them out of the corner of my eye, a constellation every bit as compelling as the starry skies above (Theagenes, says Tekle, who is the Perseus figure, lover of Andromeda). I imagine that chest rising and falling as she drifts off to sleep. No, not drifts, Lucy would never have drifted, she would have decided to go to sleep and then gone, bang. It's me who's the coward, the equivocator, the great cunctator.

As Lucy slept Ababa whispered in her ear about the *Zar* spirits that would possess a woman and want her for their own, leaving the woman restless and apathetic until they were placated by all the women getting together at night and dancing, and Lucy believed her, even though anyone with the slightest understanding of basic psychiatry and anthropology would understand that this was simply a symbolic reclamation of female power in the sort of masculine society that leaves women restless and apathetic.

And as Kebreth slept he dreamt of the dictatorship of the proletariat, I guess, tractors and milking machines, that sort of thing. Men on boats.

And as my mother slept

And as I slept, I would hear the saints in the walls, over-turning the condemnation of Flavian and Eusebius, and I would bury my head in the pillow and try to make it stop.

And my father?

My father, not given to the spirit world, or the dictatorship of the proletariat for that matter, would spend these long Ethiopian evenings getting drunk on *tej*, and discussing future land acquisition with his bodyguard, the Neanderthal Holbrook. I haven't told you about him; it's time to tell you about him. You won't like him, you're not supposed to. He's the villain of the piece! I'm not going to humanise him. Any sympathy you feel for him means you're a cunt.

Terence Holbrook was forty-three years old and as ugly as a punch in the face. He never spoke, communicating only by grunts. He was a devotee of James Cagney, and always wore short ties and high-collared waistcoats as a tribute to his hero, even in Ethiopia. The back of his fat neck always glistened with perspiration, which he was forever wiping away with an oversize white handkerchief.

Occasionally he would use the same handkerchief to blow his nose, never failing to look at what he had produced, looking long and hard as though the secrets of the universe were contained in there, held for ever in his mucus. Perhaps they were. They don't seem to be anywhere else. After his ruminations, the handkerchief was shaken once, to remove any hard bits of snot, and returned to his top pocket.

After he shot Kebreth in the head he used the same handkerchief to wipe the blood off his shoes, and his fingerprints off the gun, an unnecessary gesture, but what Cagney would have done.

What else? What else of the grunting Neanderthal Holbrook? I ENJOY HATING HIM. He wore trousers that were too short. He wore slip-on shoes. He could grow stubble in thirty seconds. For more delicate nasal maintenance he used the pinkie of his left hand, and then rolled the deposit between that finger and his thumb, before flicking it into the air. He smoked Capstan Navy Cuts. He always let his coffee go cold, and then he drank it in one draught, between cigarettes. When he wasn't guarding my father's body he was out hunting game, oryx, water buffalo, gazelles. It just wasn't a Saturday if old Mr Holbrook didn't come back with an animal's head. He died in a knife fight in prison in 1956; he was serving time for statutory rape, having married his thirteen-year-old niece. Good.

He was one of my father's four bodyguards, Holbrook being the most senior. The others came later as Kebreth's attempts at assassinating my father increased in frequency. I can't remember anything about them. Just people. One of them might have been Johnson or Thompson. I seem to recall another of them always being halfway through acquiring a moustache, but I might be wrong. One definitely wore white socks. Does that help at all? Are you getting a feel for any of this? They were a many-headed beast, that's all; they were just children too, big stupid children, and the ones who didn't shoot Kebreth in the head and then wipe the blood from their shoes have gone from my mind.

I lay in bed and listened to my father and Holbrook as the sun set across the fields, my father discussing the future acquisition of land, Holbrook grunting, sneezing, and gazing at his own mucus. The forest stood around with its hands on its hips. Humanity gave itself up in gestures.

The question of the incident at Wal Wal remains vexed, not only for historians, but also for those of us who were in Ethiopia at the time! Whether the raid on the eastern border town was a directly provocative act on the part of the Italians – still, of course, bearing a grudge for their 1896 defeat at Adowa – in order to clear the way for their future invasion, or whether it was merely an attempt to establish a new border extending Italian Somaliland westward, can only be definitively answered by an appeal to the psyche of Benito Mussolini, now dead! Subsequent events, in particular the eventual 1936 invasion of Ethiopia by Mussolini's armies, seem to favour the former more sinister motives, but the possibility that the latter was the case, that the initial border incursion was indeed a minor land grab that only escalated and led to the invasion when the leaders of the respective nations were each forced into a position of saving face, has found some support, especially among those keen to highlight the culpability of the fledgling and doomed League of Nations, which, in spite of a direct plea for assistance by Haile Selassie, found it expedient to look the other way.

The forest gave itself up in gestures, Holbrook and my father sat chatting, and I drifted into blameless sleep and dreamt about Lucy.

Oh, Lucy. If you could only see me now. Remember when you sat beside my bed during my first illness, telling me to get up, sissy boy, because you were bored, what's the worst that can happen?, you child, you're not going to die. Kicking your legs backwards and forwards, your thighs tautening and untautening, sending shivers of desire through me, wanting you to climb in bed beside me and whatever, hold me, that would have done and, Jesus, could I have imagined anything more than that?

Oh, Lucy, Ironbum Lucy, now you're just the dream of a lonely old man lying in a hospital bed, pissed off with life and the world because he can't get it up any more, and who couldn't lift his skinny arms for a wank if he could.

Sweet Jesus, to cum. To cum and cum and cum. To paint these sheets with something other than piss and skin flakes. Great big gobs of cum, I know it's in there, swirling in the little fella, I'd spray it all over the bedding, I'd make patterns, I'd draw pictures, great big fucking pictures, I'd tell this whole goddamn story in jism, the whole messy lot, it'd be a goddamn relief map, maybe that's how God made the world, why not?, and then when I'd finished, when the tale was told, I'd stand at the end of my bed and piss it all away and start again, a new story, a different story of my life, about all the people who aren't in this one, a semen

115

palimpsest, layer upon layer, behold the man, *ecce fucking homo*.

Cum Story #1 – Moira, meaning 'destiny'.

On 12 April 1955 – on the very day that Holbrook was marrying his niece, why not? – Theodore T. (Teddy) Everett, Capitalist, came in torrents upon the lovely soft belly of Moira Callaghan, Catholic, emitting, as he did, a loud groan that could be heard around the world and even up in heaven.

One week earlier he, Everett, had obtained, at great personal and financial cost, a divorce from his first wife, with whom he had spent the next three days screwing in a mock-Georgian hotel room until he, and then she. Miss Callaghan was not party to this information, being a delicate little flower, with whom, said Everett, a man not given to sentiment, was so fucking in love that he couldn't believe it. *Love love love love love.* He was in love with her as he kissed her lips, as he kissed her breasts, as he rubbed against her, as he sucked her toes through her dun-coloured stockings. He was especially in love with her as he came in torrents upon her lovely soft belly, *yes yes yes yes yes*, in love as she pushed her tiny tumtum up to meet his semen kersplat. More semen, groanspent and loving, flew parabolic through the love-filled air, hitting the undersides of her breasts, also parabolic, the bottom of her ribcage, the back of her wrist. Milk jelly, white and fecund, undulated in the folds of her stomach, warm and then cold against her panting body, rolling down to pool in her belly-button, her omphalos, umbilicus, from which once she had received her food. Teddy Everett ran his tongue down the lovely soft belly of Miss Callaghan, tasting her sweat, oh god her sweat, and tasting too, mixed with her sweat, the salt of his own cum, warm and then cold. He pressed his tongue into her belly-button omphalos umbilicus and sucked, warmtongued the sweat and cum within. He felt sweat and cum, fecund and white, roll into his mouth, roll on warmtongue and warmgum, across teeth (coffee-stained) and fillings (gold). He felt simultaneously, at the same time, there and then, mixed like the sweat and the cum, present-love and historyweight, the cum on his tongue the full stop for countless potential Everetts. Family trees adumbrated in its sticky depths. He thought, there and then, that he could feel his lost offspring swimming and kicking in the jelly, freed from the burden of existence. Presentlove and historyweight. His feet, which hadn't touched the ground since he fell in love, entangled with those of Miss Callaghan, the tip of his cock cold against her inner thigh, her head now in his hands to press lips, his mouth full of sweat and cum, mixed rolling on tongue, swimming and kicking, and he kissed her deeply, warmly, passing the sweat the cum his saliva into her soft presentlove mouth and she said please don't do that and went to get a towel.

I measure time now by putrefaction. Teeth, hair, eyes, mind.

Later that night, as Moira slept, Teddy Everett sat beside her drinking shit coffee and thinking about cum, and thinking about Lucy. Lucy Alfarez had cum in rivers for him, cum like the Blue Nile, with its source just as mysterious; he wasn't allowed to touch, but he could watch as long as he didn't tell anyone. I promise not to tell anyone,

Lucy, I promise to let all of our secrets burn inside me until they lay me down in my deathbed.

Lucy told me she had learnt to masturbate from one of the old ladies of Harar, Tekle's wife, who later took my virginity, showing Lucy how to do it, where to press, where to rub, the days are long and you have to pass the time. So Lucy, who could light her own farts and climb the tallest tree in the world, stood in front of me, tucked up her skirt and rubbed and rubbed and rubbed until *yesyesyes*, and then she went pink, gave a yelp and doused the forest floor.

Which is Cum Story #2.

Teddy put his hand on Moira's back and stroked it gently as she slept. His other hand held a lit cigarette, and he drew the smoke deep into his lungs, feeling each cilia fill with life-giving tar. He became reflective. He was a famous man, Teddy Everett. Not as famous as Hearst, but who the fuck was? As famous as Howard Hughes, maybe. He had met Hughes once, some conference somewhere, and the caption in the *New Yorker* had said, 'Coffee Magnate Teddy Everett' (his name first, maybe he *was* more famous) 'and Tycoon Howard Hughes Discuss the Challenges of Aviation' which was bullshit. They talked about girls and making money. What the fuck else did they have to talk about? Hughes could only talk about his dipshit plans with people he paid to listen. First principle of Tycoonery.

So Theodore Everett was famous. Powerful. Rich. Hung, too, you wouldn't know it to look at him now, but by Christ he was fucking –

But what of the rest of it? The guts of the matter. He was not happy. Let's be frank. He was very bloody unhappy. He spent his days surrounded by grey little men, with business degrees and no balls, who lived in grey little houses, who used their spare time to draw up more grey little graphs of projected coffee sales, devising 'neat' ideas for expanding the market, and lusting after each other's grey little wives. (And his first wife, of course. He took particular pleasure in parading her in front of them each Christmas, especially as she had spent the first one weeping, so she was an object of their pity as well as their lust, a perfect specimen for middle managers to dream of saving, their very own damsel in distress, just waiting to be saved.)

Everett relieved the boredom, his and theirs, by sacking one of them occasionally, but they were like weeds, those men: every time you got rid of one there was another one exactly the same to take his place, with the same visual aids, the same buzzwords. Christ, these people talked of nothing except work, on their lunch breaks they would talk about work, to their wives they would talk about work, and their wives would actually listen, for god's sake, and, can you imagine?, take an interest.

Jesus.

Teddy Everett, the Coffee Magnate, scratched his still full scrotum through his pressed blue-white pyjamas, a gift from Moira that morning, which he had been forced to don the moment coitus was over, pushing his belly out as he scratched to loosen the nylon drawstring that was making a red welt around his waist. He didn't like welts.

And, thought the pyjamaed millionaire, his equals (power money influence sales) were all completely fucked in the head. Hearst was about to die in a fucking castle. Hughes was about to disappear into a secret condo, emerging once a decade to crash a plane.

Everett thought about the taste of semen sweat saliva on his tongue and thought about Moira and sipped his coffee. He stared at his lover's breasts, moving gently up and down beneath her knee-length nightie. He stared at her neck, her arms, her toes. He felt himself getting hard again. He removed his pyjama bottoms. He half woke her, *mmn*, and placed himself inside her, still wet from before, and he felt her hand cupping his balls and then falling away as she dropped back to sleep. He fucked her softly, gently, as she slept, as she dreamt, and he fantasised about her dreams, maybe she was dreaming of him, of the first time they met, of him sitting opposite her at a dinner party, gradually sliding down his seat as he tried to touch her foot with his beneath the table, tried to touch her stockinged leg, while the man she had arrived with, no!, think about her legs, maybe she was dreaming about the moment when his foot touched hers and she blushed, so everyone could tell, everyone there, all the men, maybe she was dreaming about all those men, lying on her back wearing only her stockings as they sucked her breasts, feeling their tongues on her nipples, but they weren't the men they were the women, and they were touching her clit and they were yelling at him go faster go faster and cum inside her and he did, he did cum, and as he came she woke up and he said loudly, through his orgasm, Moira, my darling Moira, will you marry me?

Because you don't fucking learn. You never fucking learn.

Moira and I married on 2 November 1955, Selassie's Silver Jubilee. We divorced in 1980, which would have been his Golden one if not for. It was easier than the first time, the divorce – you just filled in a form, which was lucky, because we were old then and tired easily. Also, although I didn't know it, I was dying of cancer. I WAS DYING OF CANCER. She didn't want any money. She didn't scream or shout at me. She just sat me down one day and told me in that sweet sad voice of hers that she loved me very much and always would but she was sick to death of it, sick to death of all the lying and cheating and the rages and the sleepless nights and and and. She already had her bags packed, a taxi waiting outside, she had booked a taxi!, found accommodation. I fell to my knees, I yelled and I wept, but she was gone, gone for ever, and I was left to move figures about a map and get arrested by men who punched me.

Find her for me, Lovejoy. I want to see her before the end. I want to hold her body next to mine, her old old body against my old old body, *She: Say I love you. He: I love you. She: I love you too*, and then maybe, if she is in the mood, if the light shines through the venetian blinds at just the right angle, then maybe, just maybe, just for old times' sake, maybe

Maybe

Maybe I'm wrong about the whole lot of it, not just the old stuff, my Ethiopian bazaar, but all of it. Coffee and wives and mendicants. Lucy and Kebreth and Mr Birtwhistle. Carlo and Moira and even Lovejoy.

All I can be sure of is that there is a Bible smoking with brimstone in the drawer, placed there dutifully by my peppermint priest. I know that it's in there – I can smell it. It rests there like an accusation. It is accusative. It is always accusative. I am the accused, and I swear to tell the truth, the whole truth and nothing but the truth, so help me, so help me.

My life as a series of Bibles. I have seen so many hands weighed down by that deadweight book. Coptic fuckers wandering from place to place with it in their hands, their sleeves falling down around it. Tekle's well-thumbed copy, which he pretended to use as a doorstop to advertise his new consciousness. The one from the court room. The copy belonging to Moira's father, still more a devotional object than a book, despite Vatican II. The Bible was the key to the whole thing, the key that opens some obscure door on to some obscure mystery, allowing the devils and the angels to come rushing out and submit us to their judgment. But they never found the opening. Instead this key is passed from hand to hand, down the ages, across the nations, ossifying, becoming carbuncular, when what is needed is some sort of proof, a yes or a no, a final judgment. Is that so very hard? I am tired of this mess, this judging of myself act by confusing act. I want the door to be kicked open. I want to get my wings or be cast down.

The martyrs, Kebreth, Lucy and Kwibe, they got their absolution, they got their wings. I want that.

But if I'm wrong about the lot, then maybe I was a good man, an honest man. Maybe I, too, was a goddamn saint. Surrounded by gambolling lambs, doves alighting on my outstretched hands, basking in the glow of a heavenly light, why not?, instead of a fucked-up nicotine addict with too many terrible memories and a mouth full of his own lungs. *Lovejoy tells me I am responding well, but he's a doctor, and that's his job.* And he's thirty-one years old and has no idea what it's like to turn into a mass of shit and sweat, what it's like to suddenly panic and believe that these limbs are not mine. He has no empathy, no imagination. So when I grab his coat and tell him I want to blow innocent people to pieces, that I want to shit on the altar of a church just to get my bowels moving again, that I want to cut off his cock and burn it in front of him, he just says, There there, and adjusts my medication. It doesn't occur to him that he should punch me in the face, or drive a knife through my heart, or tear my catheter out and strangle me with it. He doesn't understand that I am no longer a useful member of the tribe, I need to be cut away for the others to survive, that I need to be staked out in the sun to die for the good of all humankind.

Lovejoy's mouth is full of dead leaves.

I am dying, Lovejoy. Don't you understand you stupid fuck? The universe is about to end. It's the Book of Revelation, Lovejoy. 666. Smell the hellfire seeping from the top drawer where that Gideons' lies smouldering. Doesn't that ever make you want to commit murder? What sort of a man can watch all those people die, Lovejoy, and not want to commit murder?

All good stories end in murder, Lovejoy. Otherwise it's just grey, formless death.

Bang.
Bang.
Bang.
Bang.
Four shots. Later they would say there were only three, but you mustn't believe them. I was there, holding a gun. That was me. I saw everything.

Listen. The fundamental physiological effect of the consumption of coffee is the neutralising of the neural inhibitor, adenosine, throughout the body. This explains the rise in nervous activity of the consumer. The body, whose task it is to sustain life, i.e. equilibrium, that is, a state conducive to living, reacts to caffeine by the creation of additional adenosine, in the expectation that a percentage of these inhibitors will, in the case of a regular coffee-drinker, be attacked by the caffeine, such that the remainder will be the normal amount required for the normal, non-anxious functioning of the body, i.e. equilibrium. The practical effect of this is two-fold. First the human body requires greater and greater amounts of coffee to defeat the adenosine and get the familiar caffeine high. Second, should an individual be denied their regular levels of caffeine the body will nevertheless continue over-production of inhibitors, such that said individual, if continuing to be denied his usual levels of caffeine, will feel fucking awful. In severe cases hallucinations may develop, and a morbid fascination with lost love.

Lucy Alfarez knew her coffee. How to pick it, how to blend it, how to combine the oils to round out a roast, how to make it more or less acidic, more bitter or less. She could do it down to the individual tastebud. She could time the aftertaste to the millisecond.

She tells me one day that she was born without breath in her, born dead, until they dripped coffee on her lips, her tiny body convulsing with its touch, her pink tongue rising to meet it, the breath entering her lungs mingled with the aroma of coffee. Never went to her mother's breast, always to the bean, tied to caffeine, like this bean behind your ear, Teddy, and she would crawl among the coffee bushes on all fours, lifting discarded beans in her teeth, rolling away the oil with the underside of her tongue, spitting the husk on the ground.

Sometimes, when Kebreth would travel into Harar for more *chat*, more ammunition, he would take us with him, and we would sit and watch the old men, cross-legged on the ground, slowly grinding the coffee in the large wooden mortars they held between their knees, a form of meditation as much as production, the heat of the Ethiopian sun burnishing their naked shoulders, sweat running from beneath their turbans, all of them a thousand years old, born of the moment when coffee was first discovered, hundreds of years ago, when Kaldi the goatherd, let him be praised, sucked on the white-flowered plant that was keeping the goats awake, right here where we were sitting, maybe, why not?, took the drupe into his mouth and suddenly felt like Jimi Hendrix, *You fucking beauty!*, that's what he yelled, the outer parchment falling from his lips, *You fucking beauty!*, the sarcocarp at his feet for the birds,

and the monks on the hilltop heard his screams, and they did come down to hear the words of Kaldi, and to suck on the selfsame plant, and they were pretty goddamn impressed too, next thing you know they are sneaking it into vespers to keep from nodding off, mixing it with butter to chew on their way to Mecca, then people are fighting wars over it, the Pope is calling it the drink of infidels, *the devil's wine*, adventurers are conquering nations to get at it, building canals to ferry the black liquid across continents, ships to drive it across the sea, they're dumping tea into the oceans, who needs fucking tea?, until coffee is the second biggest commodity in the world after oil and oil, drip drip drip, is running out, oil is running out.

Christ, but it's a good drink. I would say that, of course. Born to it and all that. Could have been born to ironing boards, so mustn't grumble. Those fucking portraits hanging around my office, gazing down at me as I made my map. Oliver, Simon, Percival, Oliver, Me, each portrait slightly more expensive, slightly better, in line with our ever-burgeoning wealth. My favourite, the only one I liked, was the founder, the bewhiskered and rapacious Oliver the First, the founding father, showing obvious signs of shock and hilarity at becoming worthy of being painted. He looked like Mark Twain had exploded. I think I would have liked him. I always think of him on the back of a railway carriage, spruiking the elixir of life. Now that was capitalism! Not the dun bookkeeping I inherited, journals of accounts into which I inserted Ethiopian holy books to read behind my desk.

The paintings improved in negative correlation with the ballsiness of the sitter. I like to think my Lucian Freud addition was a return to form of sorts. Why not?

That said, surely the greatest artifice on that wall was the nose of Simon of the Big Nose. How many nights did the painter, Walton, Weston, I can't remember, lie awake and wonder whether to show the proboscis in its full splendour, how many times did he paint it in and then scrape it off? Three minutes in the man's company would have revealed he was utterly conceited and devoid of a sense of humour. Perhaps Waltonweston simply followed the dictates of financially set propriety and drew the proportionate nose straight off – who knows? All I know is that the nose in the portrait stopped above the mouth, a fiction I would wonder at for hours as I sat behind my desk.

I knew Simon. He's worth a story. Let me tell you about Simon of the Big Nose.

Simon of the Big Nose was 190 years old and it had not occurred to him to die, although he had done everything normally associated with dying, aside from letting his heart stop. Even before he and my father subdivided the world he would appear occasionally at our house – I never saw him enter, I never saw him leave – sitting in a straight-backed chair beneath another portrait of himself, equally charitable. It showed him as a young man, sitting on a horse, which I found doubly fantastic as he had never found himself atop any horse, nor had he ever been a young man.

From this chair – a gift from the Ottomans, according to himself – he would discourse interminably on subjects of no interest, his mouth clicking below his endless nose. Were it not for the startling size of his proboscis, sitting would have been his character note. He sat in chairs, in churches, in railway carriages, in the back seat of chauffeur-driven cars, anywhere but on a horse. He might have slept sitting up, I don't know. When I was a young boy I used to imagine him being carried from place to place, like Roosevelt, by a phalanx of resolute servants with broad chests and an underdeveloped sense of the ridiculous. He would get them to pop him down in any spot best chosen for annoying people. Then they would shout into his absurdly small ears a few details of where he was and who he was talking to, press a button in his head, and make him start talking, which he would do until the other person was dead.

He was completely mad. He had forsaken language as a means of communication and used it instead as a way of keeping his mind stumbling forwards through time. He spoke in the graven tones of a man of substance, but without the substance. His brow, the muscles exhausted by a lifetime of being furrowed in what was seen to be sobriety but was probably confusion, had slackened so much that it sat halfway down his face, with only his insurmountable nose precluding further descent.

The only time I saw him not talking was those occasions, approximately five times a day, when he would eat an egg and cress sandwich, an act with a hideous poetry all its own. Simon of the Big Nose would place one end of the sandwich into his mouth and hold it there for a few seconds while regaining his strength. He would then look around the room to ensure everyone was watching (once he had to hold the sandwich hanging from his mouth for a full five minutes while one of our maids was absent-mindedly polishing a tea urn). Then he would place the palm of his right hand on the other end of the sandwich and push, with a steady motion, the whole thing into his mouth, tears filling his eyes as he did so. He did not chew the sandwich. I swear he did not chew the sandwich. The whole performance had the air of a lesson from which we were supposed to draw certain conclusions, I know not what.

His other habit was snuff, which he kept beside him in

a small wooden box. The taking of snuff did not require the cessation of speech as he appeared to have mastered the art of circular breathing. And once the snuff was in, that was it. He never sneezed it out. I assume it lodged in his brain, moist knobs of tobacco spread throughout the cerebral cortex AT NIGHT I DREAM MY BODY IS HOLLOW AND FULL OF BIRDS PANICKING AND TRYING TO GET OUT a fact that might have led to the repetitive nature of his speech.

Most of his speeches were strange homilies on the importance of bowel maintenance, or epic stories on the provenance of the Everetts. The former were more interesting to a nine-year-old. He knew and could enumerate the effects of every single foodstuff on the colon of the human. Egg and cress sandwiches were, for instance, advantageous in the production of firm stools, unless made by a woman, who tended to add sauces and pickles if not watched, my mother for instance, she's a devious woman (he did not know her name), devious, Teddy, and then your stools become moist and inclined to arrive unexpectedly. Milk caused the runs. Cake caused the runs. The Labour Party caused the runs. Tea made your urine pale. Coffee made it rich.

– Is your urine rich, Teddy?

– Yes, Gr —

– You know that no Everett has ever had boils, don't you, Teddy?

– —

– Coffee is extremely good for boils —

I would sit there transfixed, fully expecting him to

suddenly realise that he was already dead, and to get up, shake my hand firmly, and go and bury himself in the garden.

During my childhood, Simon of the Big Nose was the patriarch of Everett and Sons Coffee. His father, Oliver the First, had whisked him away from his mother's vaginal influences as quickly as possible, and ensconced him at Eton, where he could be educated in the principles of righteousness, and flick towels at Cecil Rhodes. Rhodes would later describe him as dull. On the death of Oliver the First, from a combination of consumption and general apoplexy, Simon of the Big Nose assumed control of Everett and Sons.

Simon covered his basic incompetence by employing lots of bright people to do his work. Men in straw hats, that sort of thing. Business grew strong, expanding, *wheeeeeeee!*, from a provincial concern to a global one. He used his employees as missionaries, sent into new countries with the promise of compliant tax laws and compliant women. If the country had coffee you took it from them cheaply, if it didn't, you sold it to them expensively.

In addition Simon, who liked his drinks carbonated as a method of increasing flatulence and therefore health, sniffed the breeze and realised that Americky and its soft drinks were the way forward. It is the regret of every businessman that he did not invent Coca-Cola, except Simon, who knew the man who did, who got in on the ground floor, and sat back as insane men wended their way across the great plains of Americky, selling the new carbonated medicine, pumped through with Everett caffeine to keep you coming back.

Legend has it that Simon of the Big Nose emerged from his office only twice in his working life, once to get married and once to retire. His wife, Grace (!), was a soft, doughy woman with a face like a rice pudding. She was not seen again after the wedding, the birth of Percival being the only sign of her existence. I was convinced as a child that he kept her in his snuff box, an idea reinforced by the way he would talk into it as he inhaled.

By keeping his office door locked, Simon of the Big Nose attempted to avoid the problems of the Everett family for more than forty years. His mother, Lisbeth, had decided, given the unappealing nature of male penetration, to abjure the sexual altogether and devote herself to the cause of Puritanism, campaigning vigorously against all kinds of intoxicants, not least coffee, a crusade for which she became well known by dint of her family associations. Legend has it that she would stand in the Everett's foyer, outside her son's door, and scream choice biblical passages through it, mainly, it appears, the passage on Onan, presumably revealing some knowledge about her son not recorded by his biographers.

Meanwhile, Grandfather Percival, Simon's son, having lost Adelaide to the wilds of the dark continent, had attempted to place his penis inside every orifice in England, Scotland, Wales and the Isle of Man – the mixture of glorious triumph and ignominious defeat exposing him to a life of such dynamism that he had taken himself for a new Byron, a healer-warrior apparently, and had started gadding about in fur coats and frocks, jotting down incomprehensible odes to incorrigible women who wouldn't put out and incorrigible men who would.

All of which Simon of the Big Nose found more than a little unsettling.

Simon had a world-view lacking any of the plasticity required to embrace familial madness and the like. Least of all did it allow for a gadfly son, completely unsuited to ascension to the head of Everett and Sons. To have rebelled against his own destiny simply would not have occurred to Simon – to see his own son doing so was incomprehensible. Worse – it was shameful.

Simon spent many hours staring up at the portrait of Oliver the First, which hung above his desk, as I would one day stare up at his, imagining the wrath of the founder about his producing such a flibbertigibbet to carry the Everett name. This was the portrait of a man who had built himself up from a shoeshine boy, or a bookie's runner, or a roustabout, to start the world's biggest coffee house. A man who had jumped on a ship and travelled to Americky, where he had stood before Abraham Lincoln and suggested giving his army coffee instead of whiskey, and when the troops threatened mutiny, had stood before them and said, Patriots, I share your pain, but wait until you taste it! And taste it they did, and they cheered him to a man, and then went back out there and won that war. He can be seen in the background of photographs from Appomattox, and is reputed to have taken General Lee aside moments after he had signed the surrender and given him a cup of Everett's best. Lee declared it was mighty fine!

The only hope, thought Simon, gazing up at the painting, was the next in line, Oliver the Second, my father. The kid was a porker, there was no doubt about that, but there was an unscrupulousness in him that appealed to Simon – not because he himself was unscrupulous, but because he felt that the world was becoming more so, and that a lack of scruples was probably what was required.

Simon's politics were entirely dictated by what went on outside his own window. If he saw a lady's bag snatched, he believed England to be a nation of robbers. If he saw a gentleman retrieve the bag, he believed England a nation of gents. If he saw that the lady wore a dress that stopped above the ankle he believed the moral universe was crumbling. If a priest walked by he believed it was still sound. Each of these revelations was then relayed to the editors of *The Times*, in perfect copperplate writing, who reprinted every letter, in deference to his position rather than in acknowledgement of the acuity of his mind.

Simon stared up at his father's portrait. He was, these days, seeing many more robbers and naked ankles than gentlemen and priests. Moral decay seemed inevitable. The new grandson appeared ideally suited, therefore, to the temper of the times. The boy could pursue immorality as he wished. As long as it didn't involve homosexuality or art, and as long as he didn't have to see it.

My father did not disappoint Simon of the Big Nose. He showed a more than adequate lack of morals – often leading rather than just participating in the moral decay. He married well, produced immediately, and shared a yen for hetero-sexuality and a solid distaste for art. Simon was able to slip contentedly into senility, to a blameless life of sandwiches, snuff and remaining seated, the noose he placed around my neck never once troubling his benign countenance.

Here to here to here.

I am going to tell you about my mother, Edith Everett, *née* Stanley. I want to bring her out of the shadow. I'm sick of talking about the Everetts, sick of talking about men. This place is crawling with men. I want to raise my mother from her sick bed and set her back on her feet. I want to tell a good, bourgeois, Victorian love story, the last brave spark of humanity from a condemned man, proof that the Divine resides still within even the lowliest of our criminal classes. Something for the Quakers to get their teeth into. I don't know the details of the story, so I'll make them up. A bit of melodrama never goes astray. So . . .

Edith Everett, *née* Stanley, stands beside her son Teddy on the deck of a gently rocking ship bound for Africa, incomprehensible bloody Africa, which could have been

Mars or Jupiter for all she. Her face, not attractive, not unattractive, a mother's face, is red, buffeted by the wind. Her knuckles, scarred only by a wedding band, are white, gripping the guard rail. I look up at her as she looks at the disappearing shore.

All her life she has been a lover of feeling the ground beneath her feet. She is an avid walker, Edith, distrusting all forms of transport – bicycles, cars, boats and, god save us, aeroplanes – that served to break her contact with the Earth. She trusted her feet to hold her up, trusted her legs to move her forwards. Bare feet. The grass between her toes. That sort of thing.

Since her marriage she had never found firm ground, no level space where she could stop and be herself, where she could forget herself and simply live. A rocking boat journeying to an unknown land was yet another vertiginous episode in the strange vertiginous world of being married.

She pressed her shod feet, her curled toes, hard against the deck of the ship.

Her wedding day had been a swirl of inexplicable ritual, of standing on chairs and being pinned into dresses, of being poked and prodded by teams of giggling women, who lifted handfuls of her free-flowing hair and screwed them on to her head, arabesques fastened to her scalp, tight buns and swirls, tighter than her hair had ever been tied. She felt her forehead being pulled tight, her head beginning to ache. Before her tight face women threw coded messages back and forth to each other, winking and swinging their hips. Her mother pressed flowers into her hand, tugged at her sleeves, told her how lucky she was.

My mother didn't feel lucky. She felt herself being decorated. She felt like a Christmas tree.

Then she was sitting in a cramped car, sweat toppling down her cleavage, her parents talking talking talking, muttering instructions, felicitations, warnings. The world spun past outside the car. Women outside cocked their heads to judge her, men raised their hats, judgement complete. They stopped at the lights

and she thought she saw young Theo, the butcher's apprentice, kicking leaves along the gutter and she remembered her seventeenth birthday, when he had asked, stammering, for a kiss, and she had blushed and stammered yes, and closed her eyes, waiting, her lips licked moist in anticipation, and he had leant forward, shaking, and pressed his lips once, terrified, to the crown of her cheekbone, just for a second, and then drawn back quickly, thanking her in a high, rapid voice for her generosity, told her he loved her more than the sun moon stars and then, before she could speak, turned on his heel and dashed home because his mother would have food on the table and you shouldn't waste food, and after he was gone my mother had lain in bed that night tingling all over, softly touching her face where his lips had been, and dreaming of him and the sun moon stars.

A week later she was brought into the drawing room to meet my father.

My father was Oliver Everett the Second, heir to Everett and Sons Coffee. He was a rich man, a powerful man, a man whose name had been mentioned in the House of Lords. He was the great-great-great-grandson of the bewhiskered and rapacious Oliver Everett the First, who had built himself up from a simple clerk, or a drifter, or a chicken sexer, to the founding father and subsequent head of a coffee empire with tentacles that spread from Cuba to Brazil to Ethiopia. New money, but my mother's father was more impressed by this pedigree than by old money, as he had also built himself up from a simple clerkship to the position of Deputy Vice Chairman, although he had done it by getting the Chairman's daughter pregnant.

Edith sat outside her father's study, listening to the two men talk, a small shrine to her war-dead older brother before her, fresh flowers placed beside it every day by her father, stuck with a girl. A teacup shook in her hand. Her legs itched beneath new stockings. She had prepared herself to meet him the previous night, but he had cancelled at the last minute for business reasons. Her father had told her over their cold lamb and vegetables that this showed what an important man Oliver Everett the Second was, so she should be grateful. For myself I believe he was probably off shagging a housemaid, but I do not claim to be impartial.

So Edith had spent another restless night wondering what her new suitor would look like. It's theoretically possible that she imagined him to be an obese and ugly man without social graces or compassion, but this does not explain why, the moment the door was opened and she saw my father for the first time, her translucent teacup tumbled from her hand and crashed against the polished floorboards, or why her body dropped to the floor with it, in that most delicate of mating gestures, the faint.

My father took one look at the prostrate form below him,

grunted his approval, and was gone. He did not stay for dinner. Once again the threesome ate cold lamb and vegetables.

And now, less than a month later, she was done up like a Christmas tree, being whisked across town by a locomotion not her own, to be given to him for life.

She knew nothing about her soon-to-be-husband's family. After my father had departed on the Day of the Teacup he had not called again. Too busy with business, her father said proudly. She had managed to glean some information from the side of packets of Everett and Sons Coffee (her father's new brew of choice) but that was all about Oliver the First, apart from a short statement that appeared on each pack, written by the company receptionist Gwen and signed by Simon of the Big Nose, to the effect that he was determined to retain the highest standards of et cetera, et cetera. Other information was gradually gleaned from her father, but most of it was sketchy. She knew her betrothed's father was named Percival, but he had already written to say that he would not be at the wedding, as he regarded his relations with the Everett family as being at an end. The letter was in verse on scented notepaper, handwritten in Gothic lettering. She had heard nothing about her new mother-in-law, Adelaide, as the subject was never broached.

Events of her last month of freedom remain obscure. Particularly as regards young Theo, the butcher's apprentice. Did they see each other again? Covert love played out beneath the nodding heads of honeysuckle? There was blood on the wedding sheet, so if they did, Theo's bashfulness was not overcome. Did he think angrily about my father as he cut meat? Chop chop chop? No – she was the daughter of a banker. He had been living in a fool's paradise. Life wasn't like that.

My mother felt dizzy as she stepped out of the wedding car, at least as dizzy as my first wife who had got pissed on the morning of our wedding and

Edith Stanley felt the bridesmaids take up her train. She was wearing, at her mother's insistence, high heels, her first pair, and wearing them she felt her feet being lifted from the ground, leaving her to hang from the Earth by just her toes, and her toes, aching already from the tight shoes, threatened to lose their grip and let her fall. A stiff corset pinched her waist, rubbing against her ribcage and hips. She stumbled forwards, trying to keep contact, and found herself moving down the aisle. Faces stared up at her from either side of the church, the faces of strangers. Even those on her side she didn't know – friends of her parents there to impress rather than friends of her own. They had been wiped away, and she would never have another one.

She heard honking on the Everett side and turned her head to see an old man in the front row with a huge nose, expectorating into a handkerchief.

Her breasts began to sag.

Her hair began to slip beneath sharp pins.

Her calves, holding her toes to the Earth, began to ache.

And she heard bells, church bells, ringing in her ears, she told me, as I sat numbly beside her deathbed, *They were so loud, but they can't have been bells, it makes no sense, I must have imagined them, but no, there were bells, and I wanted to press my hands over my ears, but I knew I couldn't so I just gripped the flowers as tightly as I could, but I was scared that I might break the stems, I was always clumsy, and then there would be flowers all over the aisle, like a garden, it would have been so pretty, I would have been in so much trouble.*

She felt a hand on her arm when she reached the altar, the priest, talking to her. She could not hear him above the sound of the bells. She watched him speak. There was white clag on the sides of his mouth. His tongue was light pink. One of his front teeth overlapped the other. She saw him turn away and talk to Oliver. Oliver was talking too, his head nodding. The priest turned and spoke to her again. He stopped and stared at her, and she stared back, wondering what he wanted. His eyebrows were uneven, the lines in his forehead too long for his face. She felt a fat hand on her elbow. The priest spoke again. She felt hot tears in her eyes. She heard herself speak.

She said, I do.

And that night she did.

She lay spread on her new bed, and let her husband's penis, loosed from its wedding suit, where it had rested throughout the wedding, sweating against his testicles in the House of God, push up inside her. She felt his weight moving up and down above her, his breasts flicking against hers. She gazed at her wedding dress, spread on the floor beside the bed, shoes beside it. He had told her to keep the corset on. Her hair up in pins. He remained dressed.

Edith Everett felt pain shoot through her belly, then lay as still as she could, hoping the pain would go away. If she held her breath the corset would not rub a burn into her ribs. If she gripped the sides of the bed she could push herself into the mattress and make it hurt less. She pushed her hips down and down. Her husband speeded up, flesh undulating from one side of his body to the other, pushing her up the bed until her head met the wooden headboard, hitting it with each thrust. A pin from her hair pushed itself through her skin and drew blood. She pressed her hips down and down. She heard my father roar, felt his penis harden. She felt him grip her knees, push them up, felt his forearms move to the backs of her thighs, lifting her body, her hips losing contact with the mattress, she tried to press them down, he pushed back up, she hit at his chest, he pushed her down and they are having sex, my parents, I have to tell you this because they are making me: everything in the history of the universe has been leading up to this moment, every meeting of every molecule, every war in the history of the universe has been leading to these two fucking, every kiss, every murder, death, illness, every birth of every child, every birth of every star, every planet, this very Earth, God made this very Earth for this moment, so that I could be created, created by my father, Oliver Everett the Second, ejaculating NOW into my mother Edith Everett, *née* Stanley, with blood all over her face and all over the sheets.

As he came inside her, my mother felt herself losing her balance, felt blood from the pinprick trickle down her face, her leg slip from the edge of the bed. She was being thrown outwards, into the air, and her desperate foot, in a torn white stocking, reached out as far as it could, and felt despairingly for the Earth.

I ask Dr Lovejoy about feet. Tell me about feet, Dr Death, I say. Illuminate me on the matter of peds. Guide me through the realm of the tarsal and the metatarsal, dance me through the phalanges. Speak to me of fallen arches, ingrown toenails, foot rot – wax lyrical on trench foot and chilblains. Declaim on toes, big and small, toes and the toe-jam thereof. Inform about ankles and heels. Sprained ankles first and bruised heels subsequent. Recommend to me the best in footwear. For comfort. For support. I've got all day, Lovejoy. Give me of your wisdom.

Lovejoy looks concerned, asks me what I want to know. I tell him I want to know lots of things. I tell him I want to know how many bones there are in the human foot. How many muscles. How many joints. What the average weight of the human foot is, both in itself and then as a percentage of total bodyweight. And thus of the total body-weight of every human being on the face of the Earth, ever. How much of the biomass human is made up of feet? I ask him. Of toenails? What is the scientific relationship between the human toenail and human hair? Between stockings and petroleum? Do you find the foot a more fetishistic object with a stocking or without? If the stocking has a ladder? If it does not? With shoes or *sans*. Do you get turned on by the beige stockings and white trainers of Siobhan, the red-haired nurse? Of any nurse? Lovejoy, have you ever tried to have sex with a nurse? Have you ever considered, imagined or achieved the having of sex with a nurse? For instance, the red-haired nurse? Is such behaviour common in the medical profession or is that a myth? What part does the foot play in sex outside mere fetishism? Can the placing of a foot on the ground during coupling affect the personality of the child born from said coupling? Can the failure to do so lead to a sense of vertigo in said child, persistent throughout his life, yea, verily unto death? Tell me, Lovejoy, I want to know.

My mother stands on the deck of the ship and pulls me closer. She has tears in her eyes. She is, for the sake of the story, remembering the night of my conception, her wedding night, she remembers the pain, the horror and how she reached out to touch the floor the moment her husband spent himself in her, missing it, the whole of the Earth just beneath her, but she couldn't touch a bit of it.

Throughout her pregnancy she had kept at least one foot on the ground, she had asked her maid to walk her to the hospital, walk her up the stairs into the delivery room, her bare feet on cool tiles, the shocks of her contractions running through her and being grounded like electricity, leaving, she imagined, I imagine, burnt footsteps behind her, black marks of her power, placed at great distances from each other by her stride, but then growing closer and closer, becoming the steps of her faltering, because she saw at the end of the bed the foul metal contraption that would hoist her feet above her, the straps to hold her ankles. Here the footsteps falter, turn, scrabble against the floor, but there are men either side of her, strong men, strong men in white coats who grab her by the wrists and ankles and lift her on to the bed, her ankles high above her.

As the pain shot through her womb, Edith Everett, *née* Stanley, looked up at her feet and thought of the times she had felt the grass between her toes, chasing and being chased by whooping young men who would fall beside her panting panting and stare at her awkwardly until they were ready to get up and run again, and now here she was, seventeen years old, her feet swaying above her, heaving a ten-pound mass out of her body, it's a boy!, another fuck them boy, his boy, heir to the Everett quintillions, push, get it out, push, and then blackness and then it was in her arms, and a doctor bent down, loomed, and said, What shall you call it? and she said, Theodore, I shall call it Theodore, after the boy she had kissed on her seventeenth birthday.

My mother had won the naming rights by the simple expedient of my father being absent at the time of my birth.

He was away on business.

The newborn's full name was Theodore Thomas Everett and he didn't stand a chance. She always called him Teddy, because she was seventeen years old. He was heir to the Everett quintillions, but she always told him to keep his feet on the ground.

And he tried, he really tried, but, Christ, what can you do, because you know, Mama, you only have to lose contact once and

Here on the ship, heading ever onwards to Afri-bloody-ca, Teddy's feet were so far from the ground that it made her nauseous. She had begged her husband not to make them take this trip but he'd

Who knows? Ignored her? Beaten her? Told her to stop being so stupid, the boy would be fine, that it would be good for him? Whatever. Staring across the ocean she was not thinking of him, I want her thinking of young Theo, whom she had not seen since her birthday, who had kissed her once on the cheek and whom she sometimes thought of as the father of her child.

I tell Lovejoy I have two fathers, Oliver Everett the coffee merchant, and a butcher's apprentice named Theodore. Lovejoy tells me that that is not unusual these days. He recently delivered a boy who, after all the convolutions of biology, patrimony, matrimony, foster-hood, fertilisation and sperm donation had played themselves out, had at least six fathers, no fewer mothers, twelve family trees tangling their way through history to disgorge themselves at a single point, a small child so filled with history that it will surely burst.

It's nothing new, Lovejoy – Tekle once told me the legend of the Holy Pearl, listen: when God created Adam he placed a Holy Pearl within him to be passed *hoy hoy hoy* into a series of holy men, and then into Hannah, Christ's granny, for the Holy Pearl was her daughter the Virgin, or perhaps the Holy Pearl was Christ and Mary was the oyster, something like that, but anyway, the Holy Pearl ends up in Menelik of Abyssinia, and that's why the Kings of Ethiopia are Divine, quite apart from having the Ark and all that, but leaving that aside I guess we're all related if you go back far enough, but neither of us is Divine, not like Selassie sitting there under his umbrella watched by my ten-year-old eyes as I stood in a crowd of how many thousands, and then getting home to tell Kebreth and him arguing with his father again, how could he?, and his father also had one father, history is clogged up with these men, endless men, fighting and deciding and fighting and deciding, and when you are born heir to the Everett quintillions there is not a day in your life that you don't feel them all staring at you, even when you're alone in your

147

office, you feel the eyes of their portraits judging you, and judging you false.

Sometimes, I swear, I wake and find one of these endless Everett men standing at the end of my bed, standing there silently. The founder, smoke curling from his hair, wearing some of my features on his face. He knows the lot, of course. He doesn't like me. I think if we'd met in a bar and had a couple of drinks and talked about women he would have liked me, but he knows the lot, of course, how I destroyed it all, and he doesn't like me. Other times it's Simon. He just hates me. On a good day I wake to Grandfather Percival, shaman, mystic and suicide. He's the only one who smiles. Stoned, I guess.

It's never my father. OK, sometimes it's my father, but fuck that. So it's never my father.

Lucy Alfarez walks out of the jungle, a girl without history, without father and mother, and the Everett schlong, scion of generations, stands straight up.

And my mother lies dying in Ethiopia and tells me the greatest moment of her life was holding me as a baby, I smelt like powder, she tells me.

And my father drinks *tej* with his bodyguard and talks about the natives.

And our boat moves across the North Atlantic Ocean, Southampton growing smaller and smaller behind us, finally disappearing, as my mother and I stand on the deck holding hands, made gently dizzy by the rocking of the water.

And when I sleep now I dream of this water, the ocean, dark and dreadful, taking me away. The Earth is a heart and water is its black blood. The boat scratches its flesh as would a fingernail. It is always night on this boat, I am in my cabin, holding the sides of the bed, and my cabin is below water, under the surface of its flesh, and only one sound holds in the silence, and it is always there, that heartbeat outside the fragile boat, the ocean always beating.

I sleep and dream of water, and feel it flow between my thighs, my own urine, emptying out of me on to sodden sheets, making the backs of my legs burn as it runs across my bedsores, as it eddies around my ankles. There is a button to push for help, Siobhan is at the end of it, but it takes too much strength, to lift my arm and press that button takes too much strength, I can't do it, I don't want to do it, I don't want her to see me like this. I am sick of the fuss. I fear more than anything else the fuss. The endless fucking solicitude, the endless, endless care. Yesterday I pissed myself as a nurse rolled me over to powder my sores, I pissed all over my belly, I felt it spraying up to my nipples, I had to say, Help, please, Nurse, help, and she did, that's what breaks you, she made it all better, she cleaned me up, wiped away the urine, soaked it up with sponges, squeezed it into a bucket, and told me it was all right.

Not this time. This time I won't let her. This time I will lie here in my own piss, my own lake of effluence, until I die.

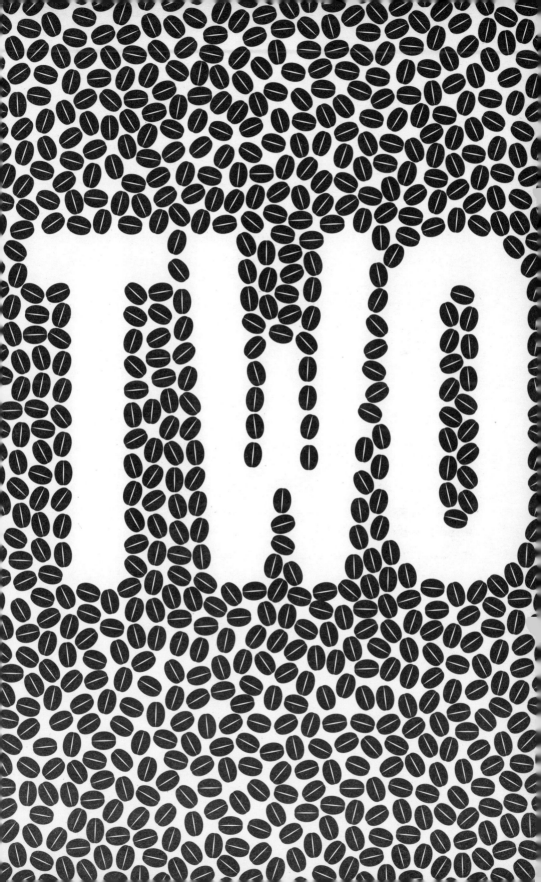

Of what doth the Glory of Kings consist, Teddy? That is the question of the Kebra Nagast. *Here, look upon its pages, this is the story of real power, not the common coin that the likes of your father peddles, commerce and whatnot, but the power of succession, the Holy Pearl passed from generation to generation, from the belly of Eve down to the mighty Solomon and the mighty Solomon down to the mighty Selassie.*

Tekle draws on his pipe and places the book before Kwibe, Lucy and me, *117 chapters!*, running his fingers across the flat Ge'ez text as though it were Braille.

Since Lucy moved in with Tekle and Ababa – did I tell you Lucy moved in with Tekle and Ababa?, Tekle taking her in because of Kidane Mehret, did I tell you about Kidane Mehret?, Kwibe and I would spend a lot of our evenings at their table, drawn there, simply, wordlessly, by her beauty, Tekle's stories, Ababa's *kai wat* bubbling on the stove and sending its odours throughout *chez* Everett. When I think of the path leading to their *tukul* I always see Kwibe and me floating towards it like cartoon characters, drawn onwards by the smell. Kebreth was always there too, writing, writing, writing. The white walls were covered with plates, bowls and baskets, blue, orange, yellow, green, with vases and bits of pottery laid into niches in the wall, broken and humble.

The floor was covered with coffee beans, so as you walked across it the smell was released, mingling with the smell of the spiced meat and Ababa and Tekle's flesh, these two huge lovers permeating their home utterly. Their sheer size and Tekle's blindness meant they seldom lost contact with each other, their hands brushing, legs touching, their coughs and sneezes joining mid-air. As a visitor you became part of this mass of flesh, you found yourself part of a many-headed beast, and if I pressed myself more closely to Lucy and Ababa that is not to say I avoided Kebreth, Tekle or Kwibe. At times it was possible to forget where one body ended and another began.

The coffee barrel in which I would lose my virginity was always overflowing, literally overflowing, as if there were a fountain at its base, a perpetual-motion machine – I wouldn't have put it past Tekle to have invented one and to have used it for something as frivolous as a coffee-bean fountain. Lucy had a cot against the other wall, built from the off-cuts of wooden Everett and Sons Coffee crates – as she grew more crates were added, the side growing to say Everevereverevereverett and Sons. After too many glasses of *tej* Tekle would call me that, laughing, Hey, Everevereverevereverett, where are your sons? and we would all roll about laughing, my cheeks burning with joy, embarrassment, love.

We would pile the *wat* on our *injera*, the sourness of the dough bringing out the spices of the meat – even now my peanut-sized stomach rumbles at the thought of it. Plus a little *tej* for each of us, CHILDREN WHO LEARN TO DRINK RESPONSIBLY BECOME RESPONSIBLE DRINKERS, and always the sound of Tekle talking talking talking, his food disappearing but his mouth, his mouth, somehow, never full. Then a pipe to finish, his own creation, shaped to match the clay silhouette of Sherlock Holmes on the front of his water-bloated copy of *The Hound of the Baskervilles*. He filled it to overflowing with two-year-old Ogden's Walnut Plug, exchanged for his redundant Bible, which was why, years later, I kept a set of Ogden's 1928 Pugilists in Action cards in the top drawer of my office desk. Jack Dempsey. Teddy Baker. Gene Tunney.

Rosebud!

Tekle's first draw on his pipe would always herald a silence, deep and unfathomable. The second was the down beat of a conductor, a minuscule lacuna, introducing the theme of the night, Tekle's gentle monologue, exposition, development, recapitulation. We would sit in rapt attention, Kwibe and I, Kebreth outside writing, Lucy staring off into the night, lighting herself another cigarette, retiring, silently, to bed.

The Queen of Sheba, Jesus, Teddy, what a woman!, visiting the mighty Solomon, David and Bathsheba's kid, the King of Israel. He had to use all his wisdom to get her in the sack, salting her food, 'You said you would take nothing from me by force and yet you take this glass of water, now I shall take what is promised on the breaking of the oath', cheeky bastard.

He takes her body and she takes his wisdom. He: Verily it is right that man should worship the one true God not the false idols of your homeland. She: OK, and, this is the important bit, his seed, his pearl, growing in her belly pop pop pop pop. And then she's off, she and her 797 camels, I cannot be your queen . . . my people . . . making that weary trip from Jerusalem back to Ethiopia.

This is a trip I have made, Teddy, hard enough for a man, let alone a woman with child. I still find sand in my clothes thirty years later.

Ababa passed each of us a coffee, blessing us with its steam.

Nine months and five days after Solomon had given her his gift, not nine and four, nor nine and six, she gave birth to a son, Glory to God, whom she named Bayna Lekham, whom she named Ebna la-Hakim, whom she named Menelik, a first son like you, Teddy, stop squirming, and the boy grew and grew, twenty-two years, Solomon's ring on his finger, and his mother told him stories of his father the King, until like you the boy could barely sit still. Sit still! So he too made that trek, reverse order, Ethiopia to Jerusalem, my princely ancestors in his train, until he found his father, King Solomon, keeper of the Tabernacle, the Law of God, the Holy Covenant, and his double, for all children are made from the clay of their fathers, all.

Ababa allowed herself a chuckle. *You too, Teddy.*

And, yea, the son did sit before the father and, yea, they did eat dainty meats, fine beasts presented in slivers before the King, no good solid wat, eh, Ababa? Menelik's favourite Tamrin, the merchant, at his right hand, Zadok the priest at the King's right hand, and the King did ask Menelik to assume his throne, and Menelik said, Nope, I have sworn by my mother's breasts, you remember them!, to return. And the King was sad, for nothing pains a father more than to lose a son, Everevereverett.

If you must leave us, then we shall build a great kingdom in the south, said Solomon, Solomon said, and he sent Menelik away with the first-born son from each of the noblest families, Fankera, Lewandos, Dalakem, Adram, even Zadok's son Azaryas, imagine that, Teddy, the mothers weeping, the fathers setting their faces to stone to hold back their own tears and failing. A whole city weeping. More sons rent from fathers, Teddy.

But there was one bond the pilgrims could not bear to break – Zion, the Covenant with the One True Father, God that is God. And so, before leaving, Menelik's new posse, Fankera, Lewandos, Dalakem, Adram, even Zadok's son Azaryas, broke into the holy place, in the dead of night, in the calm before the storm, in the darkest hour before the dawn. And, yea, Teddy, God came unto them in a pillar of fire, in a tower of smoke, what's all this, then?, and they spake, and He spake, and He said, Sure, why not, I anoint thee Ethiopes!, and they took the Ark of the Covenant from whence it sat, replacing it with a replica and getting the hell out of there.

Once again they made the trek, Jerusalem to Ethiopia,

down down down, an army of first sons pursued for a time by fathers and second sons, who had discovered the theft at dawn, at the cock crow, until the fathers and second sons saw God before them and God said, You have forsaken me, the Covenant is broken, and they had to turn back to secondbest Jerusalem. And the Covenant resides here to this day, Teddy, we are God's chosen people, not just a bunch of slaves for your arsehole father to kick around, and the land of Ethiopia will never be conquered, not by you, not by the Italians, not by anyone ever. So you have to choose which side you are on, Teddy, my son, and then you have to cling to it like death.

Tekle held the book in his hands, breathing deeply. His pipe was finished. Lucy and Kwibe were asleep.

All rubbish, of course. Fairy stories. An opiate for the people, eh, Kebreth? An opiate for the people.

Lucy Alfarez walked out of the jungle at the age of fourteen, a Queen of Sheba, a vision from afar, with a silver lighter in one hand and a coffee bean in the other. Kebreth Astakie, my father's contact with the Galla people, watches her moving into the clearing, sees her white dress catching the sunlight. His canvas shirt is drenched with sweat, the ends of his fingers sore from cuts. He sees her go towards the porch of the house where the Everetts live, sees their idiot boy sitting there whittling his idiot figures out of wood. He makes lots of little animals this boy; it's good to see the children of the bourgeoisie using their hands for a change, but he makes such stupid things, this boy, such useless things. No doubt he will grow up to be like his father, fat rich stupid. Class sticks.

He sees the girl point at the boy and laugh. Maybe she sees through him too. Kebreth starts to walk towards the house, let's have a look, she seems young but she is tall. Kebreth feels a stirring between his legs, the breeze blowing in his sweaty shirt. He sees that the girl is beautiful. She is young but she is

Kebreth stands before them, *Hello hello*. The girl does not even look up at him. She looks down at her feet, tracing circles in the dust. Teddy edges closer to her, possessive.

Then the fat man sweeps out, *Who is this?!*, and grabs her, picks her up and takes her inside. THIS IS THE MOMENT TO STRIKE, KEBRETH, RIGHT NOW, DON'T THINK ABOUT IT, MOVE! Kebreth finds himself standing there, frozen. One step forward would find him running up those steps into that room and. He doesn't move.

Later, to himself, he will explain away this moment – the time wasn't right, the will of the proletariat had not been sufficiently developed. He will believe himself. Let us believe him too. HE'S JUST DOING HIS BEST! He is not the first notebook revolutionary to hesitate at the moment of truth, nor will he be the last. His body remains tensed – that is something, he is not cowed, that can be a revolution, why not? Then the girl is coming back out to sit next to the skinny-arsed little boy. Kebreth watches her hand him a cigarette. She puts one in her own mouth, slim fingers placing it between full lips, her white dress clinging to her slender body.

I feel Kebreth's eyes upon us as we play, as she picks the coffee bean from behind my ear, the side of her hand softly touching my hair, those magic hands fluttering around me before clamping down on my wrist and twisting. I sometimes imagine this as a dance, my body as supple as hers, with Kebreth our mute audience.

Well.

They become lovers, Lucy and Kebreth. Not now, but later. I am not given to suspense. Let's make it the night after Tekle tells us of the *Kebra Nagast*, maybe that very night in fact, much neater. It happens once I go home, my head full of Solomon and Sheba, Kebreth wakes Lucy and takes her home and makes her his love, and while I am back in my bed, dreaming Lucy into Sheba's clothes and myself into Solomon's body, they are entwined together, sharing those soft words that can only be exchanged by lips near enough to each other to kiss, and then kissing. She lies beside him and pulls a coffee bean from behind his ear, and they laugh and start up again. They will fall in love, and make love like lovers.

This is my first scar, running across my chest. My heart lifted from my body by Lucy, and as I walk away each night from then on I hear the start of their lovemaking, can hear it still, and the next day the body of Kebreth is no longer clumsy, the juddering circumlocutions of this awkward youth streamlined into balletic pneumatics, and just as Lucy put gold in my mouth so she has put gold into his limbs, and as they make love I walk away and my mouth grows dry and silent again.

You walk away with me too, Lovejoy, fuck you, standing there with a hand down your trousers and your greedy eyes. You don't get to see what happens next either, you just get to sit with me under a *kojo* tree and watch Kebreth kiss those strong hands, watch their beautiful bodies fall to the ground, with only the sound of their love to fill your ears.

Kebreth, tired after a night of making love to the love of my life, of fucking her again and again and making her cum and cum while I was lying awake so so alone, works his way through the coffee bushes, talking softly of the revolutionary struggle to his fellow pickers as he does, but there's a faraway look of satisfaction in his eyes. It's hard to usher in the dictatorship of the proletariat when you're getting plenty – where's your motivation?

My father watched the pickers below as he knocked back the *tej*. He had thought that his arrival in Africa – he always called it Africa not Ethiopia not Abyssinia, my mother did the same – would be like in the movies, the white *massa* carried in a sedan chair, hoisted on black shoulders, a further sedan chair swaying behind with his wife and son. Obedience, obsequiousness, that sort of thing. Hanging with the Duke of Gloucester at the Coronation, the presentation of zebras and the peeling of grapes. Sitting on a porch being fanned by a native while the coffee-pickers turned plants into money and Ibrahim Salez turned that money into gold. A spot of big-game hunting in the evening, safari suits and pith helmets, him and Holbrook posing with rifles for photographs, while awestruck Ethiopes held the heads of lions gazelles buffalo oryx. That was Ethiopia to him, that was it, not badly made *tukul*s with builders clinging to the outside, the stupid heat, the natives who were taller than him, their muttering of words he couldn't understand, enigmatic girls wandering out of the forest and pitching camp, Man Fridays who read books and wrote things down, and what was Salez doing, fuck him, I send him a thousand pounds and get five hundred pounds' worth of gold six months later.

Not to mention that hysterical woman. Not to mention that pallid sickly boy of mine, heir to the Everett quintillions, who can't even get through the night without pissing himself. The company is doomed.

He would spend hours a day poring over his financial journals, accounting for every last coffee bean, every last penny, and file them carefully in our ridiculous travelled-five-continents roll-top desk for safekeeping, trusting the key only to himself and to me in case he died, and I would give the key to Kebreth, who would steal the journals and use the backs for taking notes.

As for big-game hunting, I do remember that my father stepped on a frog once, killing it outright, Kebreth running up to him and telling him that the spirit of the frog is sacred in Africa and that my father must pay homage to the God of Frogs lest he wake one day and find himself amphibious.

Holbrook did bring heads back, each Saturday evening, heads of lions gazelles buffalo oryx, carried in muslin sacks over his shoulder that he emptied with a heave in front of my father, the creature's head rolling across the room and ending up wedged in a corner due to the slope of the house. Holbrook's toy African boy, I'd forgotten about him, let's forget about him, scurrying across to fetch it, placing it before my father so they could contemplate one another, man and beast, and I imagined some of them diving forward and sinking their teeth into him. This, too, is my coffee story.

My father would have the heads of the beasts mounted, his name on a silver plaque below the jaw, then nail them to the unsteady wall from which they would fall after about a week. The sound of animal heads thumping against the floor was constant and unnerving, and when I returned to England they, whoever *they* are, sent the heads back to me, a large crate arriving in our storeroom, opened by an apprentice who nearly died of shock looking into that giant wooden box and seeing that many-headed beast, laughing at him. I had them burnt, all of them, and the smell of their flesh cooking in the flames smelt to me like Harar.

When not staring blankly at his books my father would be bullying the workforce into working harder, faster, his words met with mute indifference by all, an ineffectual man barely able to hold a brandy glass, a Dannemann cigar.

What a battle this is! An ineffectual slave-owner against an ineffectual revolutionary, in an obscure corner of an obscure country, and I guess it's lots of these battles that create some sort of saturation point, the greatest journey begins with a single step, but maybe it's not, maybe it was irrelevant even then, it just happened to fill my life, to belly the sails of my existence, and couldn't I have just reached my hands out once and torn a hole in it all and stepped through to another life?, somewhere where the great battles were being fought, knights clashing on chargers, tanks rolling over the tops of homes, or, even better, somewhere where there were no battles, the middle of a flute solo, pitched quietly and unending. Just that. Just for a while. But who's to guarantee I wouldn't have fucked that up too?

Great, I am going blind. On top of everything else, I am going blind. I tell Siobhan, *I am going blind!*, and even though she knows it is death getting me ready, she tells me that she will tell Lovejoy so that he can get me some drops, which will be a waste of time but at least it is an evasion. Far easier than saying the word 'death' in a hospital. Nobody says it, even though it is the one constant. All of us, the whole sad cargo, with our iron lungs and our catheters, our crutches and our bedpans and our bandages, are told we are looking better, chirpier, we will be able to get out of bed, take up our pallets and walk, at least as far as the cell door. The doctors could write flash cards with these phrases on them, holding them up at key moments, shuffling them occasionally. The word 'death' would not appear on any of them. The word 'death' is far too dangerous to let out into the atmosphere: it would take on a life of its own, it would fall from the card and into the mouth of the patient, a sickly sweet word to roll around the tongue. For some it would be indigestible and would be spat out violently. For others it would be sweet, sweet truth, snuffing out hope, that bastard hope, and would be swallowed gratefully, whole. The last breath of the free man would throw it back into the atmosphere, where it would be passed from mouth to mouth, the perfect palliative, a Chinese whisper, winding its way through the hospital, picking up a multitude of germs along the way, infections, until its cargo of bacteria would be so pestilent that the merest touch would kill you, and everyone in the hospital would be dead.

Which is why they don't say it.

But maybe they talk about death among themselves, the hospital staff, over sandwiches and magazines and tea. Maybe they talk about little else. Maybe they even sing about it, invoke it, throw death around the room and bounce it off the walls GOOD OLD DEATH! YOU GOTTA LOVE DEATH! Tearing it out of themselves with a shout of joy, making it a communal gift, getting rid of it there and then so they don't have to take it home with them, so they can have sex and watch television like normal people, but listen, they're not normal people because normal people know that the sick are to be avoided, the sick are offensive, you shouldn't go anywhere near them, and you sure as hell don't touch them, you don't clean up their shit, you don't wash their balls. Normal people know this. Nurses don't. Doctors don't.

Doctors and nurses run around looking after diseased people. Looking after patients. There must be other patients here, I have heard them screaming in the night. What I would give for the strength to scream.

Some of them shuffle past my door on high days and holidays, pushing their metal IV frames before them, trundling up Golgotha. Some of them talk to themselves as they go, some even sing, the shits, no one wants to hear that, and more than once I have considered the possibility that this is an asylum rather than a prison, but I don't remember going mad, so it can't be.

But I also don't remember arriving, I remember just before and just after, but not that bit, and I certainly don't intend to remember leaving. A window to the right of my bed lets in a rectangle of light two foot by two, and when the light is yellow it is day; when there is no light it is night. Day used to be bigger than that, I've seen it covering deserts and oceans, I've even sat in my own private Learjet and had it above me and below me, but now it is two foot by two, and soon it will not exist at all. The end of the universe is nigh, and I don't care about anyone else. There is a window box on the window ledge supporting an ecosystem of two yellow shrubs, which I presume is to give the illusion of life. I attempt, in my more philosophical moments, to regard these plants with sufficient gravity. Human life is, after all, whatever be its glories and its follies, sustained ultimately by the existence of plant life. Photosynthesis. Semi-permeable something something. *Qua thingy, ergo sum.* Thus my shrubs.

Occasionally a tall man in white overalls comes and pours a jug of water over the plants. He is completely bald but sports a massive beard. I have decided not to talk to him or acknowledge his presence. He talks to the plants, *Hey, plants, that's better, isn't it?* The plants drink the water. He tells them they are looking well, and they will be able to get up and walk around in a couple of days.

People move past my door. Mostly they are nurses. Sometimes they are tradesmen. Twice I've seen priests, but I've also seen the Virgin Mary and Henry Kissinger, so who fucking knows?

Moira never drank coffee, of course. Not because she didn't like it, because who doesn't like coffee? She said she didn't drink it because it tasted too much like longing.

To my first wife, however, longing was the most desired of all drugs. To my first wife, however, coffee was the most desired of all drugs.

If you want to know why I did what I did, I think it might be because of her. I think it might have been just to annoy her.

We were married, she and me, my first wife and I, on 6 May 1945. It was one week after Hitler killed himself, eight days after he married Eva Braun, and nine days after Mussolini was hanged, upside-down outside a petrol station, with his mistress, Clara. Celebrations were in order! The tide of Nazism/Fascism had been turned back! The world was free! She wore an ivory dress with a sixteen-foot train, four months pregnant but not so you'd notice.

I met my first wife during a bacchanal in the Penthouse Suite of the New York Hilton on 4 February 1945. We were celebrating my adoption of US citizenship, and the fiftieth/five-hundredth/one-millionth barrel of Everett's Standard Roast off the production line since the shift to America to avoid Hitler's doodlebugs and ambitions. Land of the. Home of the.

She was standing awkwardly, working-classly, beside a Louis XIV style Boulle table – wearing pink chiffon and a pink corsage. She had black lines drawn in eye-liner up the backs of her legs. Her hair was up like Barbara Stanwyck's in *Double Indemnity*. Her lips were red like Betty Grable's in *Diamond Horseshoe*. Her arse was round like Dorothy Lamour's in *A Medal for Benny*. She was a real doll!

She had been brought to the party by the youngest son of Ibrahim Salez, who had found her in a burger joint three blocks from the hotel, weeping into a thickshake because Tommy or Bobby or Johnny had been seen balling Darlene or April or Sue. I wanted her so much it made my teeth itch. I told her to forget Tommy or Bobby or Johnny, because I'm Teddy Everett and you've seen me in the papers. We drank wine from the same stiletto and danced to Perry Como, until she had to stagger to the Louis XIV-style bathroom to throw up. Then we cruised to a deserted parking lot in my Chrysler Thunderbolt, where we hugged and kissed, and I told her about drinking coffee by the Barada river in Damascus, smoking a hookah and watching the boats go past, mine included, stolen by a man called Obst who knew I was too stoned to do anything about it, but then, truth be told, I had lots of boats, and I felt her soften in my arms. I was in! I bent down and licked the eye-liner from the backs of her legs as she knelt on all fours on the sofa-style front seat of the car, my tongue ending up in her vagina, the first time cunnilingus had ever been performed in the United States!, which made her fall in love with me there and then, and when I told her I had been exempted from military duty because of the effects of childhood trauma associated with the murder of my dear dear father, she couldn't help opening her legs in a gesture so profoundly patriotic that I, in turn, couldn't help responding, entering her, profoundly, patriotically, breaking through her hymen at the precise moment, give or take, that our brave boys, also profoundly, also patriotically, broke through the Siegfried Line and saved the world!

We spent the rest of the night walking through the streets of New York, down Hollywood and Vine, past doughnut salesmen and walls covered with rain-soaked movie posters. Gary Cooper and Loretta Young in *Along Came Jones*. Rex Harrison in *The Rake's Progress*. Betty Grable in *Diamond Horseshoe*, and Ingrid Bergman looking more rootable than any man or woman before or since in *Spellbound*. We ate sixty-five-cent steaks washed down with Pepsi at Jack Dempsey's Broadway Restaurant, and caught Tommy Dorsey's show at eight a.m. at the Capitol. We kissed against a poster of John Wayne in *Tall in the Saddle*, oblivious to the fact that this was the precise moment that my most dogged spermatozoa had found itself a waiting egg, *Howdy!* We kissed and kissed, like Merle Oberon and Laurence Olivier in *Wuthering Heights*, like Greer Garson and Walter Pidgeon in *Mrs Parkington*, especially like Lauren Bacall and Humphrey Bogart in *To Have and Have Not*, and as she told me she wanted to fuck me again, like Ethel Barrymore and Cary Grant in *None But the Lonely Heart*, the egg split open and let its sticky visitor inside, *Howdy yourself!*

Listen, cells grew and split, split and grew, forged towards organhood. Helixes gripped and tore. In other news, the Russians, ferried southwards by the Trans-Siberian railway, seized two hundred villages in Silesia. The Allies entered Mönchengladbach, levelled Dresden, and crossed the Rhine. Urgent meetings were held. Churchill, Roosevelt and Stalin at Yalta; Hitler, Goering and Himmler in Berlin; and, crucially, myself, my pregnant ladyfriend and her drunk, gun-toting younger brother in my office at Everett's. Negotiations dragged through the night. Stalin, his position strengthened by recent military victories, won tacit

Anglo-US support for Soviet control of Eastern Europe. Hitler, his position weakened by recent military defeats, won tacit support for the idea of marrying his girlfriend and then topping himself. My first wife, her position strengthened by the embryo growing within her, not to mention the presence of her gun-toting brother, won explicit support for the fact that the right thing would be done.

And so, in a series of firm handshakes and the placing down of weapons, it was agreed. Russia got Poland, the Third Reich was abandoned 988 years early, and my first wife and I, *Gloria in Excelsis*, were to be joined in the sight of God and her brother, in holy, most holy, matrimony.

Sixteen-foot trains were ordered. Ivory dresses. Actual stockings, you can do that when you're rich. The blue suspenders of her strange and awful mother. My mother's last handkerchief, still spotted with blood. A corset, done up not too tightly because of the. Shoes. Whisky.

We spent the night before making love in every room in her sister's house, drunk on love and alcohol, and at three a.m. she put on her wedding dress for me to see, twirling around in front of me, I'd paid for it after all, and they say it's unlucky *but we showed them!*, and I came on her chest and watched it roll down the ivory.

I stole out of the house at five a.m. before her parents arrived, one blue suspender around my thigh beneath my trousers where it stayed throughout the ceremony.

Ibrahim Salez's youngest son was my best man, and he gave two of the three bridesmaids syphilis.

My first wife and I had our first legal coitus two hours

later in the Penthouse Suite where we had first met, shagging on the selfsame Louis XIV-style Boulle table, and as we rocked backwards and forwards on the tortoiseshell marquetry we turned each other on with our newly minted matrimonial names, *husband! husband! wife! wife!*, and she told me dirty stories about her provincial couplings in barnyards and tractor trucks, about cousins and incest and rumours of bestiality, and I told her about my father fucking my second cousin Adam on horseback, presumably on the pretext that immense wealth and overarching obesity can only combine in the lewdest varieties of corpulent activities, a story whose telling made her cum and cum and cum and cum so hard that she flew backwards off the table, *whee!*, a wide-eyed arc of tensile womanhood, accelerating towards the floor at thirty-two feet per second per second, landing flat on her back with the wind knocked out of her and me sprawled on top, the table reduced by my plummeting weight to its constituent elements, pewter, copper, horn, a gilt-bronze mount pressed into my stomach, oak and walnut clattering against my head and splitting in my ears.

The table was wrecked!

My first wife's slim left ankle was broken!

And our growing child was dead dead dead in her womb.

There is a traditional Ethiopian poetic form, Teddy, sammena worq, bronze and gold. Poems in this form have two meanings, a simple, obvious one, the bronze, and a hidden, deeper one. The words of each are exactly the same, but the meaning is different. There are some who say all stories are bronze and gold. And some who say it is true of every sentence, and finally every word. Perhaps it is true of life itself.

At first it was the broken Louis XIV-style coffee-table that garnered most of the attention. The table had, no doubt, survived much in its time, the detritus of the rich and famous – clocks, coffee cups, magazines and Gideon's Bibles, shorts and panties hastily removed and flung, socks, earrings, watches, lamps heavy or light in keeping with styles glib or weighty, wine glasses, carafes, powders, tobaccos, pot-boiler novels, pamphlets on hygiene, on restaurants, on facilities (within the hotel, without the hotel), all manner of bric-à-brac and, no doubt, who could deny it?, couplings legal or indictable, strenuous or refined, brief, extended, Olympian, disappointing, vigorous or slow.

But it could not escape the plummet of my bridegroom body, still frozen in a rictus of ejaculation, trying to gather my thoughts and my facial features into something unified and useful nor could it escape the terrible destinies of the family Everett, who will eventually break everything they touch, themselves included.

(The coffee-table in my current room is made of re-assuring stainless steel, smooth, shiny and bright, allowing the possessions of each patient to be swept quickly away when they die, mine next.)

Porters, bellboys, concierges were summoned to hoist my fallen angel from the kindling and pronounce on her dis-abilities. One bellboy took particular interest, and would find himself summoned again and again by my wife to attend to her bandages, massage her calves. My wife, unused to such servility, would test the gilt of its edges, complaining of infirmities previously unnoticed – calves knotted by the stress of the fall, knees scraped by the kindling she had fallen into, thighs bruised by the impact of the table – infir-mities requiring the bellboy's touch higher and higher until

until she came to one ache in particular, an ache, dear God, in her womb, troubling her most, and which required filling by him, and by so many afterwards, trying to fill the gap that now existed inside her, and between her and her grieving man.

He wasn't to know, of course, he was seventeen, dumb as dogshit, just a boy with a pair of slim grown-up lady's arms around his neck, a hand holding the back of his head, pulling him down on to a hotel bed, a mouth against his, eyes that never closed during lovemaking, unlike those of the girls he was used to balling, staring confidently into his. Just an act, fifteen minutes of a blameless life, he can probably barely remember it.

But I can torture myself with these moments for ever. I pick at it again and again.

The moment the bellboy entered my first wife she gave a silent scream, letting irredeemable poison into our marriage. It was a scream so utter and so huge and so female that it could be repeated throughout our marriage, torn off in fragments and reused, an accusation that damned me utterly, you have ruined my life, her eyes becoming red and

How many dead children has Lovejoy held in his surgeon's hands? How many have passed through this hospital, transported here in ripe bellies and leaving as tiny corpses, little seahorses? You could pickle them in brine and watch them through the glass. And they will watch you because, as every man or woman who has staggered out of a disinfected mausoleum knows, there is no escaping those eyes.

Hey, Everevereverevereverett, where are your sons?

Where are their portraits? Where is that famous Everett DNA now? Where is your coffee business?

All gone. It all stops with me. I am the end of the line.

Lucy Alfarez walked out of the jungle at the age of fourteen with a silver lighter in one hand, a coffee bean in the other. It is morning, my mother is in bed. She sleeps late now; the days hold such terror for her that she shortens them with sleep at the beginning and sleep at the end, until there is no day left. Africa is so big. I sometimes imagine her screwing up a handkerchief in her hands, and the thought fills me with terror – other times I think of her hands lying passively on her lap, and I am no less scared. When your mother is a stranger then

Then

Her skin is yellow now. Her hair has grown long, her face without makeup. Africa is so big.

She has been in bed for four months, will stay there for three years, and then die. She had lain down on the day of the Coronation of Haile Selassie, the day we found out about the suicide of my grandfather, her father-in-law, Percival, whom she had never met. It wasn't until I was given her personal effects on my twenty-first birthday that I found the letters they had been writing to each other. From him the week after her marriage, but meant to be read before, warning her of the horrors of the Everett family, *I don't presume to know you, but a word of advice, save yourself, my dear, they will crush you as they have crushed me*; from her, by next post, enquiring as to his habits and where he found such beautiful notepaper; from him, *I have taken the liberty of including a small collection of my poems, they are nothing much but*; from her, *Your poems are very beautiful, I used to love poetry, but who is she, the woman you write about, are you all right?*; from him, *Her name is Maria, but she is every woman trodden beneath the feet of uncaring men, an angel, and you know they are trying to kill me, don't you, I am an embarrassment to them*; from her, *She must be beautiful, at least they are killing me to my face tee-hee, there is talk of Africa, I am scared*; from him, *She has gone, warned off and I am alone*; from her, *I will write when we arrive*; from him, *Please do*, and then nothing.

Never keep any records. Never ever ever. Because later someone will find them and. Then they'll. And you'll.

My mother sits staring at the wall as Lucy walks out of the jungle. She has been unable to send Percival the promised letter, nothing has come from him, he has no doubt forgotten her, that's what happens, isn't it?, whatever the promises of new friendship or love, there is always death wrapped up in it, not sudden death, just the slow rescinding of promises, the gradual onset of neglect.

Lucy comes to sit beside me. Who was she where did she come from? People come running. My father. Lifting. Shouting. The belt. The whistling of the belt. Could my mother hear the whistling of the belt? Did she react? How did she react?

I don't know how my mother reacted. I play out the scene again and again, but I don't know how my mother reacted. Did she tense with each blow? Put her hands over her ears to stop the sound of leather on flesh? Bury her head in the pillow, hide under the sheets? Was she just glad it wasn't her, glad it was the impertinent girl she understood at a glance?

I know how my mother reacted. She sat there, her hands lying passively on her lap, without moving. Gone.

177

Time passed! 1931, 1932, 1933, and I am eleven, twelve, thirteen. As I lie here dying I try to separate them out, find some distinction between them, but they agglomerate, refuse to come apart. Birtwhistle was right – this is a timeless land! Kwibe is growing with me, perhaps we have the same birthday, that would make things easier, we grow at the same rate too, sprout our first pubic hair simultaneously, have our first wet dream the very same night! About the very same girl! You know, underneath their skin, people are pretty similar! We both watch Lucy with growing aware-ness, she watches us with growing scorn. She is fourteen, fifteen, sixteen – a hundred years older than a fourteen-year-old. Her curves become more pronounced, and she removes them from us more frequently. My arm no longer burns from her twisting, there are no more coffee beans hidden behind my ear. She spends more time with Kebreth, working beside him, sharing his cigarettes, sharing their musk.

Kebreth is getting older too. How old is Kebreth? The man who bowed and scraped as we first arrived in Harar looks no different from the one who hangs from the *kojo* tree four years later. He spends his time attempting to lead the employees of Everett and Sons into insurrection; there have been assassination attempts unnoticed by his intended victim, cheap guns that failed to fire, bullets that flew two feet too high, a gas pellet that turned out to contain nothing but oxygen, and a hunting accident that claimed the lives of three dogs, but he spends less and less time working for the revolution, at gathering the crowds. He still makes the occasional attempt on my father's life, but more as a way of impressing a chick than of inspiring Pan-Africanism. Given that he eventually dies for the Cause I think we can allow him this period of reflection.

My father spends these days becoming more indolent, a seated version of my mother. The *tej* has taken control, a draught in the morning before settling down to his papers, one at lunchtime, and then more to wile away the afternoon. Company records show that the greater part of his interest remained in the prospect of foraging gold from the plain of Egypt, as promised by Salez, and the pair communicated by a steady flow of telegrams, Salez eking ever more money from my father, my father falling for ever more outlandish schemes, none of them coming to fruition, but none of them foundering with the sort of haste that might cause suspicion. Salez would occasionally wire my father about some fictitious piece of a fictitious pharaoh's jewellery sent back to England, the delays in correspondence causing a useful amount of confusion. My father would occasionally wire Salez to tell him he was a robber, an extortionist, a blackguard, and that he was going to go to Cairo personally and wring his neck, but then the *tej* would kick in, and the heat would get hot, and my father's eyes would moisten as he explained that Salez was his greatest friend on Earth, and the best salesman of Everett and Sons in the world. It was good, decent, Edwardian charlatanism that Salez practised, smoke and mirrors in Savile Row suits, and Salez's son would repay the debt in the 1940s by giving me a bottle of Glenmorangie, and introducing me to my first wife.

My mother stayed in bed, attended by her silent familiar Kwibe. She neither gained weight nor lost it. Whether she gained or lost wisdom I am not to know. I don't seem to be gaining any lying here, so let's say not. She would stay sitting up all day, and into the night, until my father stumbled in and dropped on to the mattress beside her. Then she would lie down, facing away from him (and he from her), until he woke, stumbled out and pulled on his pants, at which point she would sit back up, and resume her quietude, waiting for Kwibe to bring her morning tea. They were like marionettes, the three of them, sliding from place to place along perfectly engineered grooves.

My eyes are fucked. Sweet Jesus, my eyes are fucked.

Mrs Smithers took my father's increasingly static condition and commensurate lack of libido with good grace, quickly making an emphatic female decision to stop having sex for ever, hanging up her desires as simply as hanging up her coat, a genetic adaptation engendered by Christ alone knows how much female suffering. Her housekeeping became minimal – there was no point trying to keep things clean when the floor kept moving, no point trying to dust when there was a builder hanging from the eaves. As for cooking, who could eat in this sort of heat?, and the boy seems to prefer the darkie food anyway. She allowed herself to slip gracefully and gratefully into superfluity, wearing her obsolescence like a hat.

Holbrook spent three years cracking his knuckles and poking his willy in and out of a hole in the wall while singing 'Jesu Joy of Man's Desiring'. I don't know what Holbrook spent three years doing.

What else? Hitler was elected, Bradman took 103 off Harold Larwood and Bill Voce to show that Bodyline could be faced down and defeated. I learnt to speak Amharic better than I could speak English and spent my evenings in the flesh of Tekle and Ababa's hut, more skin pressed against mine than in the louche orgies I would host in the late 1940s. I whittled 375 stupid stupid wooden animals making me the god of some realm where stupid stupid wooden animals roam free. An accidental first orgasm made me leap from my bed and run the length of the room in blind panic, stepping on a gecko halfway across, which helped not one little bit. I climbed to the top of the *kojo* tree one day and fell all the way down, landing on my back and receiving no injuries. I spent days living on cigarettes and coffee to see how it felt, and it made me feel depressed and horny, my first encounter with the weird thrill of self-hatred that underlies every addiction until it becomes itself addictive. I embraced God, rejected Him, and embraced Him again, as teenagers are wont to do. I fell ever deeper in love with Lucy Alfarez, as the Italians began massing on the Ethiopian border, preparing to invade and blow the whole thing to shit, and always, always, this bed in this hospital in this prison was here waiting for me, my final altar, empty for seventy years, except for every other poor fucker who has lain here waiting for death.

Lucy Alfarez, seventeen years old, sits on my bed, swinging her feet, and tells me she is bored. *Bored bored bored.* It is 1933. I can work that much out at least. I am thirteen and in bed with a fever, and Lucy is bored. Kebreth is working and she does not want to work; today she is a girl not a woman, and she has no one to play with. I have been in bed for a week. Everyone hopes it is not malaria.

The smell of me, my smell, fills the room, fills the house. It winds its way through every room, under doors, sticking to windows. It enters my mother's room, my parents' room which is my mother's. It enters her nostrils, she breathes it into her lungs, it rolls around her maternal heart, and she finds herself swinging her legs out of the bed, my baby is in trouble, and she finds herself getting out of bed, the first time in three years, getting out and coming to look after her baby.

Twice a day my mother comes and changes the sheets, flinging the set covered with sweat and urine into a corner, an arc of sick discharge curving across the room, while I sit watching and shivering in a wicker chair beside the bed, wrapped in a blanket. My father stands in the doorway and tells my mother that she is stupid, there are plenty of niggers who will do that, sit down, will you, woman, but my mother doesn't meet his eye; here his words carry no weight. We are in the realm of the domestic. My mother has found a purpose. She remakes the bed with clean sheets, sheets she has washed herself, and she pops me back inside them. She lays her hand on my forehead. She tells me that soon we will be going home, and then everything will be all right, Angel of God, my guardian dear.

I remember.

I remember being embarrassed by that hand on my forehead. My god. Her presence. Her constant crappy changing of the sheets. I sat in the wicker chair, watching her heaving and huffing and puffing, and one end would always be tucked in too far, and she would have to spread-eagle herself across the bed to pull the far end and make it fit, and another corner would jerk free. She could never get the whole thing straight. All she had to do was get the fucking thing straight.

Jesus, then I wouldn't have had to sit there squirming, hoping that no one would see her there, her backside in the air, pulling desperately at the crooked sheets, saying to me, saying to me like nails on a blackboard, that she'd soon have it fixed.

And when I was back in bed, lying there on wrinkled sheets, she would flutter around me, getting me glasses of water, making me sit up or lie down according to her anxiety, putting her hand on my forehead to see if I was still hot, her hand would be on my forehead and her brow would crease and she would say, Better or worse?, like she fucking knew, and white shame would run through me and I would hope like hell she would just go back to being locked away in her room.

Sometimes she would just sit on the chair and tell me

everything was going to be all right and tell me I was her baby, and that was more embarrassing than anything.

Oh, my inept mother. Live your life again. Come back to the Earth and live a life of freedom, without a child, without a husband, without the fucking Everetts. Run away from home at the age of fifteen and marry a film star, you loved the movies, Mama, or the apprentice at the butcher's, Theodore his name is, and leave bed-sheets to those who have no skills beyond bed-sheets.

Lucy is bored. All the boys, all the men are picking beans, making coffee. The men always ask Lucy to leave. It is no job for a girl, they say. Besides, they say, smiling, the work rate seems to drop when you are around, Lucy, some of the boys are reaching an age where

Lucy is bored. All the girls, all the women are cooking or washing clothes. Lucy hates cooking. Lucy hates washing clothes.

She asks me if I would like to watch her play with herself and I say, Yes, and she says, Fuck off . . .

And then she is beside me, on the bed, her body alongside mine, the length of it running along the length of mine, both of us on our backs, staring at the ceiling. She lifts the top of my pyjamas above my belly. Pulls the bottoms down to my knees. I lie beside her, unable to move, feeling myself stir. Lucy licks the palm of her hand and moves it, glistening, above my crotch, kissing my ear as she does. Then, staring into my eyes, she reaches down and squeezes my penis just once – just once – laughs, and is out of the door.

And I am following, desperately pulling the drawstring on my pyjamas, howling, primeval, howling.

Oh, Lucy, did you know how much trouble I would get into, did you know how sick I was, did you take the time to look at my face as I chased you through the trees, did you see the fever there, did you see the tears in my eyes, hot, hot tears, because of the pain of my illness, and because of the thrashing I would receive? Did you not see my red face as I held you to the ground, my hands pressing your wrists against the earth, my heart thumping at the thought of my mother opening the bedroom door and finding the bed empty, my heart beating at the thought of your slim body beneath me

as I tried to kiss you, remember it was the first time I tried to kiss you, tried to kiss anyone, and I tried because I was burning, because I was helpless and angry, I was angry, Lucy, angry at my hopeless fucking mother, angry at my cruel fucking father, but mostly angry at you for being so fucking beautiful, for fitting into the world so exactly, twisting me so easily, I was angry at you, which is why I bit your lip, why I hurt you, and then you rolled me over and freed your wrists and slapped me hard across the face.

Because, you said, I was full of germs, because you didn't want to catch my fever.

But you did.

And for a week I couldn't see you. For a week you were in bed, somewhere else in bed, and during the night I would imagine I was there with you, holding you and keeping you safe, and then I would remember that you were Kebreth's lover and then I would remember that Kebreth was your lover and I would burn with shame. And for a week my father thrashed my backside, the leather strap whistling through the air, each blow launching from me a howl, hot salty tears, making me burn with shame.

My mother also caught the fever. But unlike you and me, Lucy, my mother knew the word 'death'. She had seen it in the newspapers beside the name of her precious brother, had heard it murmured by aunts and uncles as she watched his coffin sink at the age of seven, had seen it bubble out at dinner parties followed by the heavy scraping of cutlery. She had written it in her diary on the day of her engagement, wrapped in the poem of a seventeen-year-old girl. It had come screaming around the globe at her, the day before the Coronation, I will always be there for you, and lodged in her frail heart. And now she found the word sitting in her mouth, as she lay again in her bed, me up and about so she redundant again, truly redundant, stuck in this incomprehensible country, sweating, shaking, and it was her saliva that death was wrapped in, not her brother's or her mother's, and it tasted of fever, was full of germs.

Should I have looked after her on those last days? I was only a boy! It was Kwibe's job! I would peer around the door frame at this sweating creature, watching it shake as it reached for a glass of water. When I think of that time my mind tries to find a symmetry: it has me placing my hand on her brow, fussing with her sheets, being as inept for her as she was for me. But I didn't. I just watched, watched her get smaller, watched every bead of sweat that rolled down her face and dropped to the floor subtract a little of her, until she was worn down to nothing.

Such long nights, those Ethiopian nights, listening to my mother dry-retch in the other room, willing Kwibe at three a.m. to take her a glass of water, where is he?, why isn't he here?, she needs water! Such long nights again now. It's the waking that stretches them. Then, the warm piss, the night terrors; now, the warm piss, the night terrors, plus a needle in my arse at eleven and four, some viscous and anonymous liquid that aches its way through the muscle and into the bloodstream. The nurse who does this is always different. The night staff terrify me. Why are they the night staff? During the day it is Siobhan, the red-haired nurse, who pierces me, except when it is the jolly one, she does the occasional afternoon, I think, perhaps to keep her hand in now that some husband has gone back to work. Siobhan is somewhere else, doing something else when she is there. THERE IS NO TORTURE GREATER THAN KNOWING YOUR BELOVED ISN'T THINKING ABOUT YOU! NOT EVEN CANCER! Siobhan is never there at night, and I think of nothing else.

Mostly.

Last night after another anonymous needle from an anonymous nurse, after this stranger had injected me and left, I cried for an hour, proper howling, teeth into the pillow, that sort of thing. Nothing like a good cry, my mother used to say, did she, did she ever say that? I was nothing but a hard kernel of despair.

But tell you what, I felt a million bucks afterwards! King of the fucking world! Nothing like a good cry.

So when Siobhan came in this morning, *Where have you been, my love?*, I was so full of myself I could have sat her on my lap and told her funny stories, I felt that good! Did you know I spent four years in Ethiopia when I was a boy? Yes, you see my father sold coffee! No – not a shop! – he owned the whole plantation! I had a friend called Lucy, very mysterious, and one called Kwibe Abi, who was a local I tried to teach to play cricket. We would play all sorts of games together, the three of us, oh, the fun we had! Then there was this guy called Kebreth, you would have liked him, he had these crazy ideas, the establishment of a proletarian government in Ethiopia that would have led to a Pan-African revolution! I know! And, get this, there was another guy, Tekle Tolossa, who was blind but could predict the future. I slept with his wife a couple of times – he didn't see that coming! – so I hope you don't mind, you're not my first. When all of this is over I'll tell you more, I need someone to listen to me, I'm dying and I'm full of stories, and when they die the others will be gone too, and I've already killed them once, I don't want to again. So, my little chickadee, my honey bunch, my sweet child, just sit here and listen.

The day my mother died, Kwibe Abi and I had spent the day fighting the Italians with stick guns, shooting them out of the air and watching them fall, Kwibe signalling a cease fire every few hours so he could take my mother her food, or collect her still full plate.

At dusk, when he should have been taking her dinner he stopped, squatted down on the spot, and stared at me, with those big accusing eyes of his. Stand up, Kwibe! Please go to her! I don't want to. Even that day I didn't want to. Even now I don't want to.

The sky was hung with stars, the *tukul* was hung with builders, crawling across its walls and roof on all fours, wet like lizards, and they revolved their eyes and watched me as I entered, flicking their tongues in and out, one brushing cold against my arm as I went through the door.

Pews slid along the hallway as I walked up it, candles flamed and guttered, the eyes of angels carved into miseri-cords turned from wood to jelly and followed me. The Patriarch walked at my shoulder chanting the Trisagion, *Lord have mercy, visit us and heal us, cleanse us from our sins.*

I peered through the door frame at her, my dying mother. The ghost had entered her, the saints of the Orthodox Church, Raguel, Samuel, Libanos had come out of the walls to surround her and then become one with her flesh, the flesh of this white woman, this woman as white as marble, the girlish red of her cheeks now a white pallor, sunken, sculpted, white. It was fascination not compassion that brought me to her bedside, I'm reconciled to that, I wanted to look at this thing, this sepulchral thing, beneath its sepulchral cross, to compare it to my mother, compare it to Edith Everett, *née* Stanley, whose pink cheeks a butcher boy had kissed and had felt hot beneath his lips. I pulled up a chair, sat beside it, sat beside this thing. The peace around it drew me in, made me calm. It stared straight ahead, like my mother, it had her outline, but sharper, the skin as white as the bones beneath. In the distance I could hear Lucy playing, laughing, and this one time I didn't want to go to her.

The thing was breathing, shallow breaths, its chest rising and falling, without sound, the silence as deep as a pause in music. Its hand reached out for mine and I took it; it was neither hot nor cold, it was as it should be.

You know, Teddy, before I married your father, there was another, a boy named Theodore, who worked as a butcher. I gave you his name. I was very young, but I think I was in love with him. I think I loved him more than the sun moon stars. He was handsome and very kind. On my seventeenth birthday he asked me for a kiss. I let him, and he kissed my cheek, just once, and blushed. I can still feel it.

I saw him on the way to the church on my wedding day, why not?, kicking leaves along the gutter. He was off to his life, I was off to mine. They were different lives.

Mine led up the aisle to an altar. A priest. I remember watching him speak. There was white clag on the sides of his mouth. His tongue was light pink. One of his front teeth overlapped the other.

There was the sound of bells.

The priest. His eyebrows were uneven, the lines in his forehead too long for his face. He asked me if I do. And I said, Yes, I do.

I have done, Teddy. I have tried. But I can't any more. Your father. Your father is not a bad man, Teddy. Life is hard. Remember that. It's important that you remember that.

Her final absolution. A lie to smooth things over.

And I let go of her hand, her cold cold hand, and I knew she wanted me to say something, a last word for her, a lie to help her too, but nothing came, the Patriarch nudged me, *Say something!*, but I found myself backing out of the room, the Patriarch watching me go, and I saw my mother's eyes fill with tears and then with terror, and I sometimes comfort myself with the thought that they were looking beyond me, into the gathering light or the gathering darkness, but I know they were looking into mine, and what they saw wasn't on the outside, her eyes saw deep deep inside me, to the things only a mother knows, because there are some things only a mother knows, and we spend the rest of our lives finding them out, and that is the job and the horror of life.

When I went back out, *Breathe, Teddy, breathe*, the builders were, for the first and last time, gone, the house quiet and still. Kwibe was on his back under the *kojo* tree, his eyes closed against the world, the terrible pressing world. I lay next to him and did the same, listening to the nothing, its emptiness and sorrow.

The silence was only broken by a final piercing scream

as the ghosts and saints left my mother's body, her soul flying upwards, through the space where the outline of the cross was burnt into the wall above her bed, up and away to meet its judgment, as if any, dear God, were needed.

Kwibe and I lay there, and the silence – basic, original and untouched – returned.

Insert here the goddamn Magnificat, for my soul does exalt in the Lord, and my spirit does rejoice, *Hosanna, hallelujah*, just not every day, just sometimes, and by Christ, isn't that enough, Lovejoy, the odd moment of epiphany between the arrival of lunch and the changing of my catheter? Between the arrival of love and the moment we climb the cross? The rest is just life, easily documented. And shit.

It was the Zar spirits that got her in the end, of course, Ababa tells me as we fuck, her large arm covering my ear, her sweat running down my cheek, my other ear against her chest, listening to her beating heart thunder with life.

It was the Zars that got her, forget your crosses and your

saints and your martyrs and your white-boy epiphanies. Right from the start, baby, it's the Zars. It's married women they want, they attack them and possess them, make them hysterical, mad, tired, all of those women things. Something exotic like your mama was sure to attract a strong one. But because she didn't know, because none of you knew, you didn't know what to do. Do you know what to do, Teddy? Appease it. That's right. Make it happy, make it content. It's not going anywhere I can tell you. I think Kwibe knew that. He was trying to make it happy, keeping it fed, telling it stories, but he was just a boy. The Zar waited for your mother to make it happy, it waited to be invited to the dancing ceremonies of women and their Zars, then it grew bored and sent her to bed. And when she got up to look after you the Zar got jealous, and killed her, they don't normally do that, she must have really pissed him off. So I guess it's your fault little man, haha. But I got you now, so give your mama a kiss.

Our hot mouths together, my tongue reaching shyly in and touching hers, her tongue so big against mine and then our bodies doing that thing again, almost by themselves, and then she beat me up to teach me some manners, boy,

and then her husband who is a blind man and a seer comes home and beats me up too, you know, Teddy, one of the three wise men was a King of Ethiopia, Jaspar or Caspar or Balthazar, no one is sure, Bazan maybe, let me get the book, Kwibe and Lucy will be here in a moment, fairy stories of course, but as has been shown the structure of folk memory is is is and and and is is is.

And we eat *wat*, the shack becomes peopled with kings

and emperors and I see Kwibe taking them into himself, absorbing their triumphs and defeats, he needs them now for our games and later for when he becomes a hero himself and and and is is is and and and

And I think about the Zar spirits and wonder if the one that took my mother from me has found another lover, and whether this one puts out for him, and whether they are there together dancing as I watch the women in their night rituals around the fire, which even now Ababa is preparing for, washing between her legs where I have been, and going out into the dark.

Siobhan combed my hair for me today, an embarrassing procedure for both of us, for me because there is so little there, for her because it's obviously beneath her. Five years of training for this! She might see the whole box and dice as beneath her. Maybe she wanted to be an astronaut. Now all she has is a cheap comb and my love. Hair combing does, however, give me confidence, as it is the sort of activity one submits to in a hospital, not a hospice. Nurses in a hospice are gently guiding you towards the exit, but in hospital there is, presumably, hope. My hair is being combed for human folk, not St Peter.

Are you watching all of this, St Peter? Are you scribbling in your goddamn book? How's the ledger looking?

As she combs little flakes of skin fall lightly down to rest on my collar, like it's Christmas. Perhaps it is Christmas, who knows? I used to employ my own barber back in my heyday, a blessedly silent Hungarian with a shiny bald head and a long drooping moustache, who in fifteen years of haircuts only spoke once, telling me his life story through a storm of tears, how he had escaped three minutes ahead of the Nazis, his family left behind, coming out of the bushes and into the arms of the Russians with his hands above his head like Mickey Mouse ears, and now he is wiping his eyes on the gown around my neck, bawling into paper towels, until finally collapsing on to his knees, broken, defeated, and yet, brave soul, slowly and resolutely raising the small square mirror above his head so I can see the back of mine and give my approval. He never spoke to me again. Good.

While Siobhan combed what was left of my hair, I thought about death. I tend to these days, what with. My favourite Everett death is undoubtedly, indubitably, that of my grandfather, Percival, who took his own life before God could get to him.

News of his suicide arrived by telegram in Harar the day my mother died, which was not ideal. It was the Great Suicide Scandal of 1933! The newspapers were full of it, despite all efforts to suppress the story by the Everett family on one side, bless them, and the family of his final love Tatiana on the other. Both were confounded by the efforts of the Order of the Silver Star holy holy holy to proclaim the martyrdom of their founder, and to follow his example.

He had taken an overdose of mescaline and barbiturates,

and stabbed himself in the stomach with a bone-handled letter-opener (a wedding gift from Simon of the Big Nose, who gave a matching one to Adelaide of the Suitcase which she would use, legend has it, to cut the throats of lions and tigers in deepest deepest darkest darkest Africa), hacking away at his belly and then submerging himself in the steaming waters of a Renaissance-style hot tub in the Sicilian Abbey of St Thelema, former headquarters of the Order of the Silver Star – Aleister Crowley having been asked politely to leave nine years earlier amid rumours of orgies and infanticide. In my grandfather's possession at the time of his death was a collection of sepia prints of himself, captured in a number of imaginative and compromising situations with most of the populations of Hammersmith and Bath, the Countess of Luxembourg and, fatally, with the exquisitely beautiful daughter of a Mafia don. He had met her three-quarters of the way through a performance of Wagner's *Ring*, sweeping her away as the *Götter*s began *Dämmerung*ing, and writing for her three Quattro volumes of execrable sub-Yeats poetry (self-published), an Orpheus to her Eurydice.

The last of these poems, unfinished, was found under the insole of his left boot, and described, in terms more epic than lyrical, their first fuck (while Brünnhilde was busy immolating), with details so graphic and powerful that it was agreed by all that Percival had finally found his poetic voice, that he had thrown off the shackles of Yeatsian metre and Frazerian imagery, and that, had he lived, he might have been a worthy successor to his Great Aunt Fran whose poetry-filled stocking had just been found by

Sylvia Pankhurst, soon to be protector of the Emperor Haile Selassie, when Ethiopia was overrun by Italians.

My grandfather had, since the birth of his behemothic offspring and the departure of his suitcase-carrying wife Adelaide, drifted far from the noble mercantile mission of Everett and Sons Coffee, and given himself over to the task of self-discovery, and, those being the days when Jung and Gurdjieff had more or less a monopoly on both the Self and Discovery, he soon found himself knee-deep in the occult, by which I mean the Occult, throwing himself rapturously into a heady regime of goat-slaughtering, absinthe-drinking, opium-smoking group sex and golden showers, his id being given more or less free rein against the quickly rejected Simon-of-the-Big-Nose-shaped superego.

He became a great favourite of newspaper feature writers, who interviewed him once every three months, as much for the photograph of him dressed in a caftan and rooster plumage as for the interview, which he inevitably powered around to the topic of colonic irrigation, a subject on which he was held to be the pre-eminent and most enthusiastic authority – a shaman of sorts, who could recommend the most effective method of purgation for any given case, which was invariably a combination of croton oil and deep knee bends, a reading from any sections of the *Brihadaranyaka Upanishad* that dealt with poo, and a quick dose of rumpy-pumpy, with Grandfather Percival himself only too happy to oblige. The results spoke for themselves!

Legend has it that the family attempted to have him killed on more than one occasion, Simon of the Big Nose losing his favourite bodyguard, the rhomboid Great War veteran Haines, in one such attempt. Haines was a stolid and slow-witted man, an ur-Holbrook, acquainted intimately with violence and its benefits, who Simon charged with the task of infiltrating the inner sanctum of Percival's endlessly purgating salon, in order to poison Percival and thus end the embarrassment he was causing the company. Haines dutifully complied with the first of these imperatives, donning a caftan, first over, and then instead of, his double-breasted suit; allowing Percival to perform various layings-on of hands; drinking the liver oil and performing the deep knee bends; reading out ponderous passages of *The Golden Bough* to the assembled minions; performing with admirable dexterity at various orgies and bacchanals and, finally, going down on his battle-scarred knees and receiving on his forehead the gift of micturition that cast him as one of the adept. This, one speculates, gave him a considerable amount of opportunity for emptying the vial of strychnine he had about his person into Percival's morning coffee.

The reason that Grandfather Percival survived this attempt on his life, and was able to live long enough to commit suicide, has been the subject of some controversy. Three theories have been put forward. The first states that strychnine had been discovered sewn into the lining of Haines's caftan during one of the endless series of disrobed activities to which Haines was dutifully giving himself, being replaced by an acolyte with a non-toxic substitute that Percival was able to drink without ill effect. Percival then feigned death until Haines went away.

The second theory states that Percival, having spent a good fifteen years under the influence of various cocktails of drugs, from absinthe to opium, from cocaine to mescaline, had so fucked up his central nervous system as to make it impervious to further chemical intrusion, and that the strychnine was simply incorporated into Percival's system and disappeared.

The third theory seems the most likely, being backed up by compelling documentary evidence. This theory states that one night, in the Sicilian Abbey of Thelema, Haines – his brow moist with the urine of numerous acolytes, his caftan stained with a glorious rainbow of bodily juices, and his backside singing with the after pain of male member insertion – experienced (while watching one of the innumerable Leni Riefenstahl nature films that Grandfather Percival was in the habit of screening), an epiphany, which rent the veil of *maya* that was his former life, and revealed to him that the pleasures of nature worship and anal sex were not transitory, but were, alleluia, the very truth of his being, or possibly Being, and that far from being antithetical to the violence he so cherished, the Occult could actually embrace and channel it, could harmonise it, indeed, with the violent impulses of the Earth, our Great Sweet Mother; he would be the microcosm in the macrocosm, and thus violence would be for Good and not Evil

which meant for Haines, and many other members of the Sect, attempting to wipe the Jews off the face of the Earth, our Great Sweet Mother. And so it was that Haines – allegedly – swapped his copies of *The Golden Bough* and *Isis Unveiled* for the far easier to read *Spiritualism* by Carl du Prel, *The Sin Against the Blood* by Artur Dinter and, decisively, *Bolshevism from Moses to Lenin* by Dietrich Eckart, morphine addict and doctor, copies of which he sent to Simon of the Big Nose, and which would sit ominously among the archives of Everett and Sons Coffee, for whom Haines, the rhombotoid Haines, Great War veteran, had once worked, for Simon of the Big Nose, then head of Everett and Sons Coffee, grandson of the founding father, the bewhiskered and rapacious Oliver Everett the First, great-grandfather of Percival who committed suicide, later attempted by his grandson Teddy Everett but he doesn't want to talk about that right now, he's sorry he brought it up, sorry for everything, but they keep giving me injection after injection, it could be anything, my nervous system is fucked,

but Haines disappeared. I think they found him in Hitler's bunker at the end or maybe he was Himmler's lover, I can't remember the story, but they certainly discussed Hörbiger's Cosmic Ice Theory and Teed's Hollow Earth Theory on more than one occasion, Haines and Himmler, Himmler and Haines, according to the archives anyway, but you can't believe what you read, the Cosmic Ice Theory states that small fragments in the universe are captured by larger fragments, and that the Earth, Great Sweet fragment, has already captured many small planets and the Moon is made of ice, everything is made of ice, the Moon is the next small fragment to crash into the Earth, ending all life there and then, which is all right for me because I'm dying of cancer

and the night was as cold as ice in the Sicilian Abbey of

Thelema as Grandfather Percival unsheathed the bone-handled letter-opener that had been his wedding present a lifetime ago, when he had been married to Adelaide of the Suitcase and they had made love in a Trans-Siberian railway carriage producing that fat son of theirs, who was in Ethiopia now if he remembered correctly, except it was still called Abyssinia then I think, he thinks, with a son of his own, Theodore, and a wife with whom I exchanged a few letters when I was feeling down, Ethiopia, born if I remember rightly, of the union of King Solomon and the Queen of Sheba, thus the true home of Christianity, also first refuge of Muhammad after the revelation, thus the true home of Islam, home of Axum, diocese of Prester John, now ruled by the saviour of the Negro races Ras Tafari, land of the Coptic texts, the *Kebra Nagast*, the *Fekkare Iyasus*, not that that idiot son of mine would know any of that, the fool, without an ounce of poetry in him, not one ounce, maybe his son will save us, maybe not,

and he looks one last time at the photographs of him and Tatiana, captured in beautiful congress, and I can only think now of Lucy, was she like Lucy, Grandpa? did you find some peace there, just for an instant, in the memory of her arms, a peace you could draw on and hold, a still centre to this wild, incomprehensible universe, a place where time stood still, stood still and waited, waited, tensed, for one endless instant, before you opened your cheap inglorious shirt and drove, god help us, a real knife into your actual stomach before those Wicked Sisters, the proper Mafia, could emerge from the shadows, *ta-da*, and riddle you with hard lead bullets?

Percival Everett, blood pouring from a self-inflicted wound in his belly, lowers himself into a Renaissance-style bath tub in the Sicilian Abbey of Thelema and dies, gazing calmly at half an erection, and becomes, despite many subsequent attempts by yours truly, the only Everett ever to die for love.

My father had more or less lost interest in his own father by the time the news reached Harar; besides, he had more pressing matters on his mind, the possible intransigence of the new regime in Brazil, for instance, who were threatening to undermine Everett's coffee interests by moving from a monoculture to something more varied, which for my father meant nothing more nor less than Creeping Socialism. It was left to Mrs Smithers to inform me of my grandfather's death, which she did while wearing one of my mother's blouses.

The predilection for suicide in the family of Everett and Sons was put forward by my first wife's lawyers during our divorce proceedings as a good reason for us to break up. They had a point! It was possible, they argued, that suicidal tendencies were genetically predetermined and therefore culturally unpredictable. Kebreth said that my grandfather's suicide was historically determined by the pressures of being asked to perform a role in the Theatre of High Capitalism to which he was constitutionally unsuited, and which had forced him to seek solace in the opiatic effects of religion, not to mention casual sex, which was a bourgeois substitute for meaningful interaction, not to mention homosexuality, which was a bourgeois substitute for interaction with women, women having been downtrodden or trodden down by the Theatre of High Capitalism, not to mention Crowleyism, which was a reification of the general crisis of values, all of which could only be overcome by the institution of a socialist state so, deep breath, my grandfather's suicide was a martyrdom of sorts, it had totemic significance in the decline and fall of capitalism, which was why he was going to kill my father, notwithstanding assassination being illegitimate revolutionary behaviour (Lenin) because structural adjustments in the March of Socialism were being dictated by necessity (Stalin) and were, anyway, geographically specific (Lenin) such that, although lessons could be learnt from previous revolutionary activities, one should not be bound by them (Stalin).

And he needed my help. Think of your mother, Teddy, think of how he treated her, look at Mrs Smithers, you see why he has to die, don't you, Teddy?, be brave, Teddy, that's all I need you to do, but you'd better take this, just in case, it's a gun, Teddy, things could get ugly, blood could be spilt, Everett blood, dark and thick like Turkish coffee, like the coffee you will drink with the mullahs of Tarsus and

Ankara, running down your palms and along your finger-tips, staining your briefcase, your financial plans, you can't look away, look at the tendrils of your veins waving in the gash, spitting out their dark liquid, everything is so quiet now, Teddy, only the gentle sound of your wife sleeping in the bed behind you, you will never be whole again, Teddy, the skin has been breached, and you call out for Lucy, Lucy, Lucy because the hole won't stop bleeding, even now, and the bed is filling with blood, and get out of my head, Kebreth, get out of my head.

I am so scared, Christ, I am so scared.

Lovejoy, *naif* that he is, tells me that he believes suicide can only happen with the free will of the suicidee and to see it as inevitable is to fatally undermine the notion of personal responsibility, which is why he gets pissed off with failed attempts that take up time you could be spending with people who don't actually want to die.

Lovejoy is looking tired. He has taken to coming to see me last thing in the evening, barely glancing at my chart, before sitting in the chair beside my bed. I ask him how I am doing and he tells me I am responding well. Then he falls silent, for an hour sometimes, staring at the wall. Perhaps he is in love with Siobhan too. He doesn't stand a chance.

The night after my mother died Kebreth Astakie places a hundred pounds of gelignite in a three-inch hole beneath my father's window, pressing the putty into the aperture with long slender fingers, setting the timer to go off the moment the sun crosses the horizon. He breathes through his nose, there is sweat on his forehead, his forehead is creased in concentration. He is a man intending to kill another man. This is not random: it is a political act, an assassination. It is, as Trotsky would have it, the propaganda of the deed, a cataclysmic act that catapults us from the absolute present into the immanent future. 'He who aims at an end cannot reject the means.' As he moulds the putty into the aperture, Kebreth thinks about my mother, who is dead, and about my father, who is to be killed. He thinks about Haile Selassie, the newest member of the Solomonic line, running begat begat begat from King Solomon and the Queen of Sheba, tidal waves of regal reproductive juices rolling down the pages of the Coptic calendar, eddying here at Axum, there at Meqdela, finding new streams, carving new paths, rolling ever onwards, to gather now, sixteen years after the death of Lij Yasu, three years after the death of the first empress, Zaudita, pooled now in the person of the 225th emperor, Haile Selassie. And Kebreth thought, Bugger that. It was time to stop the flow. The death of Oliver Everett the Second would be the opening salvo, the shot across the bows. The revolution has begun.

How many have there been like Kebreth? How many are there now? Failed revolutionaries, planting their bombs, polishing their rifles, preparing to save their country, creed, religion from the yoke of repression, dropped out of history, meaninglessly dead. There are always more failed revolutionaries than successful ones. They are the majority. They always will be.

So the night after my mother died, Kebreth Astakie placed a hundred pounds of gelignite in a three-inch hole beneath my father's window, and I don't think I have had a full night's sleep since. The exhaustion of my mother's death, the wailing of the women who barely knew her, wailing at one remove, pretend wailing. My father grunting above the prone figure, as he grunted all those years ago. The body taken away and buried, I guess. I don't know what happened to my mother's body. And then falling into bed, shattered, finally drifting off at five a.m. Then the explosion, timber falling, and no one hurt because stupid Kebreth had assumed that my father would be sleeping in the front room out of respect, not in the bed my mother had died in eight hours before, but that was where he was, the bed to himself at last. The stars have a bloody cheek coming out some nights.

And my father emerging from the dust, red-faced and screaming, throwing rubble across the room and it smashing above my bed, raining its fragments down on me, and it's not true that your life flashes before your eyes when you're dying, *it falls down on you in clumps*, like rubble in an exploding building, thumping against your skull as your mouth fills with the swirling dust, and figures loom towards you, people half remembered or not remembered at all. Kebreth must have told me about the bomb, someone must have taken my mother's body away, people must have come running when the house exploded, but I don't have those bits any more. Lucy was there, I guess, but when I'm sobbing for my mother it's on a pillow, and I can't remember which night it is, and when I'm sobbing on Lucy's lap it's about something else. I know someone was shot for the bomb in the house, but it wasn't Kebreth. It might have been the night I heard the man tied to the tree and beaten, maybe he was beaten not shot, maybe it was Kebreth, but Kebreth was never beaten but later he was shot. My mind is tangled like the limbs of lepers, like Ethiopian trees, and I want to get out of here, I want to fly above these Ethiopian trees, like I did when it was all over, I want to feel all that happened fall away and I want to be sitting behind my desk, safe and sound, in a suit, in a tie, my first wife demurely in front of me, her calves crossed, telling me that if I didn't marry her then her idiot hick brother would blow my goddamn brains out.

That moment will do, any moment but my father heaving rubble at me and screaming that he will kill them all, any moment but that.

Carlo!

Have I told you about Carlo the Cuban Revolutionary? I must tell you about him before I die. I'll keep myself alive by telling you about Carlo! I saved Carlo's life once too. Listen.

Carlo the Cuban Revolutionary was a passionate and ugly man with darting eyes set deep below a single thatched eyebrow, eyes that could pick out a well-turned ankle or a nice piece of arse across any bar in the world. He had large lips and spat into his hands constantly SCHRUNKKTH SCHRUNKKTH, depositing a livid green substance on his palms and down his wrists, the phlegm of the revolution, the mucal offerings of a man for whom no sacrifice was too big, no cigar too long, no woman too married. He was that most fearsome beast of seduction, the dick on legs, who has not read works on etiquette, who doesn't understand the economics of the thing, but who has a gun and will shoot any man if it offers the possibility of fucking their wife.

My first wife met him in a bar in Havana in 1953 and found herself in the missionary position three and a half minutes later on a half-inch-thick bug-infested mattress spread on the floor of the bar's cellar, the top of her head against a wall moistened by rising damp, stained brown by spilt beer and spat cigar tops, her feet pressed against the dusty bottles of a wine rack, its shaking causing a rattle of bottles that was greeted with cheers and group singing in the upstairs bar, group singing that came down muffled to the lovers, and that Carlo took up in time with his thrusting.

This was the revolution, this was it, dirty sex in a cellar surrounded by beer and cigar butts, with the wife of a capitalist, and Gramsci notes that all phenomena should be open to revolutionary interpretation, no matter how base, all phenomena should be respected as an expression of a particular desire of the masses, which can therefore be harnessed as a tool of revolution, by aligning that desire with a desire for revolution in the first place and complete social restructuring in the second, or maybe vice versa, I can't remember, but, writes Gramsci, from prison, consider jazz, consider the dancing of Negroes, consider notions of repeated physical movements, such as sex, such as those, writes Gramsci, Gramsci writes, of the Negro around his fetishes, or of the white bourgeois dancing the Charleston, or of Carlo as he moves backwards and forwards inside my wife

and also consider syncopated rhythms, such as those of jazz, such as those of my first wife as she tries to move her head from against the wall, and manages by curling her toes around the wine rack and drawing her body down the mattress, making Carlo miss a beat, forcing him to slip from constant to syncopated rhythm, confusing him for an instant, disrupting his natural desires and forcing an irruption in his thought train, like a Zen *koan*, like

writes Gramsci, the influence of Buddhism on Western civilisation, allowing my first wife to use his own weight against him, to use the power to undermine the power, the Tao that overcomes, to flip him across her body and then underneath her, his legs caught up and forced to cross by the trousers now around his ankles, caught and passive, still singing but now like a daydreamer, as he finds himself falling unrevolutionarily, unideologically, unceremoniously, in love with the slight American woman lifting herself up and down on his hipline and multiple-orgasming with the syncopated rhythms of continual revolution, after the Leninist model, the Buddhist imperatives, the teachings of the Tao and of the Holy Ghost, to whom Grandfather Percival dedicates a tabla solo, in a small temple outside Greenwich, YVHV, Shakti and so forth.

Oh, my Lord, cried Carlo, his knees lifting upwards, his scrotum tightening, semen preparing to burst forth, the jizz of the revolution and then

everything.

slowed.

down.

and. my. first. wife. said.

not.

yet.

hold on   I haven't finished with you yet   roll over on to your side   stand up   bite my shoulder   don't bite my shoulder   pass me a beer   light my cigarette   hold this slow down   kiss me here   stroke my hair   kiss my shoulder blades   take me from behind   don't cum   turn over   don't cum   suck my breasts   pass me a beer   suck my fingers lie down flat   OK, cum   cum for me   cum for me now cum and cum and cum   good boy   good brave boy now sleep   sleep   sleep.

And Carlo the Cuban Revolutionary did sleep and he did sleep deeply, and he dreamt of a small house on a hill, where he kept chickens, and where my first wife would wave to him from a window and tell him his dinner was ready, and he would skip up the path, pausing only to pat the dog, and my first wife and Carlo the Cuban Revolutionary would sit on the sofa and eat paella and watch baseball, while their little bearded kids ran around spilling Coke on the dog and then my first wife and Carlo the Cuban Revolutionary would take each other to bed and make passionate bourgeois love – and in his arms my first wife slept too and dreamt of making passionate revolutionary love deep in the Cuban forest, the voices of Carlo's comrades around a campfire in the near distance, talking about the day's victories and defeats, and my first wife and Carlo the Cuban Revolutionary would hold each other through their green battle fatigues, their boots entwined, Carlo's trousers around his ankles, Uzis slung over their shoulders, and they would start up again and make syncopated, staccato love, subversive, undermine-the-basis-of-society kind of love, and then fall asleep in the warm Cuban night.

Which was how I found them at three a.m., the bar long closed, a few *callabreros* snoozing on the porch, empty bottles in their hands, the bar owner sleepy and annoyed, leading me through the broken furniture and smashed glasses down to the cellar, watching me as I descended and stopped to gaze at their entwined bodies, Carlo's trousers still around his ankles, my wife's head rising and falling on his chest, her body completely naked, one foot now back in the wine rack, cobwebs between her toes, and I woke her softly and she smiled at me and placed her lips against mine, her tongue against my tongue, and told me I tasted of cigarettes and coffee, and I told her she tasted of beer and cigars, and we removed her foot from the wine rack, leaving her shoe behind, caught in the dark metal, and we stepped over Carlo's still sleeping body, which stirred slightly and then didn't, and we went up the stairs together arm in arm and into the bar where we drank a shot of whisky and leant against each other while the owner righted furniture

and out into the street where *callabreros* wound their way home pausing only to raise their empty bottles in appreciation of my wife

and into the arcade where my wife pressed me softly against a wall and kissed me and stroked my hair and lost her train of thought and asked me to take her home

and back to our hotel where the doorman slept soundly behind the desk

and up the stairs, pausing only to lift my now unconscious wife into my arms

and into our room to place my wife on the bed and gently tuck her in, to kiss her forehead and watch her fall deeper and deeper into sleep and then go to the desk, still covered with financial reports, to pour another glass of whisky, and because of the heat, or because Carlo made me think of Kebreth, or Lucy, or perhaps because business wasn't so good, or perhaps just because of the mood, to take a razor blade from my travel case and open both of my wrists.

Christchristchristchristchristchristchrist.

I am in so much pain and the fuckers won't give me so much as a cup of coffee.

The evenings have become cubist, a series of planes and ledges; my dying eyes only have enough strength for simple shapes, triangles and squares, circles, intersecting lines, all piled on top of each other, senseless, the world reduced to wallpaper. Colours push out against the white frieze of the ward, making me nauseous. The flat sheet of the world hangs a millimetre from my eyeballs, soft breezes press it against their taut jelly, blurring the images, scarring their surface. I cannot lift my arms to rub them.

Siobhan appears at the end of my bed, standing in profile, watching me with both eyes. She speaks to me, I think she speaks to me, and her words are smeared across the air, like oil on canvas. She carries needles, tubes of glass, bottles, which are always blue, always too small for her hand. The watch, upside-down against her pointed chest, is a glittering prism, time bent, crystalline, reflecting time here, never linear, anything but linear, sometimes time screeches from evening to evening without touching the day, sometimes yesterday comes round again and again, curving back on itself and starting at a different moment. To try and hold on to any sort of sequence is to be cut by its sharpened edges, torn open ruthlessly as by a surgeon's knife.

When time tears you open, it infects you. It makes you sicker. Time has broken through my flesh, passed on its bacteria, caked it all over my chest and lungs, and Lovejoy bends down close to me, appears from nowhere, bends, and is close to me, and tells me they are going to have to go in again, going to have to cut me open and pull apart my chest, because the infection time has left there speeds things up, brings my death forward, and Lovejoy doesn't want me to die because he's a doctor, and they, whoever they are, don't want me to die because they are paying Lovejoy to be my doctor. And I hate them and I don't know who they are.

Siobhan takes my pulse and tells me I will be all right. I tell her I don't know what all right means and she laughs and I tell her I really don't know. She says I will be well again, but I don't know if I can trust her. I try to trust her because I love her, but I don't know if I can. There are gaps in her motion, she leaps between frames, she never describes a perfect line. And sometimes she repeats herself, sometimes she arrives three times in a row, And how are we today, Mr Everett?, and then she is beside me and the steel shaft goes into my arm, and the bottles are always blue and they are always too small for her hand.

And some nights, when my eyes soften to take in form, I see her pale white arms come towards me through the miasma, and she places two fingers in my mouth, dropping pills, capsules, diamonds. She tells me this will make me feel better, two fingers in my mouth, her hand salty with sweat, sweet with disinfectant. I feel my slack lips move up around her wrist sometimes, my teeth a bracelet of pearls, and I feel the delicious terror of not stopping, but pushing upwards, upwards, her arm moving down my throat, soft hair and freckles moving inside my gullet, until her hand reaches my stomach, and she rolls it across her palm, moist and curved, then squeezing, gently, firmly, forcing a stool out of me in a perfect measured dose, squeezing me until I am empty. And I would be soft against her, looking into her pale blue eyes, as she slowly drew back out, running the fingers of her other hand through my sweaty hair. Her hand would come to rest in my mouth, and I would suck from her fingers my internal juices, my cancerous black liquids.

But it's enough to feel her fingers against the tip of my tongue, because touch is so precious to me now, so so precious, you could pull all the tubes from my body, and cut all the pills and injections, you could stop feeding me and giving me water, if only she would sit beside me all day with her fingers in my mouth, stroking the underside of my tongue; that would be enough to survive on for a billion years.

A billion billion.

A billion billion years after falling asleep, Carlo woke and found himself on a half-inch-thick mattress in the cellar of a bar, surrounded by beer bottles and cobwebs, with his pants around his ankles. The American woman was gone. He thought for a moment that she had not been real, that she had been an angel, a cherub a seraph, so beguiling were her ways, so lithe and supple her body, but he found scratch marks across his chest and smelt her perfume in his beard so

Carlo's penis was red and sore, the foreskin still pulled back, and he set himself about the task of putting it back in place, pressing the hollow between his thumb and fore-finger along the skin to try and roll it back down.

Empires rose and fell. Galaxies were born and died. And still the foreskin of Carlo de Jesus failed to come to a lip, no matter what he tried.

He was in love.

Carlo gingerly pulled his trousers over his tender appendage, wincing at the rough fabric against its exposed head. He was sweating. His bones ached. He was thirsty, nauseous, tired. He found the cellar oppressive, found himself throwing his feet up the stairs, wincing with every step to the rub of the trousers. Then he was running, through the bar, out into the cool night air, which he breathed deeply into his smoke-filled lungs, letting it swirl in the furthest reaches of his foreshortened bronchioles, and then expelling it with a roar of joy that filled the sky and set the stars afire. Fuck, it was good to be alive. Carlo ran through the streets of Santiago del Cuba singing my wife's name. He sang it in the street, he sang it in the middle of the road, he climbed on to the roof of the local police station and sang it there until his brother the police officer fired three shots above his head and sent him scurrying down the drainpipe and full pelt down an arcade towards the hotel where my wife had told him she was staying. When he found the place his heart leapt and he roared, et cetera, this is just his version, this is what he told me when he grabbed me at gunpoint in that same bar two weeks later, he told me that when he found the hotel his heart leapt and he roared, and he called her name from the street, and saw her appear at the window, a fragile slip of white illuminated by a small light, saw her beckon him to come up; then he saw her turn towards the door, saw her scream, saw the fragile white slip of a body crumpling from view, the small lamp extinguished as she knocked over the bedside table on which it sat.

Listen. At the precise moment that Carlo de Jesus kicked open the door of the hotel room to find the coffee baron slumped in a pool of blood blood blood, still gushing from his wrists wrists wrists, and the coffee baron's wife, a fragile white slip in a dead faint across the room, a cord from the lamp on an upended bedside table twisted around her ankle,

a terrorist group headed by local lawyer Fidel Castro attacked two army barracks in Moncado, five kilometres away. The plan had been to take control of the barracks and then bring the army on side, precipitating a revolution and deposing President Batista, who had staged a coup the previous year. Carlo grabbed a glass of water from the desk of the coffee baron and splashed it on to the woman's face, bringing her back to life. This was a reflex action caused by him being in love with her. This was a mistake. It meant that when Carlo pulled out his pistol a moment later to finish off the filthy capitalist coffee baron, a further reflex action, this time on the part of the woman, forced the gun upwards, approximately three inches above the coffee baron's head, the sound of the bullet cannoning into the wall causing him, the coffee baron, to regain consciousness. He, the coffee baron, heard his wife say, *Help him help him*. He thinks a debate ensued. Maybe not. He heard another gunshot and flinched. He didn't want to die any more. But this gunshot sounded further away, and was followed by a volley of shots. Castro had attacked the army barracks with a small group of terrorists. This had been a mistake. It was a night of mistakes. Carlo heard the gunshots too. What was he doing here? Castro had taken him aside a week earlier and told him about the attack, told him to join them on the twenty-sixth and now he was in this hotel room, his arm held aloft by a fragile white slip of a woman, help him help him, the coffee baron rounding on him slowly, a wave of blood rolling across the desk, reaching out his arm, help me help me.

Fifty-five members of Castro's revolutionary army, including every member of Carlo's division, were killed at Moncado, falling in a hail of bullets as Carlo the Cuban Revolutionary carried Everett the coffee baron with white SCHRUNKKTH SCHRUNKKTH handkerchiefs around his wrists down the stairs, into the taxi of his brother the taxi driver, and took him to hospital. Had my wife not opened her legs that night and had I not opened my wrists Carlo would have been shot dead too, or captured, tortured, and then shot, like many of the others. Which was how I, Theodore Everett, head of Everett and Sons Coffee, saved the life of Carlo the Cuban Revolutionary, leaving him for ever in my debt.

He shot himself five weeks later when he found that my wife had had a change of political heart and started doing for one of the Rothschilds what she had done to my life.

Messy divorce, she and I, I and her. We both wished the suicide had worked out. Cleaner. Easier. Cheaper. Bad time for Everett and Sons too. Cuba. Bolivia. Nescafé. The CEO, Theodore Everett, seems to possess an irrational suspicion of all things Italian, and is therefore slow to react to, compete with, embrace, the new Italian Italian Italian Gaggia machines that have turned your local burger joint into the perfect place for that perfect cup of coffee. The kids just can't get enough! Is this the end for Everett and Sons? Have they missed the boat? Has Theodore Everett got so darn caught up in this messy divorce with his hourglass wife that he's dropped the ball, fumbled the pass, struck out at the bottom of the ninth? Or has the old dog still got a few tricks up his sleeve, like cornering the UK market, that's where he's from after all, two thousand *faux*-Italian joints from Soho to Southwold, and then appearing on the steps of the courthouse with his lovely new Irish colleen Moira Callaghan you gotta love that. And contrary to the rumours he's happy to explain that his recent illnesses are simply some issue to do with his blood that he may have picked up in Ethiopia in his youth, and he not only categorically denies ever having attempted suicide, but would be quite happy to take on any scurrilous rag that reprints such base accusations, just as his great-grandfather Simon did when the British papers printed similar accusations against Percival Everett, Theodore's grandfather, Simon's son.

Thank you, gentlemen, I have nothing else to say.

My first wife hit the bottle from the night of my first suicide attempt, spending the next month as she was to spend the next twenty years, smashed out of her skull on whisky brandy gin, open to any sexual advances male female other that happened to cross her path, until Brother Kevin of the Scientologists found her shaking beneath an olive tree in 1976 and managed to get her in touch with her Thetan self, who now lives with her in California with her third husband and his Thetan self too.

Then the inquiry, she and I, I and her. The first one's always the hardest. Lawyers and lawyers and lawyers. The great courtroom drama of 1954, just what Everett and Sons needed after the suicide scandal and the questions questions questions, what was I doing in Santiago del Cuba at the precise moment that the Communist Castro was attempting to overthrow the President? Why the suicide attempt? Was I afraid that something might come to light about my activities? What exactly were my activities? Did I know Castro? Did I know de Jesus? Are you, let's be frank, a Communist?

I was on holiday. No, it was probably not a sensible place for an American citizen to be found but I am familiar with it because of my business, Cuba is big in coffee, I direct you to our end-of-year accounts 1952–3. I don't know why I tried to kill myself. What activities? No, I didn't know Castro. Yes, I do know de Jesus, he was fucking my wife. No, and I thank you for your frankness, I am not a Communist (Kebreth!). None of my friends are Communists (Lucy!). I have never engaged in discussions that would undermine United States security. I have never discussed base, nor have I discussed superstructure. I do not know a Mr Hegel. I do not know anyone who fits Mr Hegel's description. No, I have never overtly or covertly encouraged unionism. No, I don't know Hoffa. No. Never. None. No. Never. None.

And now divorce. She got half my money and I got half her jewellery. Including her wedding ring, which I flung off the top of the Empire State Building a week later, maybe killing someone, I don't know, but it felt good, and if I could relive one moment of my life again that would be it, but then again no, then again there is Lucy, sitting waiting for me under a coffee tree, her legs bare in the sunshine, and me crawling towards her, crying, because my mother is dead.

And maybe this time, or maybe another time, or maybe lots of times, bits and pieces, but Lucy is stroking my hair as I cry, my head on her lap, my open mouth on her thigh as I try to stop sobbing, my tears rolling down behind her knee, the sun on our bodies, a gentle breeze, no one working today, today is *Meskel*, we are celebrating the finding of the *One True Cross*, not all the false ones the rest of us are forced to carry, the crosses we have hewn ourselves from the ever-growing tree of our failures, we find those crosses every day, and the flowers are blooming and everything is warm here, even my tears make us warm, and Lucy leans down and kisses the back of my neck, just once, and then sits back and thinks about nothing.

Lucy Alfarez walked out of the jungle at the age of four-teen with a silver lighter in one hand and a coffee bean in the other.

The ten-year-old boy, Kwibe Abi, watches her from across the yard. He is drawing patterns in the dirt, mean-ingless hieroglyphs imitating letters from a thousand different languages, none of which he can write. Like Lucy he is an orphan. His back story is unknown to me because I never asked. I never asked anyone – I'm not sure anyone knew. Kwibe Abi was just there. He had always been just there.

Did he know his own story? He would invent ancestors, emperors and kings, names imbibed at Tekle's table. He is a direct descendant of Ezana, greatest of the Axumite kings, builder of the Axum stele, first convert to Christianity, and builder of the first Ethiopian church, which to this day houses the Ark. He is a direct descendant of Queen Yodit, who persecuted the Christians who tore down the very churches that Ezana had built. He is an ancestor of Lalibela who built them up again.

In his veins runs the blood of Emperor Galawdewos who defeated Gragn the Left-handed, scourge of Harar, Emperor Susenyos, who changed Ethiopia from Orthodox to Catholic, and his son Fasil who changed it back. Of Iyasu the Great, remembered for his patient administration and his grief at the death of his favourite concubine, and Iyasu II, whose sybaritic tendencies were punished by not one but two locust plagues. And, not three generations back, the blood of Tewodros himself, the great unifier, who asked Queen Victoria's help to fight off the Ottomans and received only a pistol as a present, the very one he used to shoot himself.

Sometimes he would pretend to be an Everett, sticking his belly out and walking with the air of a man in a silk shirt.

Kwibe Abi watches Lucy approach Teddy. The stick he is using to draw with becomes a sword in his hand as she walks up; he fights the trees, repelling invader after invader for the princess, making the blood of the enemy fall like leaves on to the dusty ground. As he hears my father take the strap to her he strikes out harder, striking for every man woman and child crushed by belligerent power. He is Menelik now, staring at the Italians across the mountains of Adowa. He knows he has the support of the peasants, he knows his army is five times the size, but mostly he knows he has the protection of the Ark, and as he drives his sword into Brigadiers Dabormida, Arimondi and Baratieri, *Ebalgume! Ebalgume!* he knows God is watching and blessing the battle.

Kwibe Abi watches Lucy and Teddy play. He knows that one day the boy will betray him, betray them all, but the Ark will win out in the end, there will be a plague of locusts inside Teddy's lungs, punishment for his sybaritic ways, so Kwibe Abi can wait, silently, like an emperor, like a judge.

Here's an interesting fact while we're at it: certain species of ant turn other species of ants into slaves in order to sustain their colony. This is known as helotism, which we define as a system in which one social class (religious, racial, etc.) is oppressed and degraded by another. The slave-making ants raid the nests of other ants and steal the eggs, adopting the newborn as their slaves. The slaves then feed their owner ants. Studies have shown that the victims of helotism are not thought to be aware of their situation. Interestingly, studies have shown that the perpetrators of helotism are always thought to be aware of their situation. Interestingly, studies have shown that slave-making ants which become separated from their slaves will starve to death even when food is made available to them.

No studies have ever suggested a link between this behaviour and any instinctive drive to dominate within humans.

This is my coffee story.

It was the night after I had lost my virginity that they came for me, it can't have been, it was after another night with Ababa, we were lovers, Ababa and me, and I still smelt of coffee, of Ababa and of coffee, I can't remember when, but it is my perfect moment, and here is where it goes.

Back then you could say I became a man without

blushing, and as I stared at the ceiling afterwards I had become a man. Before Ababa had thrown me into the coffee beans I had dreamt of whittling the perfect plane, of beating Kwibe at football, climbing the highest tree. Afterwards I thought about sex. Nothing else, just sex. The flesh of every woman in the world ever passed through my body as I lay there, an infinity of sensual pleasures squeezed into the tiniest fraction of time. The world didn't exist outside Woman. I was, as Grandfather Percival would have said, living an Indian cosmology: thousands were the hands of She, the tongues, mouths, and the other bits, Durga astride her lion, Lakshmi showered by her elephants, and I was lost in her warm all-embracing embrace and fell asleep reeking of sweat and semen. And

That was when they came for me, hands grabbing at me, pulling me away. At first I thought it was the lepers again, come to drag me out of the world of sensual pleasure and back into the hell of being, or whatever a fourteen-year-old calls such things. Hadn't they come every other night?, didn't they leave flakes of their skin on my pillow?, but the hand across my mouth was strong and smelt of coffee. I felt myself being lifted, the bed slipping away beneath me, up up up in strong arms, one hand over my mouth, the other lifting me between my legs, hard against the damp patch. And my captor was walking softly, out through my door, down the hallway, on to the porch and down the stairs

And then running through the clearing, into the forest, the trees speeding past me, I wanted to duck but I couldn't move, I wanted to wake up but I was awake. Leaves dashed across my face and my arms, stinging me. I had to close my eyes, as tight as I could, so tight they hurt.

And then we were there. The man stopped. He was panting. I remember, can still feel, his chest heaving against mine. Sweat dripped from his hair on to the back of my neck. I kept my eyes closed, I was scared to look. Maybe I had been taken by gypsies, my father had told me that could happen if you were bad, if you wet the bed, they liked bed-wetters, they would take them and cut them from ear to ear, they called it a smile and they would dance around and sing.

I felt myself being put down slowly, but my legs couldn't take the weight and I fell. I pressed my face against the ground, it was hot, sparks hit my arm, there was fire. Voices. Laughter.

– Teddy

– . . .

– Stand up, Teddy. Come on, my little prince.

I stood and spat leaves out of my mouth. I lifted my head and opened my eyes. I looked into the face of Kebreth Astakie.

He was laughing, the fucker. They all were, they were all there. Kebreth, Tekle Tolossa, the fourteen-year-old Kwibe Abi, ten or fifteen others, all standing around laughing.

Lucy was there too, kneeling on the ground, her knees against the hard ground. She was wearing one of my mother's old pink nightgowns, torn at the shoulder. Her face was red in the glow of the fire, her black eyes black with sleep. She was shivering.

I tried to catch her eye but she wouldn't look at me. She was staring at the fire. Lucy knew how to stare at fires.

The laughter continued, Kebreth's loudest of all, but then he raised his hand and they all fell silent. He spoke over his shoulder in Amharic to a man I had not seen before, a tall man, strong. The man walked around the group until he got to Tekle Tolossa. He whispered in his ear, took him by the arm and led him towards us. He stood next to Kebreth and started to chant, very softly. Kebreth came over and dragged me to my knees beside Lucy. Then he stepped back and reached inside his pocket, and I knew then that he was going to kill me, he was going to blow my brains out with the gun he had made me hold, because I was the son of the father, and the demons get passed on, all thirty-six of them.

Instead Kebreth pulled out a small bag of coffee beans. He pressed his hands into them, rubbing the oil against his coffee-coloured palms. Then he came over to me and rubbed his palms on my face, my white skin turning brown under his hands.

Then he pulled out a notebook and spoke. Are you Theodore Thomas Everett? I nodded, unable to speak. And are you Lucinda Maricina Alfarez?

Yes.

Then repeat after me.

I, Theodore Thomas Everett

I, Theodore Thomas Everett

Being of sound mind and body

Being of sound mind and body – oh, Christ, the patch between my legs, they will all see it, Lucy will see it

Do solemnly pledge allegiance

Do solemnly pledge allegiance

To Karl Marx

I heard tittering from the back of the group. I pressed my legs together trying to hide the dampness.

To Karl Marx

To Friedrich Engels

To Friedrich Engels

Tekle Tolossa giggled. Oh yeah!

To Antonio Gramsci

To Antonio Gramsci

To, who else?

Someone shouted, Tolstoy, and everyone laughed, Lucy was laughing too – who the fuck was Tolstoy? She had seen it, my shame, my cheeks were burning, and Kebreth kept going, to Tolstoy, to Stalin, to Gorky, to fucking Chekhov, Bukharin, Lenin. I could hardly make the words come out, my throat was so dry, but no one was listening anyway, they were all laughing so hard, so loud. I felt dizzy, nauseous. I wanted to run away, to crouch in the bushes and throw up, but I couldn't move my legs, couldn't stop the world spinning.

Kebreth raised his hand again and they fell silent. He stepped forward and put his hand on my head. Theodore Thomas Everett, he said, I now pronounce you a Communist.

I felt like my throat had just been cut. That was it. They had done it. I was a Communist now. It was that easy.

Kneeling here on the cold ground, in piss-stained pyjamas, surrounded by dark rows of coffee plants, I was a Communist. A goddamn no-good threat-to-civilisation

Commie, the devil incarnate. And so was Lucy. I heard her recite the same names, Tolstoy, Stalin, Lenin, but no one was laughing. Kebreth's hand was on her head, as it had been on mine, anointing her. And her eyes were black and they were fire.

How many of these men were there, the coffee Commies, thirty, thirty-six, fewer? Ten, maybe, of the hundreds working the fields. Not just ten that night, but ten total, twelve if you included me and Lucy. Maybe twenty with the women who weren't there, someone had to look after the children, that's who the revolution is for, the children, and one day the men will look after the children too but not now. And they would meet like this and talk and talk and talk, turning everything over with their words, every part of the power structure down to the language and the gestures, seeking the echoes of history in the way you slept, the way you sat.

I hoped like hell they would take me home, let me sleep. I was scared that we were going to have to fight a war that night and I would be killed. I didn't want to be killed, I knew that if someone was killing me I would cry like a baby in front of Lucy, it was all bad enough without that. But when the ceremony had finished all the men sat down around the fire, Lucy too, and they passed around the *chat* and coffee beans. I can still see my hand shaking as I took a bean and placed it in my mouth. My wrists were so thin.

The tall stranger's name was Mebrahtu, and he had come from the eastern border or from the depths of hell, I know not which. He was, Tekle told me afterwards, a follower of the Cult of Mary, an observer of the thirty Marian feasts, and may not have been real, he may have been a product of our collective will, I mean he probably was real, but but but.

He spoke quietly, forcefully. Kebreth translated his words into Galla, into Falashan, into English, the sentences repeated again and again in different languages, like looking into a broken mirror. The proper names were always the same, or nearly, so they stuck in your head. The Italians are eyeing up Wal Wal, he said. They need water, stuck in the Somali desert. They are only a small army, the Italians, but that can be worse. A big army you can predict, but it only takes ten malcontents in a small army to get the others belligerent. Selassie won't do anything, he's in the palm of the Europeans, didn't he give them a pack of zebras a few years back? Kebreth shook his head, fucking zebras. But that was the Germans, said someone else, but the Germans and the Italians, well.

I looked over at Lucy. She was quietly scratching the bottom of her foot, smoking a cigarette and listening, listening.

I heard the name Gramsci and my heart leapt. I think he also said Mussolini, he must have done, and the name of the Italian general, what's his name, whatever.

Listen – April 1930 we arrive in Ethiopia, November 1930 Ras Tafari is crowned Haile Selassie in front of no lepers. December 1934 the incident at Wal Wal and I sleep with Tekle Tolossa's wife and I am made into a Communist. January 1935 Haile Selassie appeals to the League of Nations for protection against the Italians. October 1935 the Italians invade. May 1936 Selassie flees and
and

and so they're all doomed. That's the point. Everyone around that fire is marked for death. Do they know that? I can still see Lucy, Ironbum Lucy, sitting in the glow of the fire, twisting three coffee beans between her fingers, pulling them from between her toes. Did she know? She didn't know, how could she? She was immortal, she could do magic. She could walk out of the forest wearing only a torn dress and break the heart of Theodore Everett.

But the others, did they know? History was grinding onwards, they all knew that, but what would it do with them? The tall man knew, maybe. His face was weary, even when he was laughing, he had seen some things, you could tell, and not only as they happened, but before they happened, you could do that if you looked closely enough. History followed an inevitable, inexorable course, thesis, antithesis, synthesis. History came to a point and the point was sharp. The tall man had watched it moving, so that every new thing was already a tragedy, because tragedy is the end point of inexorable history.

It was nearly two years to the invasion, but he could see it. He could make the necessary connections. He could see the decision to be made. If you defended Wal Wal you were defending Selassie, whom you wanted to overthrow, but Christ, that was better than trying to overthrow the Fascists, wasn't it, isn't it, maybe? He could see the long nights trying to work out whom to fight first, what the correct tactics were, he could see the inevitable decision, there were no Lenins here, and he could see the slaughter to follow. He could see his own death, and that of every man there.

Jesus Christ, in three years everyone around that fire would be dead. Except me.

But I'm dying now, and that's the main thing.

The cancer will die with me, of course, the stupid fucker. If it would just stop where it is now we could live together for ever – I have some bits of my life I can spare, the bad dreams, the broken memories, the failures, the cowardice. Let the cancer slew them from my ageing body and live on them, I don't mind. They are as solid and meaty as the lung it is chewing away at, and they multiply themselves every time I close my eyes, so they can never run out. But once my lungs are gone, my little malignant friend, that's your lot. We're both going to hell together, sunshine.

But you can't tell it that. It won't listen. It likes the conditions. Give it a bit of moist lung to settle into and it goes crazy, whatever the consequences. Can't get enough of it, eats like a fucking horse. The first time they operated on me, the shit they scraped out ate through the wall of the operating theatre, and was off down the street before anyone could move.

Lovejoy tells me I'm looking better, again and again and again, but that's his job. He knows as well as I do that once it starts spreading the whole box and dice are inevitable. Every day a new tube is inserted, more fluid drained. The human body is seventy per cent water and I'm down to about thirty.

I don't know how much of what remains is me and how much is the cancer now. Perhaps it's only the cancer that keeps me upright when I sit, and if they removed it I would be like a rag doll. They're not going to remove it. They haven't told me that yet, there's no need to, it would bore all of us to go through the rigmarole. One day I'll be dead. QED.

Tekle Tolossa, who is a blind man and a seer, knows that he will die too. As the tall man talks I watch him, sitting with his legs crossed, rocking backwards and forwards, backwards and forwards, chanting under his breath. His shirt is tight across his chest, the buttons look as though they are about to pop. I remember thinking, *The buttons are about to pop.* He is the last of a line of princes, a line of princes so fucking glorious, so fucking glorious, Teddy, that your father would not be fit to lick their arses. But Tekle can't keep the line going – Christ, how he has tried but

It is said that his wife brought him a child once, but he could sense a another man's progeny with his fingertips and

He rocks backwards and forwards, keeping himself

awake. He is older than the others, the night weighs more heavily upon him. During the day he works as hard as any man there, by our deeds we will be judged, Teddy, but he gets less and less done, the others have taken to helping him with his tasks, running ahead of him to strip the coarse cover off the bean so when he arrives it comes away more easily. Sometimes he tells them to stop, but more and more often he pretends to be unaware.

His house is tiny, and he and his wife fill it with their tremendous flesh, their endless songs, and cigar smoke. There is a single table, three chairs and a cot, all built by Tekle Tolossa. There are coffee beans all over the floor, and when you walk on them they break open and the smell of coffee fills the room.

I sit at his table some evenings and watch as he slowly takes off his work boots, more hole than leather, and washes the pulp from his hands. His palms are black from the coffee. Ababa makes *injera* and *wat* for me, for Kebreth, Kwibe and Lucy. She is in her forties, twenty years younger than her husband, and she has the face of a fifteen-year-old, swear to god, and she sings as she cooks. She and her husband communicate in songs, in touches, in the movements of their bodies in space.

When he is there I try not to look at Ababa, my ears burn with the fear that he knows I think of her as I go to sleep. When he passes me bread my hand shakes.

He has not always been blind.

Kebreth tells me that Tekle Tolossa was here before everyone else, before the plantation, not blind. He had been a holy man, born in Abiche, born in El Obeid, born in

Madagascar, who knew at the moment of his birth that God was in all things and all things were in God, and as many were the children of God as were the sands of the desert, the desert where he lay on his back as a child and stared up at the stars, and as many were the graces of God as there were those stars. And he had also seen in those stars, as he lay on his back as a child, that time was not linear, it is always now, the present contains its own future, you could read the fate of the forest by looking at one leaf, turning one clod of earth.

He had left his parents in his youth, leaving behind a race of princes so glorious, *so fucking glorious* and he had spent his years wandering across the deserts of the Danakil, taking up handfuls of sand to divine the future, and the sand told him that his future was where his past had been, where his princely ancestors had supped with the Queen of Sheba, the land of the burnt ones, the Ethiopes. The sand took him south, through Gonder and Welo, east to Lake Abbe, where he drank a mouthful of water in which was contained the whole history of the lake, and the whole history of water itself, of every river and ocean and sea in the world, and then he turned south again, south again, through Dire Dawa to the holy city of Harar, where God sat mysterious and adjutant in the seven-walled city on the hill, gazing down at the coffee fields below.

And Tekle Tolossa thought, This'll do.

He would make his own coffee back then, picking a few beans from the wild plants, grinding them down with his teeth, making a paste to chew. He would chew the paste lying on his back, gazing up child-like to the stars, and he

would imagine himself in the purple robes of his ancestors, chewing those same beans, looking at the same stars.
He thought of the ancestors who would follow him too,
thought of them in a thousand years' time, still chewing
the same beans, and he saw through God's eyes for the
first time everything that had ever happened, would happen,
exploding at that one point in the universe, and the Earth
beneath his back felt hard and deep and absolute.

He lay there for two days, chewing more and more coffee,
shaping more and more ancestors and descendants out of
the clay beneath him, watching them gather around him
in their own purple robes, kings of the Earth doing the
work of heaven, and on the third day he rose, walked twenty
paces to the north, twenty to the east, his body leading his
mind, following the lea of the land, until his body and the
ground said here at the very spot where we gathered around
the fire, and at the very spot where, thirty seconds after
he had hit the ground, a huge beautiful woman, twenty
years his junior, came and stood above him and asked him
if he wanted a cigar.

Ababa tells me one day, as I lie panting against her
breasts, that she had found him sitting among the coffee
bushes, cross-legged, chatting to himself and giggling,
looking like he hadn't eaten in days, which he hadn't, and
she took him home and made him *kitfo*, her famous *kitfo*,
and all the thanks she got was for the strange man to tell
her he had seen through the eyes of God, God had brought
him to this spot, and, listen, Teddy, I was the one for him,
baby. I thought he was mad, everyone thought he was mad,
but, that said, once I'd fattened him up he was quite a

looker, and, baby, if God had said I was the chosen one, then who was I to argue?

As soon as he could stand up she threw him down and made love to him, thinking of God gazing down on them from the clouds as they banged each other behind bushes, on rooftops, in lakes, in the desert, stopping long enough to get married and then banging in their own tiny house, on their own floor, on his newly made table.

Months passed. Eight, nine and, migod, ten.

And nothing happened. No swell of belly. No fruit of womb.

He took her in the morning, at nightfall, she took him over dinner, in the middle of the night, when he was sleeping, when she was waking up. They made love in doorways, windows, they screwed among the coffee bushes.

They fell to prayer like Abraham and Sarah, crying, O Lord, why have you forsaken us?

But the Lord did not answer, He just sat silent and mysterious within the walled city, so one morning Tekle Tolossa left the sleeping body of his wife and walked back through the fields, back to the spot where he had lain that first day, because if the answer wasn't there, there was no answer. He placed a coffee bean in his mouth and began to chew, felt its acid in the cavities of his teeth, then chewed another and another. He watched the sun move up across the horizon, saw it burning across the ground as he chewed another bean, and again he saw his ancestors and his descendants rise up out of the clay to surround him, but this time he wasn't fooled, he knew it was a trick of the light, well, you can't fool me, sun, so he stared it down, stared at it until it was no longer a magical object in the air, stared at it until it was just a ball like the hateful Earth, and as he stared at it he watched his ancestors and his descendants burn in its flames, burn screaming back into the clay, until in the end there was him and him only, a man, lying on the Earth, blind.

In this way Tekle Tolossa proved that the sun was only a ball of fire, not a god, and the sun proved to him that he was only a man, a collection of bits, eyes teeth arms legs, bits that could break down or be burnt away, and if you have a low sperm count that's biology not cosmology, and Tekle Tolossa took the lesson, abjured his faith, and gave himself over to dialectical materialism.

Meanwhile!

Ababa had woken up to find him gone. She knew where he had gone, and why, knew by the touch of his last kiss as they fell into their dreams, the last squeeze of her hand before sleep. She got out of bed, wild, crazed, for if she did not know what he would find there, she knew what she wanted him to find when he got back. She ran and ran, following the curve of the Earth, for the Earth was wise to her idea and guided her to her goal; it took her across the fields, through the coffee bushes, and as the sun rose it saw the Earth's plan and it licked out a magical finger there, and there, through an open window, she saw the baby she was looking for, a sleeping baby, innocent as the lamb, and she knew now that there was a God, and with the warmth of the rising sun on her back she bent through the open window and gently lifted the baby out of its crib.

Ababa ran back through the fields with the new bundle

in her hands, hoping that he would be home so that she could cry, Look, a miracle, the sun has given us a son, but he was not there, so she sat down among the coffee beans and offered the baby her breast, knowing there would be milk there for a child of the sun, and milk there was . . . and Tekle Tolossa ran back through the fields, knowing he would never be fooled again, would never fall for phantoms and lies, because you don't need such things to see into the future, and he ran and ran, blindly, blind, feeling the curve of the Earth beneath his feet, which was nothing special, people walked this track every day, you just had to follow it and he did follow it, all the way home, and Ababa flips her breast back into her dress as she hears him approach, then he's in the doorway and she cries to him, Look, a miracle, the sun has given us a son, the sun, Tekle Tolossa, has given us a son!

The sun is beginning to rise, giver of everything, life and blindness. The stranger is still talking. Tekle Tolossa rocks backwards and forwards.

The tall man's words have made him sick with fear, because Tekle Tolossa is a seer, and a seer is a seer because he knows men, bugger God, he was unnecessary for the process, what you needed was to know the hearts of men, and no matter how firmly you pushed the mass of men into a group, a class, the individual was still in there, lurking, and in each man lurked the possibility of evil, that was his word, evil, come closer, Teddy, where I can hold you, vile and sickening evil, even in the best of men, Teddy, like Kebreth, even in you, and he knew this because years before his wife had brought home a baby that wasn't his, as innocent as a lamb, a tiny son from the sun, plucked from the coffee fields, and, Teddy, with tears in my blind eyes, I picked that baby up by the ankles, its tiny legs in my big dumb hands, and I dashed it down on the floor of my home, its head splitting under my foot like the crunch of a coffee bean.

You won't know you're truly in love, Teddy, until you act like a cunt for no reason. You won't know until you lie awake at night terrified by this thing, this person you can never truly own. You won't know until you say and do things that you can't explain, and everyone will want you to explain, her especially, but you can't, you just can't, and that's how you'll know you're in love, Teddy. Just like that.

Little Teddy Everett, heir to the Everett quintillions, boy-child, bean-picker, Communist and bed-wetter lies in his bed in an Ethiopian shack in deepest deepest darkest darkest Africa, rolling on his tongue a single coffee bean, Ethiopian Harar. Black spittle flows across his teeth tongue gullet, down his throat and into his stomach tummy gut. It is an hour since Kebreth brought him home, maybe an hour and a half; the sun is starting to turn the land to gold. Insects. Birds.

He is thinking about Tekle Tolossa, who is speaking to him in his dreams. In Ethiopia, Teddy, there is a promise, a covenant, called Kidane Mehret, Mary's Covenant of Mercy, allowing her to intervene in human affairs and save one of the damned. One. It is, they say, our Holy Fathers say, the Covenant above all others, the Covenant preceding all others, embodying all others, the ur-Covenant, prior to and over and above the Ten Commandments, prior to and over and above the Jewish Covenant, Teddy, knocking Muhammad's pledges into a cocked hat; they are but pale imitations, that lot, johnny-come-latelies in the Covenant stakes. Kidane Mehret, boyo, is the Mercy that contains all other mercies, the Grace that contains all other graces, the Pity that embraces all compassion, here and now and ever more. Perfect Mercy, without judgement, Mercy that is, by definition, without judgement. Just what the doctor ordered.

And when I believed, well, I.

But now I.

And so I.

But if I don't believe, I can't believe I'll be damned, can I? So that's all right.

Teddy lies in his bed in an Ethiopian *tukul* in deepest deepest. He has the bed-sheets pulled up to his chin. He feels the backs of his legs on the mattress. He is cold, shivering. He is hot, shaking.

He hears the men walking past his house, men on their way to work, breaking into laughter or song. People taking the piss out of each other. Someone bangs on his wall as they walk past. He wonders if it is Kebreth.

The house is beginning to wake. Servants move things from place to place. Someone speaks in a loud voice. A cup is broken, maybe. A fly passes through the room.

Teddy watches the men going off to work. A group of men breaks off from the main group, Kebreth, Tekle Tolossa, Kwibe Abi. They stand at his window in a triangle, Kebreth at its apex. Their shirts are open to the waist, wind blows through their hair, as the sun rises behind them. They begin humming softly as Kebreth speaks.

After the revolution, says Kebreth, we will still work here, but the money we earn will be ours, it will not go into filling the fat bellies of men like your father. Selassie has sold out his own people, because it is in the nature of power to be greedy. Power begets greed, greed begets power. What is needed, Gramsci tells us, Lenin tells us, is a new society, where no one is greedy, where greed is unknown.

That cannot come from above, as one who has tasted greed can never be truly free of its effects. It can only come from below, where the people know hunger, not greed, and who, having suffered hunger, will be unable to inflict it on others. Everyone will work together to ensure that everyone is fed. None of the tools of production will be in private hands. This is called collectivisation, Teddy. Remember that word. No one will hold power like Selassie, like your father, instead everyone will be in power, working together, maybe not today, maybe not tomorrow, but one day it will be like that. Until then, Teddy, we must organise, organise, organise. Even you. Especially you. People like you are the future, Teddy, remember that.

The heavy sound of bed-springs. His father. Teddy shrinks into his bed as he hears phlegm being drawn up from those fat lungs and spat into a chamber pot. Teddy hears this every morning, although everyone believes he sleeps for another hour. Every morning Teddy lies there and imagines peeking into the bedroom as his father wakes. His father is in a white singlet and huge white under-garments. He holds the chamber pot on his knees and retches saliva into it. Teddy tries to back away but makes a tiny sound, and his father looks up, straight at him, a line of phlegm hanging between his lips.

Teddy sees Tekle Tolossa walking behind another man, his hand on his shoulder, being led towards the coffee plants. He hears his father shouting, the servants grinding beans, and then smells the coffee in the air, setting his little neural inhibitors tingling.

Teddy stares out of his window at the men working in

the fields. They are laughing, singing, working. Some stop and roll tobacco. From his hospital bed sixty years later Teddy sees Kebreth look into his eyes and wink. A blue-bird sits on his shoulder, and the notes it sings set staves in the air.

But you fucked that up, Teddy, didn't you, you fucked it right in the arse, and everyone died without you firing a shot.

Lucy Alfarez walked out of the jungle at the age of four-teen with a silver lighter in one hand and a coffee bean in the other. Through blind eyes Tekle Tolossa watches her come. He has been waiting for her for a long time. She is beautiful, you don't need eyes to see that. The forest itself sings her praises and stones seek to cry out her name.

There will not be absolution in this girl – that he knows. Only Mary can grant Kidane Mehret, and pull him from the waiting fires. But there is no Mary. At best, some amends can be made. This is no small thing, to make amends.

He sees the girl approach the boy, Teddy, hears the whittling stop. The moment sits full, indivisible. Tekle Tolossa is a seer, and he knows that this is the moment that will haunt the boy at the end. He sees me here, now, in hospital; we nod to each other across the years. She sits beside him, offers him a cigarette. The boy's father will be here soon. Tekle sees in the near future the belt rising and falling, but he knows the girl will be okay, she is stronger than that, it will barely touch her. And tonight the girl will sup with them, with him and his wife, and Ababa will take the girl in, not letting her mind touch on why she is doing so, busying herself with practical things, making *kitfo,* adding cayenne pepper to the marinade, a recipe passed down and down, so that this arrival means only itself and refers to nothing else.

Tekle Tolossa lets his mind move forwards, tracing the contours that the girl will describe in this place, the movement of her body across time and space. She will be Kebreth's lover, he can see that, even now Kebreth is watching her in the distance; Kebreth will try and make it fit a scheme, no doubt, but. The boy will love her too, of course, but he's a skinny little so-and-so, besides which Ababa waits for him, I can feel it in her skin, the ultimate subversion, the best joke in the world. I'll beat him but understand. She's beautiful!

The girl is being lifted now, taken by the fat man, and Tekle Tolossa sees her at the fire years later, listening to the tall man, her face blackened by coffee beans, the last still moment before it all goes wrong, so wrong. The boy is there too, his mother dead, his father soon to die, his own face made black by Kebreth, the ultimate subversion, the best joke in the world. The whistle of the belt, again and again and then stopping. A pause, and then the smell of cigarette smoke.

Tekle Tolossa moves away. The house must be prepared, a cot set up to take this sleeping child. He will build it himself. He knows that after the last, perfect, still moment, the world will tear open and there will be nothing good left. He does not know what happens, who survives and who does not. But for now he can build a bed. He can make amends.

The question, of course, is whether Haile Selassie genuinely believed that the League of Nations would intervene on his behalf. Sure he had given the President of France a hoofed animal as a sign of goodwill but

The question is whether Haile Selassie genuinely believed that the League of Nations would intervene at his behest. Sure, the League had been set up, ostensibly, to deal with the possibility of hostile land grabs, but this was the first true test of the willingness to assert the powers it had been given. That its powers were independent of, and often in contradiction with, existing agreements (formal and informal) between European nation states was problematic, but it is understandable, without the benefit of hindsight, that a nation attacked in direct contravention of the League of Nations Charter, should expect the agreements made in that Charter to override the existing agreements so mentioned.

Kebreth thought that Selassie was fucked in the head. To appeal to the League of Nations was at best futile, at worst a back-door concession to imperialism by relying on foreign powers. Hadn't Ethiopia successfully defended herself at Adowa in 1896? Could she not do so again? Rather than appealing to, say, England, which still held dominion over Rhodesia India Egypt, or France, given Morocco Algeria Indo-China. We must avoid imperialism by stealth.

The question is whether Haile Selassie genuinely believed that the League of Nations would intercede at his request. He needed them to remove the threat of Italian invasion while honouring Ethiopia's sovereignty, a sovereignty affirmed by Ethiopia's unique position as the only African nation state that had never been under foreign dominion. This then is my coffee story. The position of Everett and Sons Coffee in Ethiopia was due to the goodwill of the Selassie regime, which allowed it access to the Djibouti railway line as per an agreement struck by Selassie himself and Simon of the Big Nose.

Whatever Selassie believed, Kebreth believed the

moment had come. Marx teaches us that the seeds of revolution are best planted in a time of turmoil, when everything is going to shit, comrade, and Kebreth knew that if the Italians were about to start carving things up then all bets were off.

So this is it. This is the pay-off. You can stop here if you want to. It doesn't matter, this happens whether you watch it or not.

Here's the cast.

My father is Oliver Everett the Second, the fat fucker. My mother told me on her deathbed that he was not a bad man, but I don't believe her. He was, so legend has it, conceived in the salubrious environs of the first-class compartment of a Trans-Siberian railway carriage. Cells grew and split, split and grew. Limbs emerged pop pop pop pop from four evenly spaced points on the embryo's torso. And then? Genitalia, Lovejoy, genitalia! The penis of my father. Amniotic juices. Kelp. Rock pool.

My mother said on her deathbed that he was not a bad man. I search and search for evidence of this, but find none. It is possible, of course, that she, at death's door, was granted the gift of Kidane Mehrat, of absolving him from his sins. My mother was no Mary, my conception far from immaculate, but this was Ethiopia, and stranger things. Stranger things.

My father is unarmed. He does not know what is about to happen. His heart is, however, beating quickly, the effort of getting dressed tiring him out. He is sick and tired of this place, the heat, the way it makes his fat body drench with sweat at the merest movement.

He knows that the Italians are massing on the border. Already he and Simon of the Big Nose exchange letters discussing the possibility of collusion. They love their coffee, the Italians and they'll want to be in on the action, *certamente*! He is hoping that Simon will die soon, so he can return home and take charge. His boy will be of an age in a few years to come back and take control. He doesn't see much of the boy these days, the boy is always playing with the natives, but a few years of public schooling will beat that out of him.

My father doesn't know that his rapidly beating heart will be stopped today, a bullet hitting it mid-beat, the next pulse never to come. He doesn't know shit from clay.

Second is Holbrook. This is the moment he's been waiting for. He is tying his leather shoes, slowly, deliberately. Thin laces. This is the moment he's been waiting for. He is a devotee of James Cagney, and always wears short ties and high-collared waistcoats as a tribute to his hero. He knows there is trouble afoot. He is, I suppose, good at his job. He takes his time doing up his tie. Windsor, Half Windsor, Schoolboy. In his own mind he is the hero, and the hero always has time. Let's even let him take the time to pull, deftly, his handkerchief out of his pocket, and polish his shoes. There will be blood on them soon, so let's look at them shine.

He looks up and sees me looking in at the window. He very slowly, very deliberately lifts his hand, makes a fist, and then sticks his index finger straight up. Holbrook is flipping me the bird. That stupid gobshite mouth of his curls upwards into a smile of contempt. I can still see it.

He unclenches his fist, reaches down and picks up his gun. He wipes it once with his handkerchief, as he will once it has been fired. He spins the cartridge, Cagney-style, and then puts it in the holster under his arm.

He is ready.

Third, working in the coffee fields, is the man he will shoot, Kebreth Astakie, my father's contact with the Galla people, fluent in Amharic, Harari, Arabic, English, Italian and Marxist-Leninism. Kebreth's hobby is attempting to lead the employees of Everett and Sons Coffee into insurrection by assassinating my father and placing the entire operation in native hands.

Kebreth and I are firm friends. He is in love with the same woman as me, Lucy Alfarez, but we have ridden the storms of that equitably, me by acquiescing, him by not knowing. Once, he tried to kill my father by placing a bomb in the cracks of our house, the night after my mother died, but my father had escaped, saved by his insensitivity.

In his pocket Kebreth has an Ethiopian *bessa*, the smallest currency in the world when it was given, worth nothing a year later when Selassie introduced the *matanos*. Kebreth keeps it on him for luck. The first bullet that Holbrook shoots will strike the coin and pass through it, the soft metal yielding to the hard, and enter Kebreth's heart moments after Kebreth's own bullet enters my father's, joining their blood in a cord of love.

Kebreth rubs the small scar on his forehead, which he received watching his own bomb fail to kill my father. When Holbrook shoots Kebreth a second time, the bullet will enter at the precise point of this scar, because nature seeks out patterns, space is curved. The bullet will then enter the *medulla oblongata*, initially destroying the part of Kebreth's brain that distinguishes different tastes, then moving on to the part of the brain that deals with touch, until finally blasting through the core of the brain, containing his political convictions, his understanding of the dictates of the proletariat and his extensive knowledge of post-Leninist literature. None of these things will be necessary to him after the bullet has passed through his brain, fired by the Neanderthal Holbrook, because he will be dead, and one ceases to taste, touch or foment revolution after death.

Kebreth also has a gun. He has purchased it from a Yemeni arms dealer for two hundred pounds that he stole from my father's billfold three days ago. My father has not noticed the theft, but he could have. Kebreth's plans are always half arsed. He doesn't realise this. It is about to get him killed.

Fourth, working beside Kebreth, is Tekle Tolossa, a blind man and a seer, as I am now. He has been a holy man, born in Abiche, born in El Obeid, born in Madagascar, who knew at the moment of his birth that God was in all things and all things were in God, and as many were the children of God as were the sands of the desert, the desert where he lay on his back as a child and stared up at the stars, and as many were the graces of God as there were those stars.

He is here because he does not know what happens next. The blind seer cannot see. He has led his mind here again and again, to the moment when Kebreth yells, Now!, they have discussed it many times, but he has not been able to penetrate deeper into the mystery of what happens next. I know what happens here, he doesn't.

When he arrived here he had met and fallen in love with a woman named Ababa, and they'd, but they'd, and then he. Later they had taken in a girl called Lucy, and treated her as their daughter. He is scared because this gap in his vision foretells a great calamity, and he knows that he will be powerless to intervene. His job will be to bear witness. His blind eyes will watch it all come undone.

Fifth is Kwibe Abi, sitting on the steps of our *tukul*, a boy my age, who hero-worships Kebreth and wants nothing more than to be like his hero. He will not die today, I am not given to suspense, but he will in two years' time, possibly, fighting the Italians, probably, driven into the jungle by what is about to happen next. Or he will die in forty years' time, in the last days of the Emperor, as a last defender of the royal throne, defending the dream of Menelik or Tewodros, the kings he used to imitate in Tekle's *tukul*, or as a Derg revolutionary, pursuing the dream of Kebreth Astakie, in a gun battle to overthrow the palace and condemn Selassie to his mysterious grave. Or he will die of starvation in a camp in Tigray. He will not be called on to act today, he will merely turn and run away, tears in his eyes. His fear and shame will be transformed into anger and rage, and he will die a hero, like Kebreth, maybe.

Sixth, sitting beside Kwibe Abi, is Lucy Alfarez. She walked out of the jungle at the age of fourteen, with a silver lighter in one hand and a coffee bean in the other, watched by Oliver Everett the Second who will beat her, Kebreth Astakie, who will become her lover, Kwibe Abi, who I guess loved her too, Tekle Tolossa, who will be like a father, and little Teddy Everett, who will love her until the day he dies.

Seventh is the tutor, Birtwhistle, why not? I want him here for this. He has set up camp one mile away from us, say, and spends his nights preaching to the trees the Gospel of Poetry, and his days peering into the coffee plantation, playing with himself as he watches the women work, his hatred of the world confirmed with every post-ejaculatory lacuna. He will witness everything that happens and try to make a story of it, but he will get too tied up in the politics of the thing, in the problems of representation, of race and history, and he will never get the thing done.

Eighth is Adelaide of the Suitcase. She has been here all along, a shadow among the trees, a rumour, a slip of white out of the corner of the eye when falling asleep, a white woman dancing with the Zars, a forest sprite.

Ninth is Simon of the Big Nose, looming above us, a god, the shadow of his nose obliterating Indonesia and the Philippines. He holds in his hands the telegram that announces my father's death. By the time he finishes reading it, he himself is dead, falling into the arms of the messenger boy, his heart stopping at the telegram's final STOP, and suddenly I am the new head of Everett and Sons Coffee.

Finally, Teddy Everett is here too. Look at the boy! As innocent as a lamb! He is fourteen years old, fourteen now and for ever. He has been in Ethiopia for four years. His mother died six months ago, and he no longer misses her, barely gives her a thought. He spends his days playing with Lucy and Kwibe. At night he sits and listens to Kebreth talk about the revolution. He is becoming more fluent in Amharic, although by tomorrow he will have forgotten every word. He will wake up from dreamless sleep tomorrow and not remember a single word of Amharic ever.

A week ago he was baptised as a Communist and now it's the revolution! He can still smell Ababa Tolossa on his body. She is not here, she doesn't want to watch; this woman born to bring forth life, but unable to, has no wish to look again on death. Teddy will love Ababa for ever too, even though she will never speak to him again, even though she will come screaming to his room the next day, as he lies there shaking and trying to remember a single word of Amharic, and beat him on the chest, the face, until Tekle comes and takes her away sobbing. Teddy cries as he watches her go; he has no parting words for her, he doesn't speak the language.

He can also still feel Kebreth's hands on his face, rubbing in the coffee oil, the ultimate subversion, the best joke in the world. In twenty years' time, thirty, forty, right up until his final illness, he will hide away from everyone sometimes, and rub coffee oil into his face, standing in front of a mirror, a gun, sometimes real, sometimes imagined, held in front of him, slowly sagging.

His second wife, Moira, meaning 'destiny', catches him like this one day. Call it 1982. She sits him down the next day and tells him in that sweet sad voice of hers that she loves him very much and always will but she is sick to death of it, sick to death of all the lying and cheating and the rages and the sleepless nights and and and.

Oh, Moira.

Today, fourteen years old in deepest deepest darkest darkest Africa, Teddy has a real gun, his first. Kebreth gave it to him the night before, as they sat in the dark around the *kojo* tree. The sun sinking, the light changing, the sound of the hyenas gathering. Kebreth talking, his lover stretched beside him, Kwibe and I sitting cross-legged before him. We had done this so many times. But last night was different. He had told us that the night was going to be different.

Tomorrow, he had said, we will be overthrowing Everett and Sons Coffee, and returning it to native hands. Your father will not be harmed, Teddy. He will be arrested. I will then speak from the porch of the house. You, Teddy, will then agree to hand over the entire plantation to us. This is the symbolic moment that will usher in the future of Pan-Africanism, Teddy, You will be famous for ever, worshipped as a god. A secular god.

Kebreth handed me a gun. You will need this, Teddy. I will need you to aim it at Holbrook. He needs to understand that you are his boss now, and that you agree with the Nationalisation – sweet Jesus, that was his word, Nationalisation – of Everett and Sons. When he sees that you have a gun, he will not attempt to stop us. He will realise that we are workers like him, held under the thumb of Capitalism, we are his brothers.

I have organised for a truck to pick up your father and Holbrook, and take them to the train line. They will then leave Ethiopia. You may choose to join them or not, Teddy. I am freeing you from the bonds of family, from the chains of destiny. Should you choose to go with them you can. I understand that you may not have developed a true class consciousness yet. You are just fourteen years old.

With the Italians massing on the border, neither Selassie nor anyone from the United Kingdom will attempt to intercede. This is my plan.

Kwibe and Lucy want guns too, but Kebreth will not let them. Only one gun, trained on my father, and one trained on Holbrook. Otherwise it could be messy. People could get jumpy. Somebody could get killed.

How many of them were there, these coffee Communists? Ten maybe. Not just ten that night, but ten total, twelve if you included me and Lucy. A fucking disaster. The whole thing was a total fucking disaster.

Lucy. Ironbum Lucy. I watched you stretched out beside Kebreth. A woman, eighteen years old now and for ever. Was this what you were put here for, to love this man, to ease his passage to his grave? Were you the Kidane Mehret, the Covenant of Mercy that Mary had prepared for Kebreth, to give him redemption from his sins? When he had turned his back on the religion of his family – how can the son argue with the father? – had Mary moulded you from the Earth to give him succour, to make these last years an Earthly Paradise? Did she see how closed his dipshit mind was, how the whole of his destiny was determined, historically, to end in a complete fucking disaster?

I kidded myself then, kidded myself for ever more, that you were there for me, Lucy, that it was my cosmic plan that required you. Tekle and Ababa had the same dream, the same delusion. I have told this story other times, drunk

256

on imported *tej*, to the grey men who worked for me, and those times I have left people out, sometimes even Kebreth, sometimes Kwibe Abi. But you are always there. When I tell the story and find it too hard to say Kebreth's name then you are all mine, the grey men hear about our love, the love we had but could not keep, we kissed once, fleetingly, beneath the *kojo* tree and then I sent you away, for I am a tragic hero. The grey men take you away with them too, this wild girl, their fantasy, and when they are not dreaming about my first wife, they are dreaming about you.

But this is the last time I am going to tell this story, so I want to get it right, Lucy, Ironbum Lucy. You were not there for me – you were there for Kebreth Astakie, the stupid, beautiful idiot who shot my father.

Like this.

Kebreth Astakie is working in the fields, chewing the pulp from the *tera bunna*, rubbing the black bean against his coffee-coloured palm, feeling its oil against his short lifeline, feeling its juices run down his wrists, into his shirtsleeves.

It is a beautiful day. The sun floods the sky and makes us warm. Birds flutter overhead. A gentle breeze. The smell of coffee.

In his pocket Kebreth has a gun. It is heavy. It bumps against his testicles. His pockets are loose and he worries about the gun falling out. He did not think about this when he was getting dressed. All of Kebreth's plans are half arsed. It is ten o'clock. At eleven o'clock he will Nationalise Everett and Sons Coffee.

In his room sits Theodore Everett, also known as Teddy. He is fourteen years old and drenched with sweat. He too has a gun, his sweaty hands moist against its blackness. It is heavy on his lap. In the chamber are six bullets. Kebreth has assured him he will not have to fire the gun. All he has to do is aim it at Holbrook, to show that power has shifted away from his father. It is a symbolic gun. They are symbolic bullets. They are just in case.

At ten fifteen, Lucy Alfarez walks out of the jungle, with a silver lighter in one hand and a coffee bean in the other. She has spent the night sleeping beneath the stars, away from all of this. The previous night her lover, Kebreth Astakie, had begged her to stay with him, but she had refused. Staying would have been a goodbye, it would have sealed his fate. By leaving him she hoped to take the sting out of the whole thing, to let the night be in-itself, not for-itself. She would spend tonight with him; after it had all happened, they would lie down together.

She sits on the porch outside Teddy Everett's window, and lights an ivory-tipped Marlboro. Teddy watches the blue smoke rise into the air. He is in love with Lucy. He wants so much to tell her this. In his comic books and *Boy's Own* stories this would be the moment to do so. Kebreth has told him that there will be no shooting, but in everything he has read a gun means a shoot-out, and a shoot-out means death. If he is going to die, he should go and tell Lucy that he loves her, and that when he is gone he will still be there for her, looking after her and protecting her as she moves through life, a guardian angel, hers and hers alone.

In another version, Teddy is thinking that only his father would be shot, no one else, and that he wished to tell Lucy he loved her because after his father had died he would be the head of Everett and Sons Coffee, and he would be able to whisk her away and buy her dresses like those he will buy for his first wife, and walk her through the streets of New York and Santiago, men raising glasses to her beauty; and then they will retire, together, and in love, and lie in each other's arms like he did with Moira, She: Say I love you. He: I love you. She: I love you too.

Teddy wipes the gun on the bed-sheets. He can hear his father moving about the house, talking to Holbrook. Man sounds. Teddy places the gun back beneath his pillow and waits.

At ten thirty-seven, Oliver Everett the Second emerges from the Everett house to gaze at his army of workers, his proletariat. Teddy watches him through the window. Even now I have no idea what was going through that bovine head of his. I had hoped that with age I would penetrate that thick skull, and find one thought that seemed to fit. But nothing.

Beside my father stands the bodyguard, Holbrook. Perhaps Holbrook was good at his job. As he stands there I watch him sneeze into his handkerchief, opening it to gaze at the snot. Soon he will be wiping blood from his shoes with that handkerchief. He must have had an interior life too. Was he happy? Was there a girl back home? I once saw him writing a letter, his pen making big dumb letters on the paper, his tongue poking out of the side of his mouth. No, I don't want that for him. I just want that fat neck and the sweat under his arms. That's all I want him to be.

At ten fifty-two Kwibe Abi flees. I see him through the window, running into the forest. The fear has defeated him. He runs and runs and runs. He wanted to be like his hero, but he has spent the whole night vomiting with fear, and has spent the morning clinging to a *kojo* tree to stop his legs taking him away. But the sweat on his palms makes his hands slip, and with a cry he feels himself fall away from the tree and his legs beginning to pump. Later they will call him a coward. Later, when they have all been shown to be cowards, they will call Kwibe Abi a coward.

At ten fifty-seven, Kebreth Astakie stands up and begins to move towards the house. Teddy walks on to the porch. He stands next to Lucy, hoping she will lean her body over to touch his, a furtive touch, but she doesn't, she doesn't move. My father stands in front of us, Holbrook next to him. It is about to begin. The moment has arrived. Kebreth Astakie is walking towards us, his palms black from the coffee, his right hand in his pocket holding the gun. I move slowly down the stairs, holding my gun behind my back. When Kebreth raises his gun at my father, I am to raise mine at Holbrook. Kebreth will say, Now! and announce the Nationalisation of Everett and Sons.

Kebreth walks quickly towards my father, wiping his forehead as he does. My father sees him coming, and turns slowly to face him. Kebreth often comes to talk to my father, so my father remains relaxed, his hands in his pockets.

At eleven o'clock precisely Kebreth Astakie moves within five metres of my father and draws his gun.

And shoots him, BANG, without saying a word, without making a speech, without saying a word. Kebreth Astakie shoots my father in the heart and kills him, at two seconds past eleven, his first and last decisive act.

Tekle looks up with a start. Kebreth didn't think about it. He didn't say, Now! Tekle could not see this future. It existed beside the other one, a separate reality. He doesn't know what happens next. The link has been broken. Kebreth has stepped outside the chains of history. He has entered the realms of the saints and the angels. Like Jesus himself he is outside the grip of the temporal.

My gun is raised too, aiming at Holbrook. I don't remember raising it. God's plan. Out of the corner of my eye I see my father fall, his enormous body crumpling as the bullet enters his heart, making the blood stop going to his brain, and thus the central nervous system of Oliver Everett the Second stopped for ever.

Kebreth stands, his arm outstretched. He is very still, that disorganised hodgepodge of limbs perfectly balanced for the first time. The smoke that drifts from the end of his pistol does so languidly. He keeps staring at the place where my father stood, a hole punched in the air where a man had once been.

Kebreth does not see Holbrook take his gun from his holster and aim it at him. He has stepped outside the chains of history, and forgotten that one thing follows another. I see Holbrook take the gun out. It happens very, very slowly. Holbrook is in no hurry. This is his arena we have stepped into. He knows exactly how far time can stretch at this point. I am behind him to the left. I am sure he does not know I am there, my gun trained on him. Or he knows I am there, but has summed up in a moment that part of me that I was to grapple with for the rest of my life. That I am a coward.

A word forms in my mouth but I can't get it out. The word is 'stop'. That small word that I have been condemned to mouth silently for seventy years. I wanted to say it to my mother as she left me, as she watched me back out of her room with terror in her eyes; to my first wife as she fucked Carlo in the bar in Havana, her body wrapping itself around his as it had never wrapped itself around mine; to Moira as she walked down our curved driveway to a waiting car, all that she wanted to keep in two small holdalls, her last sad kiss still there on my cheek; to Lovejoy every time he touches me, tries to keep me alive; to my red-haired nurse as she looks at the watch on her blouse and tells me she must be heading off, it's time for the night shift; and to myself, for all of it, all of it, all of it. Stop.

But the word never comes. The gun is so heavy in my hand. My finger pushes against the trigger, moving it slightly. I only need to squeeze a little more firmly, and the gun will fire.

Holbrook shoots Kebreth in the heart, once, BANG, and

then in the head, again, BANG. Just like that. That still moment, that graceful pose of Kebreth, shatters with his skull, and with the worthless *bessa* coin in his top pocket.

Lucy screams. She runs past me, brushing against my shoulder as she goes, our last touch. I'll never wash it, Lucy! She falls on Kebreth, holding him, taking that shattered skull and holding it in her lap, her white cotton dress absorbing the blood within seconds, so it seems to pour from her as much as from him, sheets of blood staining the ground around her, flowing magically outwards, a circle of blood around Lucy and her dumb-ass lover, flowing all the way to Holbrook who will have to wipe it off his shoes when it has all finished, and blood isn't red, it's black, the blood of the dying is black; I remember gazing at the little pool in my wrist the first time I opened it.

Holbrook lowers his gun towards Lucy. Stop. My finger quivers against the trigger. I see Holbrook make the mental calculations, summing it all up in the time and space that only he has available to him. At the moment the job is neat. Kebreth had shot my father, and he had then been shot. To kill the girl would make everything messier. There would be more to explain. Holbrook, ever the professional, lowers the gun to his side.

It is only when Lucy tears the gun away from her dead lover and runs towards him, only when she makes things messy, that he lifts his gun and shoots her in the head too, BANG, four shots, they said there were only three but you mustn't believe them, and Lucy's slender eighteen-year-old body drops like a stone and becomes one with her lover's for ever.

Dear God. There are bits of my flesh I can pick away now, bits turned to vegetable, soft between my fingers and coming away with the gentlest pull, exposing the bones below. I am not human any more. People no longer come to see me. Lovejoy no longer visits, Siobhan abandoned me a long time ago. They have given up the battle. There are other cases to deal with.

I can't remember the last time I moved. It is so long since I ate or drank that I no longer piss or shit. If I summon the energy to move my eyeballs down my body, I find it indistinguishable from the folds in the bedclothes. The various bags attached to it retain their fluid at an unchanged level. Nothing goes in, nothing comes out. I have attained the third law of thermodynamics.

Presumably the moment that I die I will undergo the same metamorphosis as my mother. My skin will turn to alabaster, I will become as holy and Gothic as a cathedral. If any are here to watch my last moments they would believe themselves to be in the presence of great wisdom. They will think it is my wisdom, they will think me wise, when it is really God's wisdom, his utterly mysterious and completely fucked-up plans for me having reached their end.

No wisdom hung in the air around my father, the blood

and fat seeping from his pierced heart, or Kebreth, five metres away with only half a skull, or Lucy, lying with him as she knew she would that night, her black hair blackened by blood. I stood there, my gun still pointing at Holbrook, and it got heavier and heavier, until it was by my side and I couldn't have any more lifted it then than I could lift a glass now.

Holbrook took the handkerchief from his top pocket, bent down and wiped the blood from his shoes, then his fingerprints from the gun. Whenever I think back I wonder if it would have been possible to fire at him then, but Holbrook knew it was impossible, so he took his time.

I felt the gun being prised from my hand, not prised, my fingers had no grip, I felt it being gently removed, by Holbrook, no, it can't have been Holbrook, Thompson then or Johnson – were they there? They must have been there. Someone was screaming too. Maybe it was me.

Holbrook walked back to the bodies. I watched as he lifted Lucy up, carrying her across the yard and into one of the sheds. Another body that will disappear. As he carried her, a silver lighter and a coffee bean fell from her pocket. On his way back he picked up the silver lighter and slipped it inside his waistcoat, and flicked the coffee bean away with his foot. Then he came back, holding a rope. He knelt beside Kebreth and placed a noose around his neck, pulling it tight. Then he lifted Kebreth's body on to his shoulder and carried it to the *kojo* tree. I watched as he threw the rope over the lowest branch and pulled.

There was a moment, when Kebreth's body was upright, before the feet left the ground, when he seemed to be standing, looking out across the fields, upright, strong, gazing into the future. And then Holbrook pulled again, and Kebreth Astakie touched the Earth for the last time.

And then? I don't know. A hand on the back of my collar, Thompson or Johnson, lifting me up up up, the jungle disappearing beneath me, the ocean rotating away under me, the world continuing to turn despite having lost all its meaning, millions of people trying to get to sleep, their round and intact skulls full of their own round and intact anxieties

then I'm waking in a cold sweat and Ababa is in my room, pounding at my chest until Tekle drags her away and I never see them again

then I'm on a train, twenty-six hours again, and I think I see a boy named Kwibe Abi shade his eyes and watch me go past, but he looks so different now so

then I'm on an aeroplane, tearing across the thin tissue of the sky, my father's huge body in a box in the back, making the nose of the plane tip upwards, the wings straining under the weight, Mrs Smithers dressed in black in the seat beside me, Adelaide of the Suitcase sitting on the wing like Mary Poppins

then I'm in a bed, nurses, apothecaries, pills

then I'm at the funeral, my father and also Simon of the Big Nose, dead of a broken heart on hearing the news, one casket immense, the other with a small bump to encase the proboscis, each being lowered simultaneously into adjacent plots, an expensive choir in full voice 'I Know That My Redeemer Liveth', 'Jerusalem', 'He Was Despised', 'The Pilgrim's Hymn', me in a suit, numb but upright, sweat rolling down the back of my neck, the poor boy, to lose one's parents, so young, who would true valour see, let him come hither

then I'm behind a desk, and then

then I'm behind a desk, and the man on the other side is an Italian and Ethiopia is now Italian East Africa, business is business, and I know you have some connection to the area, Signor Everett, may I call you that?, I heard about your father, well, it is a terrible thing, but we feel confident that our government and Everett and Sons could form a partnership mutually beneficial, beneficial to both, we have restored order in and around your plantations and hope to bring you on board in partnership, we Italians love our coffee, Signor Everett, and if you would be willing to sign here, we will leave your business to operate in exactly the same way as it always has, with just a small percentage coming to us to cover the costs of whatever administration is required for us to leave you alone; then I was signing the document, in a pen with ink as black as blood

I know, Lucy. I know. This is my coffee story. I should have told it years ago.

then I'm dancing through the streets of New York, the woman on my arm alive and happy, my future first wife, and she's got gams up to here and not afraid to show them, my tongue on her tongue as I press her to the wall, the throb of her body, alive and happy, bringing mine back to life, letting the thought of Lucy flash across my mind for the first time in ten years, a pang but no more than a pang, *we've all done stuff that we*, and I'm licking the eye-liner from the backs of her legs and then I'm inside her and then the coffee-table breaking

then I'm in my office for year after year after year, sitting behind my big boss desk and the right-hand drawers are full of ledger books and financial statements, but the left-hand drawers are full of whittled creatures, maps, pamphlets, and the hidden drawer beneath them holds secret bank-account numbers, contact names encrypted and effaced, covert plans for covert operations, and it is to the left of my desk I go when I am alone, wherein I keep my idealism, my love of justice, my fear of betrayal and a Colt .45 holding a single bullet

then it's Moira wiping the cum off her belly with a towel, those soft Catholic eyes moist with disapproval and me so in love, say, I love you, and then she's walking down the driveway with her suitcases, sombre and dignified, and into a waiting car, and away

then I'm dying. From that moment, until now, I'm dying.

I thought I saw her one last time, Moira, my Moira, meaning 'destiny'. It was after they had come for me, dragging me out in the middle of the night, dragging me off my relief map, two of them (also Thompson, also Johnson), putting my whittled animals, family and friends into shoe-boxes (Kebreth, Lucy, Kwibe, Holbrook!), cuffing me, punching me and catching me in the flashbulbs, scuffled and scuttled, like in the movies, *traitor, treason*, when the Cuban documents had come to light, confirming the unholy paper trail, never keep anything leading back to Castro and forwards to the Chair.

Questions questions questions, what was I doing in Santiago del Cuba at the precise moment that the Communist

Castro was attempting to overthrow the President? Is that a sensible place for an American citizen to be found? Why the suicide attempt? Was I afraid that something might come to light about my activities? What exactly were my activities? Did I know Castro? Did I know de Jesus? Are you, let's be frank, a Communist? . . .

Yes, I was clandestinely helping to fund the overthrow of the Batista dictatorship. I regard myself not as an American citizen but as a citizen of the world. Of course I was afraid – I tried to kill myself after the failure of the initial coup attempt, although I was also on a real downer because my wife was fucking another man. My activities were centred on the financial aspects, no more than that, the money was from an undeclared bank account set up by my father and great-grandfather, Simon of the Big Nose, to launder money obtained from the smuggling of Egyptian amulets back in the 1930s, aided by a man called Ibrahim Salez. After the death of Ibrahim Salez his son took over the stewardship of this account, no, I do not know his whereabouts. Yes, I knew Castro briefly. Yes, I knew de Jesus, he was fucking my wife, see above. Yes, I am a Communist, Kebreth Astakie made me one when I was fourteen. Yes, base, yes, superstructure, yes, yes, yes

all those half-arsed attempts to make some sort of amends, my fingerprints found on documents in Ecuador, Haiti, Vietnam, Ethiopia, is it true, Mr Everett, that your money was used to fund the attempted coup of 1960, the uprisings of the 1970s, and the final overthrow of Haile Selassie in 1974? Yes, yes and yes, the position of the Ethiopian peasant classes was in my estimation untenable, the Eritrean situation, the 1973 famine, the Dimbleby documentary, and as Marx teaches us, only through revolution can we.

North Korea, El Salvador, Greece, my money spread all over the world, all of it done to stop myself being seen as a total shit, I have acted against the common good, against the common weal, seeing those accusing eyes of Lucy, for no other reason, promise, just that, haven't you done stuff you're not proud of?, but it was after that, on the day of the sentencing, *Treason!*, that I saw Moira for the last time, coming down those same steps as we had years before, after the first divorce, her by my side looking sombre and dignified, that's how she looked again, I held her hand so tightly and felt the world glowing a little more golden, I turned and there she was, on the verge of tears, and as it sank in that they had told me I was going to die, I felt a lightness, a peace, because she had borne witness, my Moira had borne witness. I don't really know if she was there but I would go on believing she had borne witness.

When Lucy stands at the end of my bed now those accusing eyes burn into my soul and I feel it squirming and thus know it exists.

I was trying to make amends, Lucy. Cash for the revolution. A rich man's martyrdom.

But I chickened out on that too, Lucy. Those cigarettes you gave me, the poison you introduced into my lungs, saved my life. They don't execute the dying any more. They commute their sentences, my sentence has been commuted!, and put them in a prison hospital and, ironically, ho ho ho, try to keep them alive.

Back in Ethiopia, back in 1935, Kwibe Abi runs through the jungle as fast as his legs can carry him. He hears a gunshot and stops, swaying, part of him wanting to turn back, the other part knowing that the word 'coward' is already lit above his head. He hears a second and third shot, and knows that Kebreth is dead. More shots mean that Kebreth is dead, because he too knows that Teddy Everett is too chicken-shit to shoot. He hears a fourth shot, and he knows Lucy is gone too. He starts running again, slower this time. He is not running away from anything any more. He is just running.

He feels the blood of his million fathers coursing through him, the kings and emperors that he has absorbed at Tekle's table, Solomon, Menelik, Tewodros, Yohannes, a race of princes so fucking glorious, he has played them all, fought their battles, known their loves, their hates. They have the Covenant and cannot be defeated. As he runs, his body changes shape, he grows taller, his chest broader, I'm making this up, I don't know what happened to Kwibe Abi, a stubble forms on his wide chin, his eyes lose – in three blinks one, two, three – their innocence and grow black with knowledge. He runs and runs.

He spends the night huddled in the doorway of the church in Kulubi where the pilgrims assemble to ask for miraculous cures or the fulfilment of their wishes, but he has nothing left to wish for, and knows there is no cure.

The next day he crosses the railway line at Dire Dawa at the precise moment the train containing Teddy Everett and the body of Teddy's father pulls away from the station. Teddy sees him standing by the railway line, shading his eyes against the sun, someone anyway. Kwibe stands there, broad and silent, shading his eyes and watching the train disappear. He begins to run again, and night after night, year after year, I spread my map on the floor of my office and trace the route of Kwibe Abi across the back of the financial reports, driving him this way and that, pinning scraps of evidence to the corners of the sheets, a hint of him here, a whisper of him there.

He sleeps beneath the stars, looking at them blankly for meaning, but in the morning the stars are gone, wiped out by the bright sun.

For eight, nine and, migod, ten months he runs, north-west north-west until he reaches the Awash river, drinks, and then north north north, across that empty nothing of a desert towards Debre Sina, towards Kombolcha, towards Hayk'. I used to spread maps of Ethiopia on the floor of my office and trace the imagined route of Kwibe Abi who had disappeared running into the forest and whom I never heard of again, and at Hayk' he falls exhausted at the door of the monastery, Sanctuary! Sanctuary!, and they let him in and feed him *wat* and show him the thirteenth-century books of the Gospels, strong beneath his fingertips, and he is now a Christian, I want him as a Christian, a soldier of Christ, and he realises, looking around, that it is these places, the hidden monasteries, that can form the battle-ground for the guerrilla war, nor shall my sword sleep in my hand, God willing.

He leaves the monastery, good luck, Brother Kwibe, heading north again, to Tigray and the rock-hewn churches, hidden once from the Muslims, now from the Italians, and he moves from church to church, clambering up cliff faces, toes curled around precipices, then under mountains, into caverns, down sheer drops, and to the monasteries of Abbé Yohani, Mikael Imba, Medhane Alem Kesho, where he genuflects before the *tabots*, recites liturgical greetings, and beseeches the priests to help him with the struggle. And some see into the future, near and distant, and remain unmoved, God's got it all worked out, the sun will wipe out the night, but some intercede, agents in the great forwardness, Christ made body, flesh and *ouns*, no longer watching from the sidelines, they dabble momentarily in the temporal, muddy their hands in the stuffness of stuff, and give him, God speed, food, blessings, maps.

He takes their food, blessings, maps and heads south again, because I want him at Maychew, where the final lost battle of the Italo-Abyssinian War takes place, at the end of March 1936, and there he is, in the home-made uniform of the Ethiopian army, watching the glorious train of Haile Selassie move on to the battleground, Selassie has come here personally, the blood of the Solomonic line coursing through his veins, not coursing because he has come knowing he will lose, and Kwibe Abi belongs to Ethiopia and to Christ, same same, and with the smell of mustard gas in his nostrils, the rain from it already beginning to burn his flesh, he plunges into battle and is killed in the massacre, his body one of those in a ring around the lake, one of the eleven thousand shot, gassed, slaughtered, their bodies piled in front of the unblinking eyes of the Emperor, the first defeated King of Ethiopia ever ever ever.

Or he escapes, and now heads north with Ras Kassa's sons to try and recapture Addis and is shot within miles of the capital.

Or he survives and is there at the vice-regal palace when they try to kill Graziani, Kwibe fires one of the shots, POW!, and is then one of the thirty thousand killed by the Baby Blackshirts in the reprisals.

Or he is cheering as the Lion of Judah crosses the border, the Solomonic line unbroken, the Italians leaving, Ethiopia is Ethiopia again.

I lose sight of Kwibe Abi here. Who does he become? He is the same age as me, give or take, but I am in the papers, and he stands silently off to one side. Did he take off his battle fatigues and live a quiet life, a wife, kids, a small shop? Did the churches of Tigray take him in again and let him see the infinite, teach him to treat the things of the world as the great illusion, with only infinite God the One Truth? Or did he follow historical necessity to its necessary conclusion, Kebreth's words still haunting him into middle age, joining the Derg, accepting, without knowing it, some of my financial backing, and helping oust the Lion of Judah? He may have driven the Volkswagen that took Selassie from the palace, he may have become a minor official, or a major player, watching over his own set of massacres with the impassive face of the former revolutionary. Was he then taken out and shot? I spend years in my office crawling all over a huge map of Ethiopia, tracing my finger north from Harar to Adowa, west from Adowa to Abobo, south from Abobo to Kebri Dehar, and north again to Harar, where is Kwibe now?

I watched those faces during the famine, and yet, Mr Everett, this revolution you helped fund led to an even greater series of famines, that mass of people without a history, a country no one has ever heard of, dropping into television screens from nowhere, and looked for faces my age, wondering if that was Kwibe Abi, brushing the flies from his face with a weary hand, a toothless emaciated old man, watching babies die, impassive, old. Is that him staring down the camera lens, wondering where I am at that moment, wondering where the double-betraying chicken-shit Teddy Everett is, while he is slowly dying?

I'm dying now, Kwibe, and that's the main thing. They have stopped visiting me, the lepers, the doctors, the nurses, everyone. My sleep is dreamless, sleepless. Yesterday they turned out the light, and no one has bothered to turn it back on again. I feel my heart beating more and more slowly, each beat further apart, and soon the distance between the pulses will become infinite.

Somewhere Moira kneels before an altar and recites the Litany of the Saints, and I kneel beside her and we recite the Litany of the Saints,

> *Holy Mary,*
> Pray for us.
> *Mother of God,*
> Pray for us.
> *Saint Michael,*
> Pray for us.
> *Kebreth Astakie,*
> Pray for us.
> *Lucy Alfarez*
> Pray for us.
> *Carlo the Cuban Revolutionary,*
> Pray for us.
> *Antonio Gramsci,*
> Pray for us.
> *Percival Everett,*
> Pray for us.
> *Tekle Tolossa,*
> Pray for us.
> *Tekle's wife Ababa,*
> Pray for us.
> *Adelaide of the Suitcase,*
> Pray for us.
> *Edith Everett,* née *Stanley,*
> Pray for us.
> *All the angels and saints,*
> Pray for us.

I try to spend these last moments thinking about Lucy, that's what I want more than anything, but I don't have the strength to lift her into my mind. She is too big, too heavy. They never found the body, never gave her a shot at consecrated ground.

But I know my grandfather will have made it to heaven. I think he is my hero, in the end. Tekle once told me that the blood still flowed from the side of Christ and would for ever – how you are when you die, Teddy, is how you are for eternity. So I see the knife still limp in his belly, the bath filling with his blood again and again for ever. Perhaps some of the blood falls to earth and touches Lucy's forehead, sanctifying her and washing her clean. Perhaps not.

Carlo is in heaven too, of course. He saved my life once. I'll have a beer with him, talk about my wife, and let him know his revolution ended up happening, such a shame he went and fell in love and missed it. But that can happen.

And me, Carlo? Well, I kept the flame burning, burning brightly. The flame of the revolution, obviously, not of love – love went from me long ago, you got out at the right time, before it all fell away. I am being held prisoner for the crime of treason, and will die in jail. Believe me, it's less glamorous than it sounds.

This is my room, Carlo. Beneath the bed are steel boxes, already packed for when I go, my *tabot*, holding, I guess, all my papers, the map. In Ethiopia there is a promise, Kidane Mehret, Mary's Covenant of Mercy, allowing her to intervene in human affairs and save one of the damned. I'm not holding my breath, but you never know your luck. Goodbye, Carlo.

I saw Selassie one last time too, the day they buried Kennedy – he walked past me as he had thirty-three years before, and again that millisecond of a glance. If you follow the money there's his blood on my hands. Some cast him up now as a god, some cast him down as the devil. I never attained such heights, apart from with my wives, so he will be sitting higher or lower than me when I pass on. Perhaps he will glance at me again – perhaps, this time, for longer than a millisecond. We have eternity after all.

Will Kebreth be there? Wherever he ends up, I shall too, and I don't doubt it will be the ninth circle, for all failed revolutionaries are traitors in the end, only victory removes the stain, so it will be me and him, on all fours as we were that first day, one black one white, encased in ice for ever, beside each other but never able to touch, something erotic in it, and the only sound will be that of Kwibe Abi's feet against the desk, *thud, thud, thud*. Giants will guard us, to remind us of our gargantuan ambition, and to laugh at us for our pissant failure.

I see silhouettes moving in the shadows at the end of my bed, one of them calm and methodical, pouring liquid from one jug to another. At first I think it is the man who waters the plants, but then I realise it is young Susu, making the coffee. I am in Salez's *kahweh*; the talking has drifted from stories in English to something foreign, musical, incomprehensible and wise, it has become a hum, as slow figures move, shadows within shadows, and someone is stroking my hair, stroking, I think he is stroking, I think my father is stroking my hair.

Beside me, on the table, my final polystyrene cup, my

chalice, stained with my last cup of coffee from three days ago, or maybe three months. Instant, foul. I don't have the strength to turn my head and look, but I know it is there, weightless on the stainless steel. With my *tabot*, I leave it as my legacy. Holy holy holy. Whosoever drinks from it will be made King or Knave, Emperor or Fool, just like that. No doubt a cleaner will crush it and throw it in the bin, but if he would look closely into the sediment he might see some wonderful things, a whole universe of possibilities, a life well worth living, who knows?

I don't. Fuck it, I'm just a man dying. That's all.

Pray for me.

Acknowledgements

You know, writing a novel is. And so it's important that. The following people are. I would like to thank all of them for their love, support, encouragement, photocopying, editing, and patience – Arts Victoria, Ann Atkinson, Martyn Bedford, Alison Caisley, Rachel Calder, Chris Cleave, Charlie Davie, Jill Dawson, Louise Dean, James Friel, Lisa Greenaway, Katie Greening, Niall Griffiths, Jocasta Hamilton & all at Sceptre, Claire and John Hanson, John Hunter, Ivan Kolker, Garry Mansfield, Ian Marchant, Alex Miller, Patrick Neate, Dan Pavitt, Jason Pietzner, Penny Roberts, Guy Rundle, Ken and Val Salmon, Kate Smith, The Arvon Foundation, Julia Watson, Kerry Watson and, of course and forever, my small round things, Pearl and Olive.